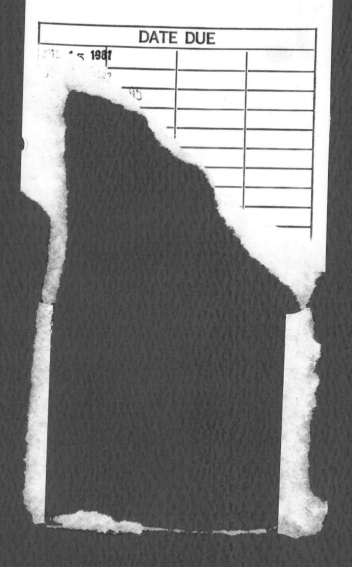

DATE DUE		
JUL 15 1981		
1982		

THE DEVIL ON THE ROAD

THE DEVIL ON THE ROAD

ROBERT WESTALL

GREENWILLOW BOOKS • New York

Published by Greenwillow Books
A Division of William Morrow & Company, Inc.
105 Madison Avenue, New York, N.Y. 10016.
Printed in the United States of America
First American Edition
10 9 8 7 6 5 4 3 2 1

Library of Congress Cataloging in Publication Data
Westall, Robert.   The Devil on the road.
Summary: While seeking shelter from a sudden
rainstorm in an old barn, a young motorcyclist
finds himself catapulted into a mid-17th
century England troubled by witch hunts.
[1.   Space and time—Fiction.   2.   Witches—
Fiction.   3.   England—Fiction]   I.   Title.
PZ7.W51953De   1979   [Fic]   79-10427
ISBN 0-688-80227-3   ISBN 0-688-84227-5 lib. bdg.

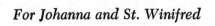

For Johanna and St. Winifred

I dreamed and behold I saw a man clothed with rags standing in a certain place, with his face from his own house, a Book in his hand and a great burden upon his back. I looked and saw him open the book and read therein; and as he read he wept and trembled; and not being able longer to contain, he broke out with a lamentable cry, saying,

"What shall I do?"

JOHN BUNYAN
The Pilgrim's Progress

1

My name's John Webster, and I'm on a drug.

Not speed or grass, or even alcohol the oldie's friend (though I like beer).

My drug's Chance.

What do I mean, Chance? Tell you what I mean. When I was a kid, Dad used to get in from the school where he's Head, switch on telly and watch a John Wayne western he'd watched ten times before. I used to wonder why, because he's not thick.

I see why now. He was squeezing Chance out of his life; for a couple of hours he was living in a scene where he knew every gunshot by heart. Keeping Chance at bay; getting a bit of peace.

I don't blame him. He has plenty of Chance at school, what with kids stuffing other kids down toilets, or getting pregnant, or shoving their hands through a glass door and running to him sprinkling blood all over the floor like a watering can.

But some oldies try squeezing Chance out of their lives altogether. Like Dad's mate, the bank manager. He insured his home, wife, kids, holidays—even the cat and dog. He had a suit for every day of the week and wore them in rotation. Used fourteen razor blades in rotation too; reckoned they lasted longer that way. Had timetables in his pockets for every train and bus that moved. If Dad

1

invited him round for dinner, he'd open a diary like a Bible. And there you'd see a mass of entries like *Dentist* or *D's birthday* or *car service* stretching years and years ahead. And three-month medical checkups on BUPA.

Fat lot of good it did him. Dropped down dead stacking money in the bank safe. Lady Chance got him right between the eyes and he didn't even have time to reach for the alarm bell.

I go looking for Lady Chance, before she comes looking for me. I fill up the tank of my Triumph Tiger-Cub, and at the filling-station entrance, I flick a coin. Heads for go left, tails for right. After that, at every road junction, I go where fancy takes me. Or else flick the coin again.

It's crazy. I once went round and round the same two-mile circuit for an hour. My mind sort of got stuck in a groove.

Best time was last Easter in Surrey. Met a pair of married vets in a pub. The husband had broken his leg and I spent the whole vac helping the wife out. Learned a lot about the engineering of calving a cow. Fascinating when you're up to your armpits in it.

Worst time was last summer; that nearly put me off for good.

The moment I passed the first-year exams, I shook the dust of University College, London, off my tires. Got nothing against U.C. Great building. Got smashing wide entrance steps, where you can swot and sunbathe. And bloody marvelous bathrooms each side of the entrance, that hardly anybody knows about. You can lie and soak all morning, after a night on the beer, listening to people talking as they go past the door.

2

That's the trouble with U.C.—the people. The rimless-spectacle types who think that just because you're studying Civil Engineering and play Rugby for the first XV, you must be Neanderthal man in person. The birds are worse. Wear a T-shirt and they start pinching your biceps and wanting to play Lady Chatterley to your gamekeeper. Or else they see the Tiger-Cub and want to do a ton. Up the Finchley Road at midnight, jumping traffic lights. To turn them on before they go to bed with me.

They don't get as far as my saddle. The Cub's not for playing Russian roulette with. I worked all one summer in a motorway café to buy her, scraping chewing gum off the floors with a knife under the direction of some middle-aged mental defective who couldn't forgive me for passing the 11 plus. Rebuilt her from top to bottom; high-lift cam, high-compression piston and roller-bearing crankshaft so she wouldn't blow apart. I can strip her in a day *and* put it all back. Tuned her like Yehudi Menuhin's violin. She can do ninety downhill with the wind behind her. Don't like taking her out in the rain.

I had her parked by the college gates; illegally, of course. Started first kick. Off I went after Lady Chance, with all July and August in front of me. Here we go into the wide blue yonder, as the marching song of the USAF has it.

The North Circular Road was blue all right; with exhaust fumes. Either the morning rush hour hadn't finished, or the lunch-time rush had started early, or all the suicidal soap salesmen were getting away early before the weekend rush. Every traffic light was a starting grid. Every kid on a Honda Fifty playing Barry Sheene; every trainee executive playing Niki Lauda behind the wheel of his Viva. I stayed alive, but it was a lousy scene for starting the Chance game. Every road I fancied was one-way—the wrong way. Or else I got forced into the wrong lane by some stripe-shirted nut in a Fiesta.

Finally, a traffic surge like a tidal wave carried me onto the A12. Just no arguing. Ah well, Lady Chance, with your permission I'll go to fabled Clacton and swim in the sea.

But the farther I went, the hotter it got. The sun climbed; the sky turned bronzy-yellow with exhaust fumes. The road turned bronzy-yellow too, shining up in my face. Every car approaching had a big reflected sun bouncing off its windscreen and a hundred little suns bouncing off its chrome. Cars in front had suns bouncing off their rear windows. *Flash, flash, flash.* Had a smoked visor, but I had to keep it up, because it was crawling with mangled flies. Had dark glasses, but they were at the bottom of my top-box.

Every crossroad, traffic jams. Creeping five yards and five yards. Brake, clutch, gear, till my left wrist and right foot were two big toothaches. I could feel the clutch swelling and catching; much more of this and it would burn out.

Tried working up the inside of the traffic jams, but it's hard when your bike's got panniers; they make it nearly as wide and clumsy as a car. And the heat was making the motorists narky. If they saw me coming, they'd edge nearer the curb to block me off. And even *touch* their paintwork with a brake lever and they'll have your no-claims bonus off you as quick as they can whip out a Biro.

Trying to work up the outside of the traffic jam was worse. The oncoming drivers were half-insane with the sun in their eyes and sticky kids wiping choc-bars all over

4

them, and mothers-in-law in the back seat saying they should have gone to Skegness instead. They were in a mood to drive straight at you with headlights on and horns blaring. And to swear after the accident that they never saw the motorcyclist, officer, even if he was wearing an orange suit and a yellow crash helmet.

And if you once left the traffic stream, the sods closed ranks and wouldn't let you back in, even if oncoming maniacs *were* trying to slice your right knee off.

The only bath I was going to get was in my own sweat. I licked thirstily at the drops running down my face. The vinyl saddle was like sitting in a puddle. Every time I changed gear, the sole of my Doc Martin's touched the exhaust and the smell of burning plastic came wafting up.

Nothing for it but try a side road on the left, make a few miles, then try the A12 again.

The side road was dreamy. Empty, shady with trees. Only the sound of my own exhaust blatting off the hedges. Rabbits lolloping out of the way; a gray squirrel streaking up a tree; harvesters in a field like a Weetabix commercial. The countryside soaked me up like a green sponge. Mile after mile of green dream.

Hell, I was supposed to be going to *Clacton!*

The moment I headed back to the A12, the road turned hostile again. Sun in my eyes. Cars coming round blind corners at sixty. One had me into the hedge, shaking all over, and didn't even bother to stop. I was a long time finding the A12. When I did, there was a jam of cars as far as the eye could see.

I tried three times, getting angrier and angrier, more and more knackered. The last time, I stood on the halt line for twenty minutes waiting for someone to give me a break. But the cars ground past bumper to bumper. In-curious faces watched me in procession from behind glass. They'd look at me the same way if I was splattered all over the road.

Suddenly I hated the whole bloody twentieth century. I turned and let Suffolk suck me in like a great big, shadowed, oak-treed, haystacked vacuum cleaner. Happy as a child.

That should have been warning enough.

2

Sudbury's nice. I had a couple of jars and shopped in the supermarket. Corned beef, baked beans, thick-sliced white, Spam and jam. Keep on thinking I ought to expand my menu, but it's too much bother. Even cornflakes are useless because the milk goes sour overnight. Eat most of my stuff out of the tin with a spoon—saves washing up.

I was stuffing the Spam and jam into my pannier when I saw the poster. Lots of guys waving pikes. Close-ups of Oliver Cromwell looking smug and Charles I looking like he knew he was going to lose.

HISTORIC BATTLE SPECTACULAR

Reenacted by the Sealed Knot
In conjunction with the Roundhead Association
In Hammer's Field, near Besingtree
(By permission of Ice-Star Frozen Foods Ltd.)
Sat. 25th June. Gates open 12 noon. Main Battle 2:30

I'd heard about the Sealed Knot. Guys who spend their spare time poncing round in Cavalier gear, losing the Civil War all over again. Suppose they need a Roundhead Association like Liverpool needs Everton. I don't dig fancy-dress, but I do like a good punch-up. And since Lady Chance wouldn't let me bathe in the sea . . . .

7

There were lots of jokey RAC signs saying *To the Battle* so I found Hammer's Field easy enough. Like a rugger-pitch, only bigger, with a ditch for the halfway line. The Cavaliers, defending the goal on my left, were busy filling the ditch with thornbushes, stripped to the waist, but still wearing their feathered hats and looking around every so often, to see if any birds were admiring their sun-bronzed torsos. But there was a guy with a real brass cannon, right on the touchline, and I couldn't resist that.

"Nice bit of engineering," I said.

He looked pleased for about ten seconds, then squashed it and said, " 'S'not bad. Old signal gun from a yacht club. Get two good cart wheels and the rest's just joinery. Japanese oak."

Lugubrious-looking guy; a born loser. Who else would be a Royalist?

"Must be worth a bit."

"Three hundred quid." He showed me his little touch-hole, and his gunpowder charges, and the little brass-bound swabbing-out bucket that swung beneath the gun carriage.

"How far can it fire a ball?"

"Dunno. We only use blank charges. *They're* dicey. Burn your face off at twenty yards. Got to be careful where you fire it. Responsible job."

"You a bank clerk or something?"

"Trainee accountant."

It figured. "Fancy your chances today?"

"No—we're going to lose."

"Why—is there a script like a film? Did you lose a real battle here?"

"Never was a real battle here. Somebody just loaned us the field."

"Why'd you have to lose then? You look a likely lot."

He surveyed his allies unenthusiastically. "Bunch of show-offs. Look at that guy." A musketeer, resplendent in lace and satin, was just getting out of a Jaguar. "He paid five hundred for that gear. Think he'd risk getting it torn by actually *fighting*? He just stands well back, firing shotgun blanks out of his fancy musket, till we start to lose. Then whips off back to his car."

"They look useful," I said, pointing to two more peacocks who were dueling with buttoned rapiers.

"They only fight one-to-one against a poshed-up Roundhead. Right on the edge where the crowd can admire them. The real rough stuff's in the middle—the pikemen. Our lot don't like being pikemen. They all want to be bishops, and pray before the battle. Or camp followers and get raped after it."

He had a point. No less than five bishops were parading up and down, giving each other nasty looks. And the female camp followers had cleavages you could have ridden a horse down. The few pikemen looked nervous, in spite of their fine red uniforms.

"Any cavalry?"

"Only in the Home Counties. Anyway, they're worse than useless. They only chase each other in circles. If they charged, they could *kill* somebody."

"What about Prince Rupert, then?" There was an elderly gent with white mustache, cantering to and fro on a solid chestnut.

"Referee."

"What, with a whistle? Offside and all that?"

He gave me a sour look. "They tell people when they're dead—try to make sure they don't get up and start fighting again. Nobody likes being dead, actually."

"Yeah?"

9

"Like to help me with the gun? My mate's got flu."

"Never fired one before," I said, modest but willing.

"*I* do the firing. Only I'll need help at the end. Getting the gun away to the car-park sharp. Some Roundheads get a bit . . . carried away when they win. Turned the gun over once; cracked a wheel."

I'd got involved with a real hero. We'd probably beat the ponced-up musketeer to his Jag.

"I'm not dressed for it," I said, taking off my crash helmet.

"Here's a hat." He offered me a shapeless broad-brimmed effort. 'Take off your jacket. You'll look OK in those boots."

Roundheads began drifting past in dribs and drabs, helmets hung on pikes, saying things like, "Not a bad day for it," and, "How's your foot, Charlie?"

"They look decent enough," I said.

"Oh, *they're* all right," said the Gunner. "*They're* local. But there's one lot . . . ." He suddenly cocked his ear and turned pale. "Oh, God, that's them now. Somebody said they weren't coming."

I listened with him. There was a sound, above the chatter of the spectators who were gathering. Might have been a marching song, or just a grunting.

> *"The ancient Prince of Hell*
> *Hath risen with purpose fell;*
> *Strong craft of mail and power*
> *He weareth in this hour . . . ."*

Two flags appeared, bobbing along behind the hedge: huge black flags with silver crosses and silver fringes. Then two sourfaced elderly men on horseback. Then a forest of pikes, all at exactly the same slope, swaying and dipping in unison.

> *"And were this world all devils o'er*
> *And watching to devour us*
> *We lay it not to heart so sore*
> *Not they can overpower us . . . ."*

They burst through a gap in the hedge, and swept past without even looking at us. Bare muscular arms in leather jerkins. Bowed muscular legs moving together in square-toed boots. Sloping shoulders and beer-paunches. Heads shaved like cannonballs, and big mouths wide open, bawling their battle hymn.

> *"And let the Prince of Ill*
> *Look grim as e'er he will*
> *He harms us not a whit*
> *For why, his doom is writ*
> *A word shall quickly slay him . . . ."*

They nearly trampled down a little kid who'd run out from the crowd. The kid's mother snatched her back just in time. They'd have trampled down the Queen, the Pope and the Archbishop of Canterbury.

"Who are they?" I whispered.

"One of the Midland Companies. From the car works round Brum. They work together, drink together, train together. Just *live* to bash Royalists. We complain to the Roundhead Association, but it doesn't do any good. Nobody can control them. Envy on the march; envy convinced its cause is just."

"Envy of what?"

He pointed to the brilliant musketeer with the Jaguar.

"They're nobbut skinheads," I shouted, fists clenched, hoping the ones at the back would hear me. But they all went marching on in step, and vanished behind a large clump of gorse at the far end of Hammer's Field, with the rest of the Roundhead Army.

"Skinheads? Roundheads? What's the difference?" said the Gunner bitterly.

I've often wondered which side I'd have been on, if I'd lived in the days of the real Civil War. Never made my mind up till now. Maybe the old Royalists had been like these Sealed Knot chaps: frivolous show-offs, a bit too quick to scarper when the going got rough. But faced with *that* load of pig-ignorance on the march . . . .

I rolled my shirt sleeves up and jammed on that floppy hat. Felt like I did before a big rugger match.

3

We then had a long wait. The crowd along the edge of the field thickened. Every second spectator had a camera, and they began discussing us as if we were animals in the zoo. The Gunner couldn't *touch* his cannon without a flashbulb going off. I found myself starting to pose like a film star. Revolting!

People began shoving kids up into the hedgerow trees for a better view. The trees were already full of loudspeakers, and the kids began playing Tarzan on the electric cables. Then the loudspeakers crackled into life so suddenly that three kids fell off with fright. The loudspeakers, in a jolly gymkhana voice, asked people not to put their children up trees, as any sudden loud noise could make them fall.

Gymkhana welcomed all visitors on behalf of the Sealed Knot. And of course our good friends the Roundhead Association. Would visitors kindly *not* put their children up trees? (Two more had just fallen out.) Would visitors not let their children stray under the boundary ropes, as cannon are *rather* dangerous? Lady visitors are warned that cannon make a *loud* noise.

An ice-cream van arrived, and soon the stricken field was knee deep in Puritan-Maid ice-cream wrappers. It began to feel like a fun-fair. Except to our pikemen, who were tightening each other's buckles and pulling up their own boots in a compulsive twitch.

Bet there weren't any spectators eating ice cream at the real Battle of Naseby. No, on second thought, and knowing the nature of the human race, there probably were people licking ice lollies at Naseby, while enjoying the sight of real human blood.

The Roundhead Army rose above the gorse bushes in one dramatic movement. Horses, guns, a forest of banners. It would have made a great movie shot, but for the factory chimney behind, proclaiming *Ice-Star Frozen Foods*.

There seemed a lot more of them than us.

All the bishops began praying and exhorting at once, so you couldn't hear a thing they said. Gymkhana-voice told the crowd the bishops were praying and exhorting.

The Roundheads looked bigger and nastier close-to. They had guys exhorting, too, only in tall black hats. You couldn't make out what they said, either.

Then a big silence. Except for a girl on our side. She wasn't a camp follower; she hadn't got a cleavage. She had a lute and she sang about "The King shall enjoy his own again." I may be a soft sod, but she had me in tears, because she made it all real: the doomed king, and all the poor buggers who had died in vain at Naseby and Marston Moor, Edgehill and Worcester.

Then the Gunner blew on his little glowing cord, and put it to his touchhole, and the cannon jumped three yards back and made a bang like the clappers, and showered the Roundhead Army with charred and burning paper, and all the ladies in the crowd screamed with delight. We were off.

Our musketeer blazed away, in between showing little kids the lovely engraving on his musket. Our pretty fencing masters chummed up with Roundhead fencing masters and wowed the girls all up and down the touchline, stamping and pirouetting. Camp followers wandered about giggling, getting in everybody's way. Odd pikemen poked at each other feebly across the thorn-filled ditch. We blew paper over a Roundhead gun and they blew paper over us. I think we made their gunner sneeze once. It was all as real as a three-pound note.

All the action was in the middle. A gap of thirty yards had been left in the thorn ditch. We had enough pikemen to hold the gap, but the Roundheads had five times as many. They were queueing up to have a go at our lot. I watched the Midland Company have a go, charging from a hundred yards back, lowering twelve-foot pikes as they came. Terrifying sight; but at the very last moment, when you expected the point of a pike to emerge from somebody's backbone, they raised pikes again, and began battering away, using them as quarterstaffs. It made a noise like a mile-wide carpenter's shop.

The Midlanders were good; but we just managed to throw them back into the ditch. Except three of them who got cut off. Our lads used *them* as trampolines, and after that they seemed content to lie still. Everybody enjoyed that bit.

It seemed as though the battle could go on forever. Referees kept galloping about, telling people at random that they were dead. After a lot of argument, the dead would lie down. But as soon as the ref turned his back, they would start wriggling surreptitiously toward the nearest bush or long grass, from which they would suddenly leap reborn. After an hour, I counted four corpses, not counting those who'd been trampolined.

But our pikemen were tiring. After every punch-up, there were more of them lying down, or showing each other their grazed knuckles.

Came a time when our lot couldn't throw them back;

till some bright lad set fire to the thorns in the ditch. That moved Cromwell's little mates, one with his backside well alight.

But setting light to the thorns was a mistake in the long run, because once the thorns were burned, Roundheads started leaping the ditch all over the place. Guess who made for us, bawling their disgusting hymns and literally slavering at the mouth? Two of them heaved the cannon over. Another got the Gunner with his back to a tree, and a pike across his neck, screwing him till he was half-strangled and shouting crap like "Yield, malignant cur, to the authority of the Parliament!"

Another looked at me, weighing up his chances. But I'm thirteen stone, and yielding's not my bag. He changed his mind.

There was a lot of carrying-about of camp followers, who were screaming their heads off and having a ball. All except one; the girl who had sung about the King. As a guy carried her past, I heard her say, "Please put me down! *Please!*"

He had his great hairy arms tight across her breasts. He was really hurting her, and loving it. She dropped her lute, and the cluddering brute put his foot right through it.

I removed his helmet and hit him on the ear.

He put her down and looked round to see what hit him.

I caught him smack on the nose; it made a *lovely* mess. He was a big kid; meaty slabs of yobbo muscle. But he wasn't very bright or fast; reckon I could have taken him—if about fifty Roundheads and Cavaliers, suddenly ardent for peace, hadn't thrust between us, grabbing every possible part of our respective anatomies. When the

Brummie saw there was no possible danger of the fight continuing, he struggled with his captors very dramatically.

"Oi'll see yow again!"

"Any time, mate," I said. "Any time."

The old ref came galloping up, purple round the gills. "You were *fighting*!" he roared. A horrible silence fell.

"It's a battle," I said.

"We never fight in battles," he said. "It's not *cricket*."

"If I'd known we were playing cricket, I'd have brought my bat."

"Where's your membership card?"

"Haven't got one. He invited me." I pointed at the Gunner.

The ref told the Gunner his membership would be reviewed. Looking at the Gunner's face, I reckoned having your membership reviewed was not a pleasant experience. I pointed out it wasn't the Gunner's fault. But the ref just started waving his hand in my face and shouting, "Get away, get away," with monotonous regularity, ears shut like watertight doors. There didn't seem much else to do.

I looked for the girl, but she'd gone. Her lute lay in pieces on the grass. I picked up the bits in my floppy hat, and shoved the lot in my top-box. Maybe I'd meet the girl again.

I put on my jacket and helmet and kicked the Cub over. The Sealed Knot and the Roundhead Association had formed up into one mass in the middle of the field, now apparently the best of friends. Then all the little play-actors formed one great big line, preparatory to charging the spectators as a Grand Finale. Big thrill for the ladies.

I had different plans.

As they started their charge, I gave the Cub all she'd got. Front wheel shot a foot into the air. Then I shot across the front of them, spraying mud like I was scrambling, and riding one-handed so I could hold up the two fingers of scorn at the whole flaming lot.

I saw the ref; I think he was having a fit. The rest scattered like wet hens.

Reckon twenty kids on scrambler bikes could've won the Battle of Marston Moor. 'Specially if they had machine guns on their handlebars. . . .

4

Can't really explain what happened next. Except whenever I get in a fight, I feel all confused afterward. It's the only time I do stupid things. If I ever mangle the Cub, it'll be after a fight. I even know I'm being stupid, but I can't stop myself.

Anyway, as I turned off the battlefield, I *did* remember to look left. Besides a totally empty road, I saw a beautiful sight. North, over Norfolk, cumulonimbus was building. High perfect anvil shapes, creamy in sunlight. I was so lost in admiration that it was a minute before I remembered that cumulonimbus are thunderclouds. That shook me. Riding in a thunderstorm's like barebacking a polar bear across pack ice.

Maybe it wasn't coming my way. Wind at ground level hardly stirred the leaves. But overhead the wind was moving south; little smoky clouds fled before the big anvils. I somehow knew the storm was coming for me.

At the same time I had the crazy conviction that if I could only reach Clacton, I'd be OK. When I was a kid, safe with Mum, Dad and rubber ring, the sun was always shining in Clacton. Could I outrun the anvils?

I couldn't find a main road going the right way. Suffolk lanes are great for dawdling, but hell in a hurry. Take one heading east and before you know it you're traveling north. Every crossroad has six ways out, and signposts, if any, carry names the RAC never heard of. Next signpost carries totally different names.

Twice I broke eastward, down lanes I *knew* were too narrow. Both ended in farmyards. Once I backed the Cub up to its axles in liquid cow dung. Had words with a farmer, who made out like I was stealing his best manure.

My sensible half kept saying get your mapbook out of the pannier, you silly berk. But there wasn't *time*, with the anvils growing and heading straight at me. Kept on hoping the road system—or Lady Chance—would give me a break.

They didn't. And every time I pulled up to try and think, the air moved like a warm soggy blanket against my face. I was sweating like a pig, and sweating makes me panic. I could see beautiful dark curving scarves below the cumulus now. Rain, torrents, washouts.

I stopped looking for Clacton and started looking for shelter. Passed the odd cottage, but didn't fancy knocking on doors. Everyone thinks motorcyclists are yobs. By the time I'd convinced some old dear I wasn't from Mars, I'd be soaked anyway.

God, this was a lonely stretch. Passed a church, but it was roofless. Passed a water tower alone on a hill, without a house in sight. But it stood on stilts, and the rain would blow underneath. Then, zooming despairingly down the side of a hill, I saw a roof below. Red pantiles; looked like a house. Then the roadside hedge hid it.

Looked ahead down the road, expecting it to reappear any moment. It didn't. Mustn't be *on* the road. I was riding past it.

Saw the turnoff just in time. Narrow. Unused. Thought it was only a field gate. But it had once been a road of sorts. Decayed to a pair of footpaths, a car-width apart. Dark hawthorn hedges closed in from each side, slashing at my face like swordsmen. Cow-parsley sprouted head high in the middle.

The twin paths grew fainter, just a zigzagging of shadow ahead. At times they vanished and it was like riding a meadow fit for reaping.

Reap I did. Cow-parsley cut at my visor, leaving splashes of trickling green blood. Plants twanged my spokes like harps. Laden grass heads and dandelion clocks exploded and swept past like smoke.

The hawthorns, whanging my helmet, forced me flat on my petrol tank. Handlebars jerked left, left, right, left under my hands like they were alive and fighting to be free. Suppose some farmer had left a bloody great stone lying . . . . My saddle gave me a boot up the backside, and I knew some bloody farmer had. My engine was roaring like a mad thing, even though I'd changed down to first. Maybe the long grass was winding itself round and round my wheels. Maybe I'd end up going arse over tip in a great big grass cocoon, and nobody would ever find my body. But I had to keep going. The shadow of the anvils reared over my shoulder and lay heavy on the path ahead. Hurry, hurry. I was desperate for shelter.

Then I was through, and idling up to the building. It wasn't a house, but an old barn. Why had I been so sure it was a house? I couldn't remember. But there were the barn doors, twelve feet high to take the old haywains. One was half-open, and dark straw inside. I pulled the open door wide, backed the Cub half-in, and cut the engine. My panic was gone. I'd beaten the storm and now I wanted to enjoy it. Since I was a kid I've loved big bangs.

The first big dark shillings of rain; the bitter-sweet smell as they hit summer dust . . . .

By God, this was a funny storm. Bright blue sky to

the left; bright blue sky to the right. Even bright blue sky behind, only looking all dim and dirty through the sheets of rain. It was as if the storm was aimed just at me. Well, hard luck, storm. I was safe and dry.

The valley was dotted with lines of trees, as far as the eye could see. Now the rain-scarves were swallowing them into invisibility, one by one. Nearer and nearer. Leaves and bits of straw flicked across the dust of the barnyard as the storm wind came. Thunder rumbling, like the MGM lion.

Wham! The whole scene turned electric blue, with trees etched white, like the negative of a photograph. Then blackness and the smell of ozone and burning, and an insanity of thunder.

Wham! A tree not fifty yards away burst into crashing smoking ruin. I suddenly realized I was sitting on the biggest mass of lightning-conducting metal for miles around. And a gallon of petrol. I was just swinging my leg over the Cub when:

Wham! I thought in the dark that followed that the whole world was falling on me.

Silence. Then a thin wail of fear in the barn behind, and the sound of blows, like someone chopping wood.

I blundered into the barn. It wasn't quite dark. There was a flicker of flame over the far side. The lightning must have set the barn on fire. And there was a guy in there going mad, flailing around with something like a long billhook. Firelight flashed on its steel blade. Was he trying to beat out the flames? But he was nowhere near the flames. He was hitting out blindly at the floor, the walls and the low rafters of the roof. As I watched, he struck a beam, and a star of raw white wood blossomed under his blade, shaped roughly like a letter T.

God, I was fastened up with a maniac ax-murderer or something!

Then I noticed his clothes. Bare arms, leather jerkin, square-toed knee-boots.

One of the sodding Midland Company. Vandalizing the place. Typical skinhead. I felt better. Haven't got much experience of ax-maniacs, but I know how to deal with a vandalizing skin.

I gently banged my gauntleted fists together, and waited for him to spot me. Maybe it was the yob who'd said he'd see me again.

But he didn't notice me; just went on dancing his lunatic dance, beating hell out of walls and beams.

Then, as my eyes got used to the semidark, I saw his dance wasn't aimless. A small dark furry ball was fleeing from his billhook, round and round the room. It turned at bay in a corner and I saw the glint of green eyes and the pink triangle of an open mouth.

He was trying to kill a kitten; trying to chop it in half.

It was obscene; it made him just not part of the human race.

As he raised his billhook to finish the kitten—and its mouth opened in one last pathetic meow—I roared like a bull. In the same instant, my visor dropped down over my face. My roar echoed and boomed hollowly even to my own ears.

He turned and looked at me. My visor's smoked, which made things pretty dark, but I could still see his face, even if he couldn't see mine. He had long greasy fair hair that looked like it had been cut with a lawn mower, and that glinting gold stubble round his chin that yobs have 'cause they only shave Saturday nights. I braced myself; a guy who'll use a billhook on a cat won't stop when it comes to humans. . . .

But his blue eyes grew as round as saucers. His mouth drooped open and went on drooping; saliva trickled from one corner, and fell to the floor in a long glistening filament, like a spider's web. Then he dropped the billhook, and began shaking all over.

What was the matter with the guy? I know I'm big, and I was feeling nasty. But he was just as big and nasty, and I was handicapped by my helmet. He had a chance to take me. . . .

But when I moved in, he didn't put up his mitts, or even try to run away. Just backed into the corner, holding himself up with his hands against the wall, babbling something like "Eleazar. Beelzebub." Then he made a funny little sign with one hand in the air.

I hit him a clout in the gut that had in it all I felt about the Midland Company. My fist sunk in to the wrist; he gave a great whoosh and collapsed on the straw. I stirred him with my foot, but he was out cold. I felt pretty disappointed.

Then I thought: My God, where are the rest of them? They work together, eat together, drink together, do everything together. I whirled and looked toward the door.

The door seemed smaller; too small for a barn door. But I didn't brood on that for long. Because the Cub was gone. The bastards; nicking my bike while I was beating up their mate. Typical skin. Where had they taken it? What were they doing to it? The top-box wasn't locked. They'd have all my gear out, kicking it around. Or setting fire to the bike by dropping burning paper down the petrol tank.

I ran for the door. There *was* another of them standing in the doorway. I could see the light glinting on his Roundhead helmet, his big thigh-boots. Breastplate all rusty; pistol in his hand. That wouldn't save him; not if he'd laid one finger on the Cub.

I ran at him. He raised the pistol. All I could see was his open shouting mouth and the big black round hole in the end of the pistol pointing straight at my face, and his fingers tightening on the trigger. If that goes off, I thought, it could burn my eyes out. . . .

There was a blinding flash. Something tightened around my throat, nearly throttling me. But I had my hands on him. I could feel the wires of his helmet's face guard bending under my fingers. Still blind, I banged head and helmet against the wall. I could feel his head rattling round inside the helmet like a pea in a pod. Then he went limp. I dropped him and staggered outside.

A cooling breeze wafted round my ears. Funny, I was supposed to be wearing a skid-lid. But I was really scared about my eyes. They seemed full of sand. I couldn't bear to open them. If there were any more skins, and they came at me now. . . .

I listened. No footsteps. No sound but water dripping from the roof of the barn. Sunlight came warm onto my face. The storm had passed.

The first thing I saw through my tears, when I finally got my eyes open, was the Cub. In the barn doorway, just where I'd left it. Funny. . . .

But I was too glad to think much. I had the Cub back, and I hadn't gone blind, though my eyes went on watering like hell.

I rubbed my throat where it hurt, and found a rucked band of fabric that hadn't been there before. A band with bits of yellow polycarbonate still attached, like a row of shark's teeth.

It took me a minute to realize it was the remains of my skid-lid. A skid-lid that had cost me forty quid, that was the best there was, that should have withstood the impact of my head hitting the road at fifty miles an hour. . . .

Then I realized the helmet had saved my life. That pistol must have been fully loaded, with a musket ball. Those Midland sods must be crazy—they would certainly pay for a new helmet.

But where *were* they? The guy I'd left unconscious in the doorway—he'd gone. Must have crawled inside to join his rotten mate. What were they getting up to now?

I wasn't going inside to find out. They were probably waiting for me. Two against one in the dark. I wasn't *that* green. Especially as my head was aching fit to burst. I realized I wasn't in very good nick. But they couldn't be, either, or they'd have come out and taken me by now.

So I waited, sitting on an old water trough. Waited a long time. When I felt a bit better, I shouted the rudest things you can shout at skins.

No effect.

The sun began to set. The eaves of the barn stopped dripping. The birds began to sing. It was so peaceful it felt nuts.

Had I killed the pair of them? That's what they'd be *wanting* me to think, so they could clobber me from behind the barn door.

At last I heard straw rustling inside. Help me, Mother, I thought, because when I got up off the water trough, my legs nearly gave way.

But it was only the gray-black kitten. She looked like a dusty Afro wig, with two bright and beady eyes stuck at one end. Her coat was staring and full of straw. She sat down in the doorway, blinking at me and the setting sun, and made a lousy attempt to wash her shoulder. From the way she sat, I knew there was nobody else in the barn. The only thing she was worried about was me.

The rotten swine must have sneaked out the back way. Who would pay for a new helmet now?

But when I plunged into the barn, there was no back way out. Only a ladder up to a loft full of straw, and they weren't up there either, though climbing the ladder gave me a nasty moment. All the windows were boarded up, and thick with cobwebs. I started looking for a trapdoor or secret passage; I was that far gone. There wasn't one, anyway.

Then I started noticing other funny things. No smell of burning; no sign of any fire at all. And no sign of the broken bits of my skid-lid, which should have been lying in the doorway. Only the kitten, scurrying away from me into the dark, then peering from some corner, eyes like two pinpoints of light.

I sat down and put my face in my hands, feeling I was going mad. Then I felt the bump on my head. Big as a hen's egg and twice as long. When that pistol ball hit my helmet, it must have knocked me cold. And the skins had sneaked off and left me lying there. Dead, for all they knew. Typical.

And those funny thoughts I'd had about there being a fire. Result of concussion. Does funny things, concussion. Had a kid in our rugger team who collided with somebody's knee at a combined speed of forty miles an hour. We had a hell of a time with him till the doctor came. He'd act normal for a bit, then he'd start walking round talking to his mother when she was two hundred miles away.

I was in a hole. Maybe my skull was fractured, under that bump. Maybe I'd keep on blacking out, from what doctors called intermittent pressure. I was a long way from home and nobody but those skins knew I was here. I might die. . . .

I was just starting to panic when I blacked out.

Looking back now, I can only give a hollow laugh. All I *thought* I had to worry about was a smashed helmet, concussion, and being lost.

If that'd been true, I'd have wakened in a few hours with a bad headache, pushed my bike to the nearest house for help, bought a new skid-lid and been on my way. Forgotten the thing in a month.

What I *should* have been worried about was that Lady Chance had her hook right into me. I'd taken the bait. I might thresh about for a while, trying to escape like an optimistic salmon. I mean, all the salmon feels at first is a pain in its mouth; maybe a dim conviction that he can no longer quite go where he wants to go; do what he wants to do. Something slender but inexplicable keeps getting in his way. He can *nearly* go where he wants to go; *nearly* do what he wants to do. He still thinks he's free, really. Hasn't a clue he's already booked for the fishmonger's slab.

Poor salmon.

5

Someone was bending over me, silhouetted against the light of the door. I flailed wildly, thinking the Midland bastards had come back to get me.

But it was a farmer; I could tell from the jut of his cap and wellies. Soon as he spoke, I knew he was a gentleman farmer.

"You all right?" The abrupt embarrassed tones Englishmen use when they have to speak to each other in a public lavatory. Later, I found he always spoke that way.

"You all right?" he repeated.

"Dunno," I said brightly. Wished he'd go away and let me sleep.

"Hurt yourself on your bike—come off?"

"Yeah," I said. Seemed easiest.

"Much damage—need a doctor?"

"Dunno."

"Better get one—on the safe side—give you a hand—come to my place." He spoke in short bursts, like an experienced machine-gunner. As he heaved me up, I realized he was very strong.

He didn't seem to notice the Cub standing there without a scratch on her. He pushed me onto the front seat of a Land-Rover and slammed the door on my side; right through my head, or so it felt. Then he got in beside me, and slammed the other door right through my head too.

He provoked the engine into life, quarreled bitterly with the three gear levers, and wrestled the steering wheel through a fifteen-point turn. He didn't drive a car; he fought it bare-handed like it was a man-eating tiger. He'd have wrecked anything but a Land-Rover in five minutes.

"Name's Derek Pooley—own all this—must change this car—too big for our needs—stretch out and relax."

I tried. But every rut in the lane banged my head like the guy with the gong in the old J. Arthur Rank movies.

"These gearboxes—not what they were—going to buy a Volvo—you on holiday?"

"Vacation," I said, faintly.

"Student? Did agriculture meself—years ago—just after the War—King's, Durham. What you reckon to Volvos?"

"Good," I said.

"Unpatriotic—buying Volvos I mean—but what can you do? Which university?"

Rather than answer, I passed out again.

The pain brought me back to life. The Arthur Rank guy had abandoned his gong for a pneumatic drill. And a thin dry male voice was saying. "Are you *sure* he crashed his bike, Derek?"

"Quite sure—saw him do it—nasty corner—wet leaves on the road—bike's a write-off." Derek sounded more like a dirty-postcard seller than ever. Why was he covering up the shooting incident? After all, I was the bloody victim, not the criminal.

"Looks like a gunshot graze to me," said the thin dry voice. "Powder burns, even. Bits of plastic—that'd be the helmet, of course. No fracture . . . but a good chance of concussion. Like to have him in hospital a couple of days. And inform the police. There are too many funny goings-on with these motorcycle gangs at weekends."

"Leave that to me—I *am* the senior magistrate—I'll have a word with the Chief Constable."

In other words, shut up and bugger off, Doctor Kildare.

"Very well." The doctor shut his bag with a loud snap of protest.

As the door closed behind him, I opened my eyes and showed an interest.

"Hah—there you are—thought you were coming round —you can come in now, dear." The last in a bull-like bel-low.

A woman came in, younger than Derek, about forty-odd. But I still fancied her. A big timeless lovely who'd always have plenty of everything. Jet-black hair, long, thick and wavy. No hairdresser could've done a thing with it. Tanned gypsy skin that would make make-up look ridiculous. She wore a man's shirt and trousers all the time I knew her, and made them look sexy in a big way. I only once saw her in a dress and it made her look like a caged bird. She made most of the girls I'd known look thin as paper. Earth mother and girl friend all rolled into one lovely big bundle. I'd have cheerfully let her teach me everything I didn't know.

"This is Susan," said Derek. "M'wife."

"Hallo," said Susan. "Better get you into bed."

I almost said "Yes *please*." And it wouldn't have been the concussion talking. Then I realized I was lying on a gracious four-poster, still wearing motorbike boots be-smeared with liquid cow dung.

"No, no—doesn't need bed—best up and keeping his circulation going—couple of aspirin—good meal inside him—right as rain. He'll be wanting to get back to his bike."

"But Derek, he's not fit—"

"Rubbish, woman. Seen a man win—Military Medal—worse wounds than that—mere scratch."

"You're not in the Army now. . . ."

That was the first of their rows I heard. Susan was forceful, outspoken, logical. Derek just knew he was going to get his way in the end. I lay there, like a court at Wimbledon, with two old pros knocking-up across me. Fascinating, because they were obviously so very much in love as well. For oldies, anyway.

But enough was enough, with a headache like mine. "I'll just take two aspirins and go," I said, when I'd found the courage to stand. "Better see to my bike. What's left of it, *after the crash.*"

Derek laughed unashamedly. "Didn't think you were the sort of chap—who would want the police involved."

They gave me a lot more than two aspirins. A dreamy dinner—soup and fish and chicken, all mucked-about with wine and spices so you couldn't tell half the time what you were eating. Then a few glasses of Benedictine, which had a kick like an international fullback.

A dreamlike dinner, too, because Derek kept talking about my crash; daring me to contradict him in front of Susan. He almost had *me* believing I'd crashed the Cub—after the third Benedictine. What the hell was he up to, lying to the doctor, lying to his wife? Even willing to lie to the police, and him a senior magistrate. Why was he covering up for the Midland yobbos? Did he know them?

"How did you come to find me at the barn?" I asked. "Seems a lonely place. . . ."

"Heard a shot down that way," said Derek. "Thought it might be poachers."

"Barn?" asked Susan, puzzled.

"Better be getting along, young man—gettin' dark," said Derek.

I was too sloshed to argue.

He drove me back to the barn. The air was soft and gentle. Rooks circled against the last of the sunset. Everything smelled fresh after the thunderstorm. Peaceful. A little stream gurgled close by. *Stay away*, everything seemed to say, *Sleep, sleep. Be easy*. I yawned deeply. Derek propped me against the barn wall.

"Not traveling on tonight—are you? Wouldn't advise it—get a good kip—right as rain in the mornnig. I'll get your sleeping bag—plenty of straw—make you as snug as a bug in a rug."

How the hell did he know I had a sleeping bag? I knew it was no good asking him—he'd just laugh. Derek's laugh was as impenetrable as armor plate.

His hands were deft and gentle, as he made a rough mattress of straw and arranged my spare pullovers as a pillow. Was he a pouf, geting ready to take advantage of my drunken state? No, he wasn't a pouf. Girl like Susan wouldn't stay married to a pouf. Besides, I wasn't the type. Poufs like pretty-boys and I was as ugly as sin. I giggled at the thought, then the sound of my own daft giggling startled me into silence.

To be replaced by rage. If he cared so much for my welfare, why wouldn't he let me sleep in his house, in a proper bed? Wasn't I good enough? Putting me to bed in a barn, like I was some old tramp! Who did he think he *was*?

But the rage faded into the soft country silence, like the giggle before it.

Yet I knew Derek was using me for *some* purpose. . . .

He straightened up. "There—all shipshape." He came

toward me. Now I would find out what he wanted to use me for.

"Good night," he said, with abrupt embarrassment. "I think you'll manage now."

I watched the lights of the Land-Rover twinkle down the lane, then crawled into my pit.

Something was climbing on me; using me as Mount Everest. Something very small and cautious. It gained the crest of my hip, ventured carefully down into the South Col of my waist, then traversed onto my shoulder.

A little cool breeze sighed in my ear, then a pinpoint of cold and wet thrust into my ear hole. Something tickled gently on my cheek.

Rats! All barns had rats! People got bitten as they slept! Rat bites turned septic!

I sat up with a screech. The small thing fled, a series of tiny rustles in the straw. Then, from far distant, a tiny defiant meow.

I stopped having a fit. I'm a sucker for cats.

6

A church bell wakened me, tolling down the valley. Sunday. My watch had stopped. Narking. It was supposed to be self-winding. What service was the bell tolling for? Evensong, for all I knew.

Or cared. I lay a long time, watching blue sky through holes in the roof. Flies dancing in dusty shafts of sunlight. I felt great, so long as I didn't move.

No reason to move. Nothing to do; nowhere to go; no one to see. Well, there was one place I had to go, but the nearest hedge took care of that. On the way back, I got thick-sliced white and corned beef out of my pannier. Had breakfast in bed.

I was just starting to snooze again when I felt a pair of eyes boring into the back of my skull. The kitten, peering out of shadow at the far end of the barn, nose twitching up and down dramatically, in the general direction of the corned beef on my knee.

Threw her a bit. She mistook it for a stone, and fled. She ran fast, but with a rocking-horse motion. There was something wrong with her legs. She was a mess altogether; dark gray coat full of tats, like the sheep's wool you find on barbed wire. Too young to wash herself and no mother to wash her.

We spent half an hour failing to make a relationship. I flung her smaller and smaller lumps of corned beef.

That only baffled her. She couldn't tell if they were stones (reckon she'd had lots of stones thrown at her in her young life) or mice rustling among the straw. Her ears splayed every way; her eyes were never still. She went round and round me in a series of dashes till I felt like a covered wagon being attacked by redskins.

Dizzy, I lay back, watching her through half-closed eyes. She relaxed and sought out the farthest-flung piece of corned beef.

I faked a snore. She knew what snores meant. Began to work from piece to piece of the beef, carrying each to a patch of clear ground to eat it. Very thorough, searching the ground for dropped crumbs afterward. She worked nearer and nearer me, while I faked snores better than Laurence Olivier. She found every piece I'd chucked. Ten in all. I'd counted them.

Then she threw back her head and sniffed again; bit like a wolf baying to the moon. She located the empty tin, lying two feet from my face. Stalked it cautiously, wiggling her backside before every move, putting down paws like velvet and pausing to throw keen assessing glances at my face. It was hard to keep snoring; hard not to burst out laughing. But it was deadly serious for her; the old drama of food, flight and death. She'd known some very cruel people.

I'd have her in a minute. The moment she poked her head inside that tin . . . .

But she was too smart. Turning her head delicately sideways, she took the tin by its key, between her teeth. Dragged the whole thing back several yards, her eyes never leaving my face. Only then did she shove her head inside for a good lick, her tongue rasping the metal. God, what an appetite. Nearly seventy pence of Fray Bentos' best, and I could have stuffed her inside the empty tin! I've known women cheaper to feed!

I decided it was time she paid for her breakfast. Waited till her head was well inside the tin—ears laid delicately back—and dived for her. By the time my hands closed round the tin she was at the far end of the barn and coming back for seconds. That narked me. I don't like being made a fool of by something no bigger than my fist. I went after her in earnest.

I might have spared the effort. She could turn at right angles, and knew just when to turn. She knew the straw, too. Where it was thick and where thin; where she could streak through and where she had to jump over. Worse, her dark gray fur absorbed the light. Later, when I tried to photograph her, she always came out blurred, though the stool she was sitting on was in perfect focus. She could sit in a cupful of shadow and be invisible—till you saw the glint of her eyes, watching, watching.

After ten minutes I gave up, puffed. After her experience with the bloke with the billhook yesterday, I wasn't doing our relationship much good. Besides, I didn't want her throwing up seventy pence' worth of good Fray Bentos. Can't stand waste.

The moment she heard the Land-Rover grinding up the hill, she vanished.

"Hah—you're awake," said Derek. Ever a master of the obvious. "Brought you—spot of breakfast." He opened an elaborate picnic basket and poured coffee. "Hope you take sugar—Susan made sandwiches—chicken—chicken-stuff, anway—survived the night then?"

I almost said no, I'd become one of the Walking Dead. But Derek wouldn't have seen it was a joke.

"Have a sandwich—take four—save my arm. Plenty

more—reach up when you're ready." He made it sound like an order.

We munched in a silence that Derek clearly found uncomfortable. He kept shifting his bottom on the log he was sitting on. Kept staring at the corners of the barn like he'd never seen it before.

"Going to pot—this place—must get it seen to. Wouldn't like a job, would you? Keeping an eye on things—sort of caretaker?"

"Doing exactly what?" I couldn't believe my ears.

"Oh, this and that. Tidy up—make it shipshape." It must have sounded pretty thin, even to him, for he added, "Get vandals round here at weekends—might set fire to the place—motorbike gangs—bad lot—present company excepted, of course. Very attached to this place— been in my family donkey's years—can't pay you much, I'm afraid—twenty quid a week?"

I studied him carefully. He didn't *look* insane. Solid, sensible, backbone of Old England. Bristling red hair and mustache, ruddy face. Pale blue eyes; soldier's eyes: mixing a sort of innocent violence with very real embarrassed kindness. He looked as straight as a die, yet guilty—like the Head Boy caught with the gym mistress.

"Thank you very much," I said politely, "but I think I'll be moving on. I was heading for Clacton."

"You can't go—without a crash helmet." He said it almost triumphantly.

"I'll have to buy a new one."

"Won't get one—this side of Sudbury—fifteen miles— no bus service."

"I'll hitchhike."

"Wouldn't advise it—not today—anyway it's Sunday. Tell you what—my boy used to ride motorbikes—prob-

38

ably there's an old helmet round the house—come down for a bath and a meal—no, no, can't do that—tell you what—I'll fetch it up here."

I couldn't help smiling. He didn't even want Susan to know he was giving me a crash helmet. But I never knew a worse liar. It didn't come naturally to him.

"Don't you want to know what happened to my old crash helmet?"

"Yes—if you like—haven't got long, though."

I told him about the fight, as we walked back to his Land-Rover. He didn't really want to know; or maybe he knew already. He tapped his fingers on the wing of the car and stared across the valley.

When I'd finished, or rather trailed off in despair, he said triumphantly, "Ruffians—trying to set the place on fire—see what I mean?—that's why I need a caretaker—finish up those sandwiches—build up your strength—see you later." Then he roared down the track like Kojak after the Boston Strangler.

Oh well, I thought, can't be bad. A day's doss, good nosh, and a free helmet, even if it was the old chinless type.

If I'd known then what I know now, I'd have *pushed* the Cub all the way to Sudbury.

7

I spent a couple of hours cleaning the Cub. What a mess.
The liquid manure from that farmyard had dried solid;
had to wet the wheels with water from the stream and
scrape them clean with a stick. Never use a knife near
chrome! Rest of the bike was all green gunge from my
ride up the track. There was dead drooping cow-parsley
under the mudguards and top-box. Talk about Birnam
Wood!

When I tried the engine, the timing was a mite out;
saw to that and tightened my chain. Chain was full of
grass seeds, so I washed it with Gunk and re-oiled it.

Then I tried to clean myself up. Cold water from the
stream didn't give the soap much help. If I stayed here
much longer I'd be in crap-order. Caretaker, indeed!

All this time I'd been watched by a certain party. She'd
fled the first six times I started the bike engine, but she
was soon back in the barn door, making her lousy attempts to wash. We were well-matched, a right scruffy
pair.

By the time the church clock down the valley struck
three, I was ready for the road and feeling peckish. Sat
on my saddle finishing off Susan's chicken-stuff sandwiches and flicking bits for the kitten. Got her to come
within three feet of me, but she always retired to eat.
Still, she obviously knew her rights. If I was a bit slow
throwing her a bit, I got that silent meow. I knew I'd get

her in the end, because she was so eternally hungry. God knows what she'd lived on till I came. Beetles; she was too small to catch mice.

The clock chimed four. I suddenly knew I was going to spend another night in this hole. A kind of cosy despair settles over you on hot afternoons in Suffolk. The blue distances swaddle you like a blanket. You feel nothing is ever going to happen again. Might as well explore the place.

It was old. The red pantiles had bent the rafters, so the roof sagged in a series of gentle loops. There were ferns growing on the gable ends, where the guttering had cracked and fallen, leaving dark wet stains down the walls.

The walls were huge blocks of dark red sandstone. Unusual. Any stone in Suffolk is buried under a hundred feet of clay. This stone had come from a long way off. In horses and carts. Expensive way of building a mere barn. . . .

I touched the worn stone with my hand, and it crumbled away like sugar icing. How many years of rain and sun and frost . . . ? In places, forests of lichen crawled over it; mostly pale green stuff, but some outbreaks of orange, and brown bits with long dark hairs sticking out and bobbles on the ends. Still, crumbling as they were, the walls were all of two feet thick.

There were three doors. The one on the left led into an old milking parlor, with rusty chains to tether the cows still swinging from worm-eaten stalls. The floor was cobbles. Funny thing, that floor. In dry weather it just smelled dusty; but in wet weather, ghostly smells of cow dung and spilled milk came up from it. Above, through cracks in the wooden ceiling, I could see the hayloft where I'd searched for those yobbos yesterday.

Then came the main barn doors, and the main barn, two stories high, up to the bare rafters of the roof. Not much in there, except a huge pile of logs against the right-hand wall. And a huge harness board nailed to the back wall. Long square handmade nails, and bits of leather and chain still hanging from them. The leather was hard as iron, and the chains were thick with a soft grainy rust that added red stains to my already black hands.

The third door was up an outside staircase of stone. It was pointed at the top, like a church door. Cripes, that would make it twelfth-century. . . . No, daft. Plenty of Victorian landlords faked Gothic doorways. This door was locked, but the padlock was new and oiled. Been used recently.

What intrigued me more was that, long ago, someone had gouged a pattern in the stone beside the door. I rubbed away the lichen, and saw a big cross and

It wasn't a mason's mark—too complicated. Besides, mason's marks are small and neat, because masons are always proud of what they've done, but modest about it.

This had been gouged out by some lunatic; deep and savage as wounds. Scored wildly into the stone, like somebody had hated the owner of the house but couldn't get in to get at them. Wild, jagged; you could see where the tool had slipped.

And there it was again, above the door, and on the other side of the door. Crosses and

Some had been carved right across others. Some were newer than others. Even though wind and rain had softened them, it was nastier than the worst graffiti in a public lavatory.

"Eeurgh!" I said, and shook myself. But I copied it down with a stub of pencil on a piece of paper.

As I turned away, I startled the kitten. She was sitting halfway down the outside stair. She slipped sideways through a slit in the wall and vanished. I examined the slit; long and narrow like an arrow-slit. But that doesn't mean a thing—all barns have slits like that for ventilation. I peered into the slit and got an eyeful of draft and dark. This would be the ground-floor room, below the room with the pointed door. But how did you get into it? I walked round the side, I walked round the back. No door into the ground-floor room—just more narrow slits.

Must be a door. From inside the main barn? I was immediately faced by the mountain of logs. Well, I wasn't moving logs on a hot afternoon like this. Stuff the kitten; she'd come out when she was hungry.

It was then that I remembered the Midland yobbo of yesterday. Flailing around with that billhook, leaving that great white wound in the beam, shaped like a T. Where was it, now? Should be about *here*.

My hands groped in the semidarkness. Felt a deep gouge in the wood. A T-shaped gouge. Deep, rough—but not fresh and white. As dark as the rest of the beam; dark with the soot and grime of a hundred winters. Unless the yobbo had rubbed muck into the scar, to hide what he'd done . . . .

Bu that didn't make sense. Why bother to hide a scar, while I was lying there, at death's door, for all he knew? Or getting ready to jump up and belt him, or call the police?

It made no more sense than his gathering up the bits of my broken skid-lid. No more sense than there being a fire, and then no trace of any fire.

Cripes, I was *going*. To Clacton and candy-floss and birds wearing *Kiss-Me-Quick* hats who were just looking for a ride on a motorbike and a roll in the hay. I was *going*, skid-lid or not. Not many panda cars round here, and if one caught me they'd probably let me off with a warning.

I heard the Land-Rover grinding up the hill. Well, I'd tell Derek and tell him *straight*.

He got out, grinning. "Found you that helmet." He reached inside. I waited for some old Kangol, without even a visor. Instead, he pulled out a brand-new AGV AGO. He'd rubbed some crap on it, but the stupid berk hadn't even taken the wrapping off properly. There was still a bit of polythene sellotaped on the back. It had a smoked visor and all. Forty quid's worth.

"Your son's, is it?" I asked innocently.

"Yes—he hasn't used it—five years—in the Hong Kong police—doing well—Chief Inspector."

"It may interest you to know," I said, "that that helmet wasn't being made five years ago—or even three. It's bloody brand new."

He stared at the far side of the valley. "Tried to find the old one—couldn't—promised you something—there it is."

"I can't take *this*!"

"Take it or leave it—it's no use to me."

"You must be *mad*, spending forty quid on a total stranger."

He tossed the helmet down, like it hadn't cost two pence. It rolled along the cobbles, making a hollow noise. You shouldn't treat helmets like that.

I picked it up. A sudden thought struck me. "Hey—those yobs I had the fight with—they weren't friends of yours?"

He looked me full in the face. "I never saw them before in my life." I knew he was telling the truth for once, and glad to be doing so.

"Well, why did you buy me the helmet? You don't owe me anything."

"It happened on *my* land—that makes me responsible."

"Why? If somebody picks my pocket on King's Cross Station, that doesn't make BR responsible."

"Doesn't it? Maybe they should police their stations better—as I should police my land better."

I just gaped.

"We've held this land five hundred years. If you'd poached—my grandfather would've had you transported. *His* grandfather would've hanged you and no comeback. . . ."

He was standing, legs astride, hands on hips. Built like a tank. His sport coat bulged every button. Not with fat, but a kind of brute authority. Like Henry VIII in his portraits.

Then he stared away and said, "Please take the helmet—I feel an obligation. Pay me back with work if you like—seeing to the barn. Need more young people around here—valley's half-empty—all weekend cottages—Londoners."

I thought I saw it all. Must be rough having your son away for five years, halfway round the world. Probably all his kids had left home and he missed them. What those eggheads at U.C. would call the "empty-nest syndrome."

Ah well, I thought, what the hell? Two weeks' work would pay for the helmet, and I'd got three months vacation. Only I'd have to watch it. These wealthy middle-aged couples whose kids have gone—they try to take you over. My landlady in London's a bit like that.

"I'll stay," I said.

I like being spoiled; in moderation.

He banged me on the back. "Good lad—must find you —better place to kip—upstairs." He led the way up the outside staircase, produced a bunch of fifty keys. The ninth one he tried was right. I kept staring at those scratches round the door.

"Much snugger—in here. Sleep better, off the ground. Use the barn—for cooking. Can't bear sleeping—with cooking smells."

"Isn't the barn dangerous for cooking? All that straw?"

"Clear it out—dump it. Your first job. Second job—clear this room out."

It couldn't have looked less scary. Drums of diesel fuel, standing in their own oily rings; radiator of a Fordson tractor, circa 1940; long nesting boxes for chickens, the sort you push round on little wheels; and, in one corner, a huge contraption with a cast-iron wheel on the side and a big wooden funnel on top. I instantly christened it the mangel-wurzeler.

"Be all right in here," said Derek.

I stared at some holes in the roof.

"Get a fellow over—fix those—needed seeing to for ages."

"What's in the room below this?" I asked. "It doesn't seem to have a door."

"Course it's got a door—bound to have a door." But the pale blue eyes had swiveled away to the horizon again.

"The cat goes in there—through that slit on the stairs."

"Cat? It bothering you? We've got too many damn cats —buy two to keep the rats down—soon got more cats than rats. Want me to shoot it for you?"

I thought of the pathetic bundle of fluff and shuddered. "No, no, I like it. Good company."

"That's all right then—must go—milking time."

The Land-Rover was halfway down the track before I realized he hadn't answered my question about the downstairs room.

In the middle of the night, something small and purring used me as Mount Everest again. Purred so close to my ear it sounded like thunder. Then it walked round and round on my neck and ear like it was trampling out a nest for itself. Finally, it settled, pounding my neck with velvet paws full of needles. Then a small mouth began sucking the lobe of my ear.

I had finally convinced her I was her mum.

My last thought, on the fringe of sleep, was how the hell she'd got in. I was in the upstairs room and the door was shut.

I called her, and she came leaping across the barnyard and into my arms, where I sat on the outside staircase. I gave her her breakfast; corned beef and bread-and-jam. She was partial to jam, especially apricot. I studied her as she ate.

After a week she looked surprisingly bigger. But no fatter. She'd eaten me out of house and home, but her shoulder bones still stuck through her skin like sharp bits of plastic. I'd tried combing her coat, but it was such poor stuff I was frightened of combing her bald. Her breath stank, and the third membrane was still up across her eyes; the triangular translucent skin that means poor health in a cat.

I watched her guiltily as she finished the last smear of jam on her plate. Today I was going to abandon her. I felt terrible because she loved me; followed me everywhere.

But I'd had enough of Vaser's Barn. Oh, Derek and Susan couldn't have been nicer; had me down for dinner twice. Susan was always popping over with a pie, or offering me more baths than I cared to take. She was nice to talk to, though she was always wanting to know about my girl friends. But I had a feeling Derek didn't like Susan and me talking too much; or my going down to their house too much. He had this obsession I should

48

always be at the barn. He'd started referring to it as "your place."

It wasn't my place; it was his place.

And there was nothing to *do*. I'd chucked the oil drums and hen coops out of the top room on the first morning. They made the barnyard look a right tip. He'd had me shoving straw round the barn proper, to no purpose whatever. Every morning he'd breeze up in the Land-Rover and storm about the place, moving this and that, tying bits of rope round gates, kicking the odd brick bad-temperedly. Trying to invent jobs for me to do.

There weren't any.

Only the cat made it bearable; riding my shoulder like Long John Silver's parrot; rubbing her cheek against mine at every opportunity. But you couldn't center your life on a cat. Besides, it was the weekend again. Those Midland yobbos might come back with a few mates.

But what could I do with the cat? If I just left her, she'd starve. Her nearest food supply was Derek's, quarter of a mile away, and he'd probably shoot her.

The RSPCA looked after stray kittens; you could contact them through a vet. The nearest vet was in Besing-tree, three miles away. I'd looked him up in the phone book.

How did I get her there? In my top-box she'd be in the dark, and tossed around at every corner; probably throw up—and smells linger in top-boxes. All I could do was pop her down my bike jacket.

She wormed down near my navel, purring like a nut-case. Then developed a fit of galloping claustrophobia and took a lot of skin off my ribs before she settled, like a baby kangaroo, head just peering out of my neck-zip.

I should have had the Cub idling over beforehand. I had to do five kick-starts and lost more skin.

Otherwise, there was just one bad moment, when we met a Belgian juggernaut on a sharp bend, and she decided to abandon ship at sixty miles an hour, by way of my face. For ten long seconds I thought I was dead, till I ended against a field gate, still upright. Then I thought I was blind in my right eye, where she'd planted her foot. But it was only blood from the eyebrow clogging the eyelid. I wiped it off calmly with spit and a filthy handkerchief. Loving cats demands a few sacrifices.

When I could see with both eyes again, she was sitting on the saddle, giving her famous impatient meow. Real little motorcyclist.

Neither of us looked too impressive by the time we reached the vet's. Called itself an Animal Hospital. Formica-faced, flat-roofed, radio aerial on top and a huge car-park for the customers' Jaguars. The smell of money was stronger than the smell of anesthetic.

The cool honey-blond at reception regarded us like something a naughty dog had left in a corner. The vet wasn't in; the vet wasn't likely to be in all day. I sat in one orange plastic chair, put my bike boots on two more, and ostentatiously began to count my wad of notes. When she saw the notes, her nose began to twitch like the kitten's when it smelled apricot jam, and she made a call on one of her three telephones. Miraculously the vet had returned.

I picked up the kitten from where she was assaulting the RSPCA plastic-spaniel collecting box and Came This Way.

Wish I hadn't. Hated the vet on sight. Young guy.

50

Tweed suit with waistcoat and a long white coat over the top. Those TV hospital series have a lot to answer for. He had dark waving hair, dead-straight nose, which he wrinkled delicately at the kitten. He had the kind of laughing Irish eyes that laughed at everybody but himself; especially, at the moment, my bloodstained eyebrow and the oil stains on my jacket.

I put the kitten on the table.

He touched her briefly round the hindquarters and said, "One pound."

"What for?"

"Painlessly destroying her. She's got sub-clinical rickets —her bones are deformed. That's why she can't move properly. I would also guess she has worms, ear mites and some generalized infection, probably feline enteritis. Certainly—fleas." He wrinkled his nose again, and shoved her fur up the wrong way. She looked wretched and meowed at me pathetically. "Hopeless case—had a hopeless start. Probably got worms in her lungs too—hear her wheezing?" He squeezed her cruelly again.

"I want to find her a good home," I said. "I'll pay for treatment and a fortnight's keep. . . ."

"Good *home*? A kitten like *that*? In *July*? We're putting down dozens of healthy kittens every week. Everybody wants spring kittens, and they're very popular round Christmas. But summer kittens—you're wasting your money. Even if she lived, she'd die having kittens herself."

He picked her up absently. Rather like I've seen my mother pick up an empty paper bag and screw it into a ball—while she was thinking about something else. He began to turn toward the door and the incinerator. I almost let him go.

The kitten looked at me, and gave one last protesting silent meow.

Of itself, my hand shot out and took the vet's wrist; the one holding the kitten. I slowly drew him back to the inspection table, and ground his wrist bones together till he dropped her. She scratched him then flew to my shoulder. I went on squeezing the guy's wrist. He had guts. He turned pale, but he didn't flinch or ask me to stop it.

"Give her a shot of antibiotic," I said. "And make sure you put your syringe into the right bottle, or I'll come back and give you a shot of the same, personally." I let him go and watched him do it, making sure he didn't hurt her more than he had to.

He turned back to his bottles, feeling his wrist bones to see if they were broken.

"Right," I said, "and I'll take two hundred Canovel, and a Nuvan-Top aerosol for the fleas, and a puffer-bottle of Sevin Carbery for the ear mites." Blessing my old friends, the vets in Surrey.

"You a student?" he asked. Meaning a veterinary student.

"Just finished my first year," I said sweetly.

"You young know-alls," he said bitterly.

"How much?" I asked, getting out my only ten-pound note.

"Nothing," he said. "We'll treat it as a *charity* case. There's another injection I could give her. . . ."

"No thanks, Herr Doktor. Give my love to Buchenwald."

He really loathed me, but he wasn't treating me like a joke any more. I swept out. It was a pity I had to go back for my helmet and gloves. . . .

I stopped at the village shop. No more corned beef; she'd have cut-price Kit-e-Kat in future. I was going to make her the biggest, fattest cat in the world.

Rode back like the wind. Kitten settled against my chest, shaking all over but absolutely fascinated. Kept giving little chirrups, like she wanted me to go faster. It was funny, riding with company. Almost like having a girl on the pillion. Dad reckons it was great in the days before crash helmets. Girls would put their cheek against yours and say I love you, while you were doing a ton. Crash helmets ruin all that. They're part of the great anti-sex plot.

Settled the kitten in the barn with a whole tin of Kit-e-Kat. She turned up her nose and asked for jam. Left her to think about it and went to tell Derek how I'd stubbed out the vet.

9

Derek was in the kitchen; it's a real space-age effort. Susan's got so many split-level gadgets it looks like the bridge of the starship *Enterprise*. But Derek still insists on sitting there, with his muck-spreading boots on a piece of rug his granny made.

There was an old guy with him, drinking tea; checked shirt and khaki slacks tucked into wellies. Thought it was the cowman, so I just said how-do and launched in about the vet and how I'd nearly broken his wrist and how could guys be that cold-blooded?

Old Derek nearly had a *fit*; kept twisting in his chair till I thought the legs would drop out. Kept interrupting me, saying why didn't I go down to the cellar and get myself a beer; or Susan was in her sewing room and wanted a word with me.

Couldn't make out what was up with him, till the old guy laid his hand on Derek's arm and said, "Steady, Derek. Don't you think I appreciate getting someone else's view of my own son?" He had a posh voice. Too late I noticed the leather bag at his feet, with something for disembowelling cows hanging out of it.

Another vet; father of the first one. Why do these things always happen to *me*? I blurted on, trying to make things sound not so bad and only making them sound worse. When I'd finally run down into silence, he just said, "My son has lots to learn. Too long at university; too many experiments on white rats. He understands what goes on inside test tubes, but not what goes on inside animals or people."

I couldn't believe my ears. Anybody criticized my relatives, I'd kick their teeth in; even if what they said was true. Blood's thicker than water.

The old vet got up and said, oddly humble, "Would you mind if I had a look at your cat? She may need another injection—don't worry, not the sort they gave at Buchenwald. . . ."

I followed his Volvo up to the barn. My track was looking all chewed up with all the coming and going. Much more, and it would be wide and clear as the M6. I realized that before I came, no one must have been up it for years.

The kitten came bounding out, as soon as she heard the Cub's engine stop. Complaining bitterly about the Kit-e-Kat.

"Here's the Daily News," I said.

The vet's mouth dropped open, then he recovered. "*News?* That's a curious name for a cat."

"She always gives the impression she has so much to tell you, if only she could talk."

"Ye-es," said the old vet, in a very meaning way I couldn't understand. But before I could ask what he meant, he went all brisk and called, "Come here, News." She came, straightaway, purring. He spent a long long time going all over her, like he'd never seen a cat before. But gently, almost reverently, like she was some kind of cat princess, rather than a moldy old tat-bag. A phrase came into my mind as I watched him: *Reverence for life.* I admired him for that; he was so unlike his rotten son. He even gave her an injection in a reverent sort of way. She went on purring, then started rubbing around his legs.

Then he turned to me. "This is a very important cat. Look after her well, won't you?"

"Important?" I said, incredulous.

"Important to me; and my son. You see, my son's diagnosis *was* correct. Only he's left out one thing—love. Not only your love for the cat, but her love for you. She has someone to grow big and strong for now—somebody who wants her. Don't be surprised if she grows in a rush. She's older than she looks . . . been held back by malnutrition since birth. Now she has all that she needs. . . ."

I blinked. Was he talking about a cat, or some bloody woman?

"How much do I owe you?" I asked abruptly.

"Thought my son said it was a *charity* case?" He smiled —at his son's expense, not mine. "Just do one thing for me. When this is all over—when she's a big strong cat, I mean —bring her and show her to my son. It might teach him something. I think I'll have a bet with my son . . . fifty pounds. When we win, I'll take you out to dinner on the proceeds. You'd like that, I expect?" He smiled again.

But I couldn't get used to the way he was talking to me. All respectful, yet sad. Like I'd won the V.C. or something, but he knew I was going to die of my wounds. It was unnerving. I'd rather he'd lost his temper and called me a silly bastard.

But he'd moved farther down the barn.

"Curious old place you've got here. *That's* a fine piece of carpentry." He was pointing at the harness board.

"Just a Victorian harness board!"

He ran long fingers over the wood. "Nails are Victorian —blacksmith's best. But look at the paneling." He tried to dig his thumbnail into it; the thumbnail bent. "Oak. Oak lasts forever. The older it gets, the harder it gets. Looks like the back of something. . . . Well, must be off. My wife thinks I'm antique-mad. Good-day to you."

The sound of his car faded, but I went on looking at the board. It was six feet high by eight feet long. I could see where the blacksmith had hammered his nails in crudely, splitting and bruising the fine paneling. Hadn't even got 'em in straight. Must have been in a hell of a hurry.

I couldn't help laughing. Take the back of something, hammer nails into it, hang harness on the nails and everyone blindly assumes it's a harness board. Throw some darts in it; and everyone will assume it's a dartboard.

Then I stopped laughing. If it wasn't a harness board, what *was* it?

I got my fingers behind the left-hand side and heaved gently. What a laugh if it fell off the wall and turned out to be just a harness board after all.

It moved; but not in a falling way. With a heavy grating across the floor. It was much more than a board. It still stood upright, three inches away from the wall, revealing a slit of dark. I put my hand in and waved it about. No wall behind—empty air.

Immediately, all that tripe about secret passages and priests' holes swept over me. There's a kid inside us all. I heaved again, enough to give myself a rupture.

The board moved three more inches. Something wooden fell down with a hell of a rattle inside. Something else went *clink, clink,* like a metal chain swinging. A little cool draft came out of the hole, smelling of soot and something else; musty, animal. It cooled my skin; I was sweating like a pig.

One last heave opened a foot-wide gap. I struck a match and plunged in.

Wish I hadn't. Match went out in the draft. I crashed

my bonce into something swinging, barked my shins on something sharp, and ended on my hands and knees, on a heap of thin things that crackled and broke, making a stink like . . . .

"*Aargh!*" I shrieked, like the heroine in a horror movie, and backed out quick.

Soot, straw, twigs, cobwebs; and the tiny perfect skull of a bird clinging to the pocket of my jacket.

"Take the strain, Webster," I said. "Let's have more light on the subject." Opened the barn doors as far as they would go, and heaved the harness board right back into the room.

The opening in the wall was also eight feet wide and six feet high. It was a fireplace and chimney. I got inside and looked up; patch of blue sky with little clouds going over.

A kitchen fireplace; the kind they roasted a whole ox on. And the gear for roasting the ox was still there, on dirty big hooks. And something like a cauldron, with a tap on the side. All black as pitch with burned-on soot, and near-buried in bird droppings and the skulls and rib cages and bone-and-feather wings of generations of birds. Sparrows and starlings and jackdaws.

And the harness board was a high-backed settle. The kind you used to see in farmhouse kitchens, and are now in posh guys' houses, stripped to the bare wood and set against Vymura. It was intricately carved, seventeenth-century, and worth a bomb. Its seat was piled with three-legged milking stools, jugs and things.

Somebody had been a cunning sod, I thought. Gather up the contents of a kitchen, bank them in the fireplace, shove the settle across, knock in some nails and hang some odd bits of harness on them, and bingo, you have one useful barn instead.

Somebody had knocked in more nails round the fireplace. On them hung a rusty pair of tongs, and bunches of frail gray twigs, that broke like ghosts of dust under my fingers, letting out strange sweet smells. Herbs. *Here's rosemary, that's for remembrance.* . . . Under the twigs, someone had scratched a name:

John Michael Briarly
Magdalen College Oxford
7.8.1877

What were you doing here, John Briarly, you crafty sod? And why did you leave in such a hurry?

My first impulse was to run and tell Derek. It was his stuff and worth thousands. Any American would go mad. . . . Genuine Olde English kitchen, circa 1650. They'd probably cart the whole barn off to America to the last stone.

Barns? Barns didn't have kitchens. It was a house.

Not Vaser's Barn. Vaser's House.

I was seized by a crazy impulse to get the whole place back to its original splendor, before I showed Derek and Susan. Sneaked down and borrowed a shovel and barrow from their cowshed. Felt a bit guilty, crossing their farmyard, because I saw their bedroom curtain twitch. But nobody came to ask what I was up to. Maybe they had better things to do on sunny afternoons. . . .

I found big bent plates that looked like pewter. Knives and spoons but no forks. A potbellied jug I scraped through to copper. All chucked into the ashes any old how. And a hawk's skull, a kestrel I think. Must have dived on the jackdaws, missed its stoop and broken its neck. There were still half-burned logs embedded in the white wood ash; they were riddled with woodworm.

And the floor of the barn was not trampled gunge. Good stone slabs, under four inches of gunge. The gunge came up easily, like slabs of turf, once I got my shovel under it. By the time I'd finished, the sun was setting.

News returned from her siesta. For once she didn't start yowling for the old Fray Bentos. Instead, she went crazy about the settle and fireplace; sniffing and rubbing against everything and purring like an outboard motor. Then rubbing against me till my jeans were black with soot to the knees. Cats are like that—any new nook or cranny drives them nuts.

I was whacked. Turned to start the old camping Gaz, to make a brew. Then stopped. Why bother with the camping Gaz? I had a whole new kitchen now. I piled twigs and logs from the log mountain into the fireplace, and set a match to them. They roared up instantly. There was a good draft in that chimney. Then I went to the stream with my potbellied jug, and filled up my cauldron-thing, and it soon started to bubble. Only thing was, when I tried turning the tap, it fell apart in my hand, and I had to jam in a stick before I put out my fire with a flood.

I pulled the settle up to the fire and News and I ate our scoff side by side. Only baked beans and Kit-e-Kat, but it was snug. It only occurred to me when I was wiping up my bean juice with a bit of thick-sliced white, that I *had* found a secret room. A whole kitchen hidden in a fireplace.

Mind you, wasn't all that unusual. Stokesay Castle was a cow byre for a hundred years. Cromwell's Army used St. Paul's Cathedral to stable cavalry horses. People weren't sentimental then.

Then came the funny day.

I went into Besingtree to get my watch looked at. Really bombed it, because I knew the road now, every bend. Footrest just grounding on the corners, and that little vibration coming up my leg. News loved it, shaking like a jelly; a real cowboy. But the drag inside my jacket told me she was growing like weeds in a garden. Eat? She'd even knocked the tin of vitamin pills over one night and started scoffing them like Smarties.

I parked. Besingtree's only a village, but it's got a watchmaker's. "Good morning, sir, and what can I do for you this lovely day?" I pulled off my watch and gave it to him. He looked at it, and then said, "Yes?" in a baffled way.

No wonder. It was going again. Only saying midnight about two weeks ago.

I know that gag; one of Life's favorites. Like the way your tooth stops aching as you ring the dentist's doorbell. So I was firm with the guy; made him take the back off. He examined it through his eyeglass, poked it, listened to it, then told me it was perfect, had been recently cleaned, and was a very good watch. Which I knew already.

He even set the date right for me, polished the glass on his sleeve, and gave it back to me, with that pitying look.

At that point, News, who'd been having a siesta curled

round my navel, decided it was time for elevenses. She screwed herself round inside my jacket, making me look like a wombat about to give birth, then shoved her head out under my chin and informed the watchmaker that she'd had no breakfast and I was starving her to death.

I waited for the pitying look to spread to the far corners of the watchmaker's face. But he just stood staring at me with an expression I couldn't read. Stared so long I felt it could go on forever.

"How much do I owe you?"

"Nothing, sir, nothing." He bustled around the counter and opened the shop door for me. "I hope you enjoy the rest of your . . . holiday . . . sir."

He hung a card in the shop door, saying *Closed for lunch,* and hurried across the road, vanishing into a cake shop.

The time was nine-thirty.

I was still standing by his window gathering my wits when he came out of the cake shop and vanished into a cobbler's.

Quaint customs of Besingtree; maybe there was a magazine article on the subject somewhere.

I was still wondering, when I heard the scurry of claws on the tarmac road, coming up heavy and fast. Just had time to whirl before a great black-and-fawn thing hurled itself at me; a huge devil-face with flaring yellow eye and jaws as big as my head.

Thank heaven I play Rugby. Had my left leg braced back and my right arm out rigid before I knew I was doing it. Thank heaven I was wearing gauntlets; my fist went straight down its throat. Then it had me back against the watchmaker's door, pinned like a fly, with its dirty big claws scrabbling at my neck.

I hit it a couple of left hooks, hard enough to drop any

guy. No effect at all, except the sound effects of a Russian peasant being devoured by wolves. I kicked it in the guts. That discouraged it a bit, and it dropped on all fours, still having my gauntlet for breakfast. I kicked it again, in the ribs, with every ounce I could put behind my Belstaff Roadrider. It made a sound like a big bass drum, and became merely one very thoughtful Alsatian.

I was sorry, then; I like dogs as a rule.

Then the sodding thing came at me again. Had it got rabies or something? I was beyond caring; I just went on kicking it. I'd have killed it, if some middle-aged guy hadn't come up and grabbed it by the collar—which was thick and black and had as many studs as a Transylvanian torture implement.

The middle-aged guy was worse than his dog. You know the sort: built like a Sherman tank; bald head, red face, big mouth. Kind of guy there's no point in arguing with, so you might as well just go away. He actually demanded to know why I was kicking his poor little doggy. Called me a yob, a greaser, a typical young lay-about. Told me to get my hair cut and why had they abolished National Service. Army the only fit place for thugs like me.

These sociologists who talk about the adolescent problem; why don't they ever talk about the demented middle-aged guy problem?

A crowd was gathering; shopkeepers, housewives, the old gaffers you see smoking pipes on the War Memorial bench. That sort of crowd always sides with the demented middle-aged. There'd be a policeman, in a minute. They side with the demented too.

"Bloody thing could've killed me," I yelped, when I could get a word in edgeways. "Look at me gloves—torn to ribbons—cost me seven quid."

"What do you expect, carrying a kitten about like that,

you young lunatic. What do you *expect* a dog to do?"

"Oh, you let him go round chewing kittens, do you? Saves dog food, I suppose?"

The crowd was closing in, very hostile. Redface turned to appeal to them.

"Leave the kid alone," said the watchmaker.

"Disgusting, having a dog like that loose," said a housewife. "Might have been a little child it savaged."

"Should be put down."

Redface was as amazed as me; his mouth gaped wider and wider.

"Look at the kid's gloves—ruined."

"Pay him for his gloves." The crowd was really aroused now.

"*Holidaymakers*—think they own the place."

"Can't walk safe in your own streets."

"Go back where you came from—get back to London."

Redface backed away, still holding the dog's collar, toward a highly polished old Vauxhall and an agitated wife. But the crowd went after him.

"Pay the kid for his gloves."

"Fetch the policeman!"

"Pay up!"

Redface bundled the dog into the back of his car, and after a lot of bluster from the driving seat, drove off. An old gaffer came over and gave me a ten-pound note.

"I can't take that," I said.

"Might as well, Cunning," he said. "He'll not come back to claim it, not in a hurry." And laughed.

"Well . . . thanks," I said weakly.

"No bother, Cunning." He went off back to the crowd. Why had he called me "Cunning"? Was it a local term of endearment, like "Hinny" on Tyneside?

The crowd was slow to disperse. Kept on telling each other what happened, over and over again. And having sly looks at me. Not unfriendly, but nosy—like they knew me; like I was a local lad. The watchmaker was having a lot to say, but I couldn't quite hear it.

Well, Besingtree was only three miles from Derek's. I suppose they're a bit short of gossip, in a one-horse town like that.

They went on watching me till I drove away. Wasn't unpleasant, but it put me off. Why *had* they taken my side like that?

Normally, the barn at night is snug. Plenty of Derek's logs roaring up the chimney; the oil lamp burning that Susan had given me, that's just enough to read *Motorcycle Mechanics* by. And old News, having licked my plate clean as well as her own, would be flopped out on the settle like a road-accident victim, head hanging over the edge.

But I was twitchy, that evening. Kept seeing the Alsatian's face flaring at me. It was worse because dogs have eyes like humans. When a dog likes you, its eyes are soft as a girl's. When a dog hates you . . . . How much worse it must have looked to News, even if she had vanished down my jacket at the first sign of trouble. Suppose I hadn't been there? Suppose she'd been on her own? Cornered? Dog would have bitten her in half.

And Derek talked of shooting her, cool as blowing out a match. And that vet, nearly bluffing me into letting her go, blinding me with science. If it hadn't been for my vet friends in Surrey, she would have been a little heap of ashes now. Why did everyone seem to want News dead?

Shurrup, Webster. Getting morbid. She's only a cat.

Where the hell *was* she? Not on the settle; not on the hearth, roasting her brains out and covering herself with wood ash.

"News-News-News!" I heard a slight rattle out in the barnyard. She'd be here in a minute, talking her head off. She always came when I called.

She didn't come. I got up and went to the door. No moon. Total darkness.

"News-News-News!"

Another sound of movement down the yard. Was she trapped? I blundered out, falling over the Cub in the process. Listened again. More vague noises, retreating down the lane. What the hell was she up to? Or was it a fox? Derek said foxes took farm kittens.

"News-News-News!"

My foot trod on something soft that shouldn't have been there. I bent down and picked it up. Furry, warm and undeniably dead. The head waggled like it no longer belonged to the body. Warm sticky stuff clogging my fingers. I licked them and got the sweet taste of blood.

"Oh, *Christ!*" I ran back into the barn, about ready to cry my eyes out.

I made myself look.

It was a young rabbit. The big lustrous eye stared at me like it was still alive. The white fur round its throat was molded into sharp points with a mass of blood. It had been half-strangled, then had its head snapped off its shoulders and left hanging by the skin.

No fox; the work of a man. What kind of man would do a thing like that? And leave it at my door, creeping silent in the night? Was it some kind of witchcraft? Somebody once told me that if West Indians hated you, they'd practice witchcraft, voodoo—putting a curse on you by leaving a black chicken nailed above your front door with its head cut off. Was it something like that?

I had to find out quick, before I went nuts. I picked up my biggest spanner, went out and switched the Cub's headlight on, and belted after the guy. The Cub's headlight carried well, right down the lane. My shadow ran before me, long, black and nasty. It looked so nasty and powerful, it made me feel ten feet tall. I searched every patch of shadow in the hedges, where the headlight couldn't reach. I'd have pounded the guy to a pulp with the spanner if I'd caught him; can't *stand* people who torture helpless things.

But I never saw him. Behind the hedges, he had all the dark in the world to hide in.

I reached the main road and gave up. A car passed; an Allegro, I think. It calmed me down; the ordinary world was still there.

I went back up the lane, calling, "News-News-News," and wondering if the guy who'd strangled the rabbit was behind the hedge, watching me. I realized it was the weekend again. Was it the Midland yobbos come back? If they reached the barn before me, and switched off the Cub's headlight, they could take me while I was blinded by the dark.

Nothing happened. I finally switched off the headlight myself. Didn't want to, but my battery didn't last all that long. Went inside and made up the fire instead.

I didn't go to sleep at all; went out and called News every half hour, on the chime of the clock.

Because my bloody watch had stopped again. The very good watch, recently cleaned and in perfect condition. That didn't help. I hate anything I own being defective. And somehow not knowing the time, being dependent on the clock, buried me a bit deeper into this smothering green blanket called Suffolk.

News never answered. If she was still alive, she must be farther from home than she'd ever wandered before. She was out in a green minijungle as savage as the Amazon basin. It makes me laugh, these country-lovers who get out of their cars for five minutes and coo about the healing peace of nature.

The English countryside is kill, kill, kill. Bird kill insect, cat kill bird, fox kill cat. Not occasionally in anger, but every night in life, just to stay alive. Trees are pretty peaceful, but even they fight each other for the sun. Never seen a little tree other trees have killed? Never seen an ailing oak strangled by ivy?

11

She came home with the sun, cobwebs on her whiskers, and a huge feather in her mouth, which she dropped at my feet. Brown feather, alternate bands of dark and light. Some black stuff on the quill end.

She was pleased to see me. Then threw back her head and sniffed, and made straight for the dead rabbit I'd mistaken for her. Licked the blood off its neck and purred like mad. She had it off the settle twice, and started skinning its leg before I took it off her and hung it behind the door. It was just food to her. She got Jellymeat Whiskas instead.

When Derek came, I showed him the rabbit. "What kind of pervert does a thing like that?"

"Anybody," he said. "Been snared. Lots of chaps round here—set snares for the pot. Price of butcher's meat—most farmhands can hardly afford sausage. Skin it for you—if you like—won't take a minute—boil it—very nice with sliced potato—how'd you get it?"

I told him.

"Obvious—chap out poaching—catches a lot—strings 'em together—passes your door going home—one drops off —has too many others to notice."

If it was *so* obvious, why was he looking bothered? As if in answer to my thoughts he said, "Know who the chap'll be—if it worries you—I'll have a word—after all—it's my rabbits he's poaching—got this place shipshape, haven't you?"

"Look," I said. "This stuff I found in the fireplace—I don't want to have responsibility for it—it's worth *thousands* on the London antique market—if a crooked dealer got wind of it . . . ."

He curled his lip slightly, as if what I'd said was in bad taste.

"That's not antique-dealer's stuff—been in the family for donkey's years."

"But why was it all hidden in the fireplace?"

"Sensible place—keep it till you need it—can't use the place as a barn if it's full of furniture."

"And what about *that*?" I pointed to the graffiti over the fireplace. *John Michael Briarly 7.8.1877*

"Vandalism—some people'll do anything—to get noticed —read in the *Telegraph*—people carving their initials—on tombs in Westminster Abbey."

"But what was he *doing* here?"

"Look, old lad—you're hangin' round this place too much —getting broody—need some fresh air—take a walk—tell you a good walk—see that ring of trees on the hill over there—splendid walk—appetite for lunch. Those oaks—really old—old in Queen Elizabeth's day—there's the path —just follow it."

I looked at the ring of trees up the valley, already blue and faded with the heat haze. How far away? Half a mile? Three miles? And all the time I was thinking that Derek's bluff squire act was as real as a clockwork orange.

"Shall I skin this rabbit for you? Do for lunch."

"Take the bloody thing away and bury it."

After he'd gone I thought: right, you lying bugger. For some reason of your own, you want me up at that ring of trees. So I'll go. Just to find out what's in your mind. J did wonder if he was getting rid of me, so he could get up to something at the barn. But that was a bit subtle for Derek.

I hadn't gone thirty yards when I heard the sound of pounding paws. She shot past my legs so close I felt her; and went tearing off into the bushes ahead, so fast her claws sent up little spurts of dust. Once in the bushes she'd either lie in wait to pounce on me, or lie on her back waving her paws at the clouds like a dear sweet pussy.

I found her on her back, wriggling seductively. Making it impossible for me not to tickle her tum.

I tickled it; no fool like an old fool. Immediately, twenty needle claws fastened into my hand. She kicked me violently with her back legs, laid back her ears in mock terror, and shot up the track again. *Tyger, tyger, burning bright.* . . .

Cats are the greatest hams in the world; never stop acting, except when they're hungry. I had every known ham act that morning. She chased a butterfly with leaps that would have shamed Margot Fonteyn. Even had the good taste not to catch and eat the thing.

Sniffed buttercups like Harry Wheatcroft sniffed roses.

Even meowed to draw my attention to where she was squatting under a hedge. Then gave me a look as if to say no *gentleman* would watch a lady doing such a thing. I had to stare at the horizon like a fool. Until another meow summoned me to watch while she sniffed her creation as delicately as the buttercup, disapproved it, and scrabbled earth over it from seven different directions. Then off again. . . .

Without her company I'd have given up the walk. It was a lonely continuation of my lane, in the opposite

71

direction from Derek's joint. At first, there were tractor tracks; then they turned into a field of stubble, and the lane became a mere path. Hedgerows closed in. Had to push my way through, even crawl in places. Only saw the ring of trees once, through a gap in the hedge. Looked nearer, yet somehow smaller.

When the path widened again, there were hoof prints in the dried-up mud. Somebody's darling daughters riding their ponies; Trigger and Spook and spiffing little Dapple. . . .

No. The hoof prints were too big; big as dinner plates. Cart horses.

Hoof marks obliterating hoof marks obliterating hoof marks. All fossilized in the baking sun. There couldn't be *this* many big horses left in the world.

The track got wider still. Fifty feet across. Like a motorway. A Sahara of sunbaked mud with hot little dust-devils blowing across it.

Wheel tracks too, but no tire treads. No cars, tractors. Smooth narrow tracks of iron-shod carts.

Horses and carts, wearing the land away. At the edge of the track, tufts of grass made a dusty last stand. In the middle, the ruts were three feet deep, with water and damp mud still lingering in the bottom. You could see where the carts had turned and twisted to avoid the worst patches. The track swept on to the ring of trees, a wound in the living land, a desecration like bulldozers leave.

But there'd been no bulldozers here.

I couldn't understand it. There was no possible explanation. It made me a bit jumpy; I started staring about. I wasn't looking for people; it was too *quiet* for that. I was looking for a line of pylons on the horizon, or a vapor-trail in the sky, or a no-trespass notice, or those piles of rusty junk farmers leave about. . . .

But there was nothng. Even the familiar hawthorn hedges fell behind. Instead, low railings with the bark of the tree left on them, full of knotholes. Like you see round allotments in slummy districts. But never so many —these went on and on as far as the eye could see.

And the fields they fenced were too small. Too many fields, like pocket handkerchiefs. Each with a pair of miserable cows, or a few stringy blackface sheep. The field gates were unpainted oak, with *two* crossbars. Not nailed or screwed together; tied with leather thongs.

Uneasy. Like being in France or Germany makes me uneasy, when I'm very tired. Because everything you look at is the wrong shape; even traffic lights and ciga- rette kiosks are threatening strangers.

Alien.

Worst was the way, beyond the tiny fields, the trees pressed in, as if, given half a chance, they'd overwhelm everything. Not just hedgerow trees, but a whole forest, that turned road and fields into a mere series of sunlit glades where flies buzzed and the air lay heavy.

There weren't this many trees left in England. Because they weren't Forestry Commission conifers, but beech and sycamore and living elms.

Living *elms!*

I tried looking back down the valley, to the clearer land around Derek's. But I didn't seem able to see it. The only familiar thing was the ring of trees ahead. Part of me wanted to run away, it was all so weird. But there's always a logical explanation, if you're patient. All would become clear at the ring of trees. I could spy out the land from there. See a line of pylons. . . . Still, I began to hurry, even if it did make me sweat. I looked at my watch, to see how long I'd been walking.

My watched had stopped, of course.

When I'd climbed the hill and reached the ring, I sneered in disgust. *Really* old oaks? Mature in Queen Elizabeth's time? Like hell. They were only forty-footers, not half-grown. What a waste of a walk!

Then I heard a rusty creaking, like an inn sign swinging in the wind. Not very loud, but it seemed loud in that silence. Peering into the green gloom under the trees, I saw a huge L-shaped construction of wood, planted upside down in the ground. From it, on a chain, hung an iron cage as big as a barrel. Inside the cage was a human dummy, badly made. Too thin and painted black. Long thin legs stuck down through the bottom of the cage, ending in black-and-white feet. The arms were fastened across the body, and the head was just a tarry blob.

A fake gibbet. God, what some folk will do to encourage the tourist trade. I could just see Americans queueing up to photograph it. If they ever found it, in this back of beyond.

Perhaps there was a film company at work? I walked over, to see how it was made. Clever. White plastic bones sticking out of the feet. Even close-to they were nastily convincing. Clever, like those plastic cobwebs that film companies spray from a gun when they wheel out poor old Dracula for his positively last appearance.

Black skin cracking and peeling slightly off yellow ribs; a hint of yellow teeth under drawn-back black lips. Holes where the eyes should be.

As I watched, a bird, a great-tit, flew down onto the dummy's black shoulder, making the whole contraption sway slightly. The bird flipped up to the head, clinging on sideways like tits cling to coconut shells in your back garden. It began pecking away inside an eye-socket. What was it after? Some insect that had taken refuge in there?

No. It was pulling a long thin strip out of the eye socket; a strip that gave and stretched like elastic. The tit heaved away with flicks of its tiny neck, fluttering its wings to get more power.

The thin strip broke; the tit flew away with its prize; and still I stood staring.

Then a breeze blew, and the gibbet creaked again, and the smell hit me.

My mother left turkey giblets two months in a Tupperware jar last Christmas . . . but *this* smell—this smell sent me reeling into the nearest bushes where I threw up everything I'd eaten for a week.

When I'd finished, I felt terribly cold and weak and empty. You always do, don't you? But this coldness and weakness wouldn't go away. I sat shaking all over, knowing I was on the wrong road, among the wrong fields, and that out there, in the clearing, somebody had done something unthinkable.

The only familiar thing in that nightmare world was the cat. She didn't seem to mind at all. Purring softly; the breeze blowing rings in her fur. And she was staring at something intently—up the road beyond the ring of trees.

I lay down beside her and peered the way she was peering. No need to panic if it was only a mouse or a squirrel.

It wasn't a squirrel.

It was a little girl about five feet tall, in a gray dress of thick stuff that came right down to the ground, so only her toes peeped as she walked. The gray dress would have made her nearly invisible, if she hadn't worn white collar and cuffs and a white bonnet that covered her head as thoroughly as a crash helmet.

Walking funny, for a kid. Very self-conscious, as if she knew she was being watched and someone would clout her if she didn't behave herself. Little discreet steps, planting one foot exactly in front of the other. Hands clasped together, almost as if she was praying. Shoulders hunched and head bowed humbly. But her eyes darted everywhere round the flaps of her bonnet, which were a bit like a horse's blinkers. She looked a mouse; but a crafty little mouse who wouldn't miss a trick.

So, OK. Little girl in fancy-dress, playing make-believe. Little girls do it all the time. I suddenly felt ridiculous, playing hide-and-seek with a ten-year-old. If she spotted me lying here, she'd probably run home to Mum screaming blue murder. Then the fuzz would be having me down to the station for a little chat. So why didn't I stroll out whistling, my usual breezy self, and say hello folks and what about the workers?

My usual breezy self was nowhere to be seen. I continued to hide in my bushes.

The kid came straight on toward me. Passed the horror on the gibbet without a glance. Twenty yards away, she stopped, and swiveled her eyes my way, without turning her head. News gave a huge purr; seemed on the point of running out to her. I put my hand on the cat's shoulders and pressed her flat to the ground.

The kid looked straight at me. Black fringe, big dark eyes in a pinched little face.

She *knew* I was there, and it didn't worry her one bit. But I stayed put. Suddenly she looked to her right; the way I'd come. There was a hideous grinding and screeching of wood, and a creaking and a thumping. The ground began to vibrate beneath me.

The next second, the light darkened and went greener, and I felt a sharp pain in my hip. I rolled over to see what was causing it.

I'd been lying on a Woolworth's carrier bag. Containing an empty bottle of Newcastle Brown, and half a BR egg sandwich, still in its wrapping.

How the hell had I lain on a beer bottle without noticing? I pushed it away in disgust. News ate the egg sandwich, as if she had no other interest in the world.

I remembered the kid. No sign of her. The sound of awful creaking and grinding had stopped. And there was no sign of . . . the gibbet, in the green gloom.

I stood up and stared about wildly. The green gloom was caused by the immense height of the ring of trees. *Giant* oaks, a hundred feet high, blocking out the light. Interspersed with horse chestnuts even higher. The horse chestnuts were full of the buzzing of bees; you couldn't see the bees, just hear them. Perhaps they were after the horse-chestnut blossom or something. . . .

But why were the trees suddenly twice the height? Where had the horse chestnuts come from? The bees?

Where were the girl, the gibbet? I searched the whole clearing, but they weren't there.

Then I realized the oaks were the same trees; only sixty feet higher. The same branches, only bigger. . . .

I had seen these trees in their youth.

Three hundred years ago.

Gibbet.

Three hundred years ago.

Little girl.

Three hundred years ago.

Like those two women who went on a day trip to Versailles and reckoned they saw the whole court of Louis XVI. . . .

Nuts, Webster. It was that bang on the head you got in the barn. Delayed effects of concussion. Go and see a doctor, before they put you in the funny-farm, along with women who compose new works by Mozart.

I looked for the wide-rutted road home, but it wasn't there. I somehow knew it wouldn't be. Had to crawl through hawthorn hedges nearly all the way. Would've got lost if it hadn't been for News.

As I reached the barn, the clock chimed twelve.

I'd only been gone half an hour.

12

I was very glad to see the Cub.

News gave an excited *Prooook* and ran across to the barn doorstep. *Prooook, prook-prook, prrroook.* She sounded like it was Christmas morning.

I was so shagged I couldn't make out what she was bending over. Tried pulling her off it, but she resisted, digging her claws into whatever it was. Had to give her a clout before she let go.

It was another strangled rabbit with a wobbling head. Smaller, this time, little more than a baby. Still warm. Must have been running about the fields half an hour since.

This hadn't been dropped by a careless poacher; this was *personal*, dribbling blood down my own doorstep. What did the maniac want? Had he spent half an hour running his bloody hands over the Cub, my gear, my sleeping bag? Was he watching me now?

I glowered round, but there was nothing to see except the countryside sleeping in the afternoon sun, and Derek's cows grazing two fields away, looking like an advert for Irish butter.

I was nearly in tears; there was nothing to *hit*. I didn't care if he was seven feet tall and built like an All-Blacks winger. I didn't mind if he pounded me to pulp, if only I could hang one on him. . . .

Nothing stirred. Except News going *prook* again, about a parcel wrapped in newspaper on the old empty water trough.

I couldn't bring myself to touch it. It was she who opened it, knocking it around with nose and paws till it fell apart.

Two pounds of broad-beans, still in their pods. Wrapped in the small-ads page of the *Harwich and Manningtree Standard, 24th July 1977.*

There were more things on the windowsill. Jar of honey. Cabbage as big as a football. There was a label on the honey, handwritten.

No name. Just *Clover Honey, 1977.* Middle-aged woman's handwriting, just like my aunt's, homely as pie.

Presents. Even the bloody rabbit must be a present of sorts. But not from Derek and Susan. *They* were deep-freeze Tupperware kind of people and they brought me that kind of grub.

These were farmhand, no-collar-and-tie sort of presents. The kind country people give each other. Why were they giving them to me?

There wasn't a house within a mile, except Derek's and the church.

Why were they walking all that way to give things to me?

I didn't feel all happy and grateful. I've learned one thing about presents in my first nineteen years: nobody gives one without wanting something in return. Unless it's your Mum and Dad, and even they're after *something.* They're just more devious about it.

And why did they sneak up and give presents when my back was turned?

I don't like being beholden to strangers.

How right I was.

But at the time I just hung the rabbit behind the door, to stop News doing her carnivore act. I had nowhere to put the other things, except the dirty floor or the settle.

"Hey, News, we could do with a table, couldn't we? If they're feeling *that* generous."

She was too busy playing with something on the floor. I looked to make sure it wasn't something nasty, dead or alive. But it was only the long feather she'd lugged home that morning. She looked at me furtively, the feather across her mouth like a dog carries a bone.

There was something odd about the quill end. It was dull and black and cut diagonally. Almost as if someone had made a . . .

Quill pen.

"Here. News-News-News."

But she was backing off, more furtive than ever. I grabbed for her. She fled to the door and looked over her shoulder.

I dived for her again. She fled halfway up the outside steps. Got you, I thought. I rushed her.

I'd forgotten the slit leading to the room with no door. She slipped through it, and was gone.

I tried pleading with her; tapping her Kit-e-Kat dish with a knife. Tried holding a newly opened tin to the slit. She was not to be drawn. Or else she'd nipped in that slit and out of the slit at the back, and was off in the woods by this time.

I remembered last night when I'd called and called her. Had she been playing me up then? Listening and not answering; driving me nuts?

Well, I'd had a bellyful of her little tricks. She'd not play this one on me again. I'd get into that room behind the staircase if it killed me. I blocked up all the slits with planks of wood, and set to work on the mountain of logs in the barn.

It had gone down a bit, with a week of roaring fires, but it was still half the height of Everest. Had a lovely time standing on top, heaving logs in all directions. I was soon in a sweat. Does me good to sweat. Got the rage out of me.

Until I reached the bottom of the log pile and found there wasn't any door; not even the foot-high one I was looking for toward the end. And there never had been a door; I checked the masonry carefully. If there'd been a bricked-up door, I swear I'd have smashed my way through it. But all I was left with in the end was a wall-to-wall carpeting of logs.

It takes more energy to rebuild a log pile. By the time I was finished, I was *really* knackered. Lay on my pit and was asleep in seconds. No dreams about gibbets, either. I wakened as the sun was setting, and lay waiting for the clock to tell me what time it was.

Dozed again. Wakened in blue dusk. There was a rustling outside.

"News-News-News!"

No response. I jumped up and ran out to grab her, and ran smack into a human being. Rather a small and wilting one, who gave a terrified scream. Female.

I took my hands off her, she fell back against the barn wall, and we stared at each other in mutual shock. She was very twentieth century. Her battered platform heels didn't go well with bare legs.

"Oh, Cunning, you did startle I. Let I get me breath." She put a grubby hand on her grubby blouse, which was open to the navel, revealing slightly sweaty but not unattractive fullness. I'd heard about country maidens and barns in my time, but it was all in dirty jokes. And country maidens had country fathers, so I didn't ask her in.

When she'd got her breath back and had a lot of sly quick looks at me, she bobbed and gave me a crumpled paper bag. I looked inside. Six brown farm eggs with little feathers still stuck to them.

"For me? Ta! But what *for*?"

" 'Tis Jackie, Cunning. Since he went in the army, he's lost interest. Don't want to do it with me no more."

"Do what?"

"You *know*, Cunning." She actually simpered.

I could have kicked myself.

"I think he do have a girl at Aldershot, Cunning." She pronounced it Aaaaldershot. "Give me something for him, Cunning. He be coming home this weekend."

"Like *what*?"

"You know, Cunning. To turn him on." There was a glint in her eye, a kind of frightened excitement, a smell coming from her that might be stale, but wasn't all that off-putting. I remembered again the dirty jokes about barns. She was pretty in a dirty way. Rosy cheeks and her hair would have been nice if she'd washed it.

It made me a bit short with her.

"You could try having a bath," I said—I hadn't had a bath myself for ten days. "And wash your hair and wear tights. He'll be among girls at Aldershot who do that all the time. And buy a bra and do up your blouse. Men don't like girls being *obvious*."

I thought she'd get angry, but she just said, "Yes, Cunning," like she was a little girl and I was her dad. So I added, to soften the blow, "You're very pretty really. If only you'd try a bit."

"It's these spots, you see. On my face, Cunning." She

fingered her face, a whiny tone in her voice. "Give I something for the spots, Cunning."

Now there I *could* help her. I get spots myself and I use a special kind of astringent soap. I went inside the barn. I had two bits, a new, wrapped pack, and an old bit that had rather dried out in the sun, and was all cracked and wrinkled like the Mummy's Claw. Wasn't going to give her the new pack, so I took her the old bit.

She curtsied. "Thank you, Cunning. That's kind."

"Wash with it night and morning," I said, "and rinse it off well afterward. Really slosh the water on your face. Cold water, to close the pores up." Sounding like everybody's neighborhood family doctor.

"Thank you, Cunning. I won't forget." She went flitting off down the lane into the darkness.

An approving *prook* came from the shadowed barn. Then a plaintive discourse on the need for Kit-e-Kat.

13

"One dormouse, two bank vole, three field vole and a female brown rat, *Rattus norvegicus*," said Susan, arranging the limp little bodies in a line down her ample thigh. "Quite a hunter, your cat. Does she bring all her kills home?"

"Everything she doesn't eat."

The creator of this rodent disaster area sat two yards away, washing the gaps between her front claws with great precision. She was no longer a kitten; she was a young cat now. Eyes bright, and rosettes of black and ginger fur blossoming through the gray tat that had once covered her.

"I can't get over the way she's grown," I said. "She's three times the size she was, in less than a month."

"So would you be, if you were main-lining on vitamins and fresh bloody meat."

"Saves Kit-e-Kat."

"Would you do something for me? Keep everything she catches and show me? I've got quite interested in nature, since I came to live here. Not much else to do, now the kids have all left home."

"Yeah, I'll keep a record."

Long silence. Usually I felt warm and comfortable with Susan, but this morning the conversation wouldn't flow. Something on her mind.

"Funny life you live here. For a young man."

"You don't know *how* funny."

"Tell me."

Once I started, it all came flooding out. When I'd finished, I waited for her to start chuffing me out of it. But surely this and but surely that, making me feel I was being a silly hysterical fool. Making me feel safe with her common sense.

But she was still silent, hunching over a fag, eyes narrowed against the smoke. In the end I said, "Well?" rather rudely.

"You're a town boy, John?"

"Yeah." What had that got to do with it?

"Living in this part of the country takes some getting used to. I've been here twenty-five years, and *I'm* still not used to it."

"You're not local, then?" We were like two skaters, approaching each other across thin ice, with black depths below.

"I was born in London. I was teaching in Colchester when I met Derek. He was on our board of governors."

"*He's* local, then?"

"Local? The Pooleys have been here since 1621. Sir William Pooley bought half the manor of Besingtree from the Vavasour family."

Vaser's Barn—Vavasour's Barn?"

"This was the Vavasours' manor house. Didn't Derek tell you?"

"Derek doesn't tell me anything. Except what suits him."

She smiled palely. "I know what you mean."

"I can't make Derek out."

"Oh, he's a *Pooley*. I live with twenty of them, all over

the house. Portraits from Sir William on, and they all look like Derek in fancy-dress. We brought them with us when we moved from Besingtree Hall. Besingtree Hall's a mental hospital now."

"That figures," I said bitterly.

"D'you think Derek's mad?" I didn't like the way she asked. She wasn't joking; she really wanted my opinion.

I gave a laugh as real as Count Dracula's. "After the ring of trees, I keep wondering whether *I'm* sane."

"You're sane, John. So's Derek. It's just that he's . . . old-fashioned. Very brave and honest and decent. A major in the War, at the age of twenty-five. Won the M.C. in Korea, for rescuing two men under fire. They'd fallen into an icy river when a bridge collapsed. After Korea, he came back here, got the farms straight, made a lot of money. Then . . . the last twenty years, everything he believed in seems to have gone to pot. The empire, and morality, and a fair day's work for a fair day's pay. And the agriculture inspectors interfering and the Income Tax snooping—there was a nasty scene with an Income Tax man last year. Derek nearly had to resign as senior magistrate. Since then he's gone back into himself, into the past. It's easy enough to do, round here. He's still Squire Pooley, and the locals think he's God."

We looked at each other. I knew in a quiet way she was nearly as scared as I was.

"So what the hell are they up to with me? What is this Cunning business?"

"If I asked him, he wouldn't tell me. I love him, but I can't talk to him. Never could much, but it's got worse. Specially since you came. He's restless—won't come to bed. Spends half the night walking round in the dark and then snoozes off on the couch in his study."

Silence. Then she lifted her head rather proudly and said, "Of course, you could solve all *your* problems quite easily—simply get on your bike and ride away. . . ."

"But you don't want me to?"

"I'd be grateful if you stayed a bit longer. You're terribly important to him for some reason."

"O.K., I'll stick it a bit longer—it's easier, having someone to talk to. . . . But that lark at the ring of trees—d'you think it was concussion? The doctor . . . ."

She shook her head decidedly. "No, it wasn't concussion—not after three whole weeks. But . . . maybe you fell asleep and dreamed it? You said you'd been awake all the previous night."

Now it was my turn to shake my head. "I might have fallen asleep—but not lying on top of a beer bottle."

"No—and there's the other things. Something *is* going on. Maybe we can find out together." She smiled, grateful and conspiratorial, all at the same time. It was irresistible; then.

I heard someone shouting outside. Two figures were standing in the middle of the barnyard. I went down the outside stair to meet them. One was tall and one was small, both with fair hair bleached by the sun.

"Morning, Cunning," said the tall one. He sketched a salute to his forelock, reaching about the level of his nose. He was wearing washed-out jeans and a washed-out check shirt. Nice grin and honest blue eyes. Farmhand. Two dead rabbits with bloody necks dangled from his other hand.

"Were you the guy that left me the rabbits?"

"All right were they, Cunning? Like another?"

"No thanks. Not at the moment—bags to eat," I said hurriedly.

"That's fine, then. Us've come for a spot of Paul Pod-gam, Cunning. For the boy here. Been off-color a bit recently. Wife wanted to get the doctor in, but I said Paul Podgam were better than any old doctors. Can 'ee spare a spot, Cunning?"

I stared at him, baffled. "Who's Paul Podgam?"

"Paul Podgam, Cunning. *Paul Podgam.*"

I heard Susan come out on the top of the step behind me. The farmhand glanced up at her, suddenly tense. He shaded his eyes with his hands, against the morning sun which stood over the gable end.

"Is it *her*, Cunning?" he whispered. "Has the yarb mother *come*?"

"Hallo, Matthew," called Susan.

"Oh, 'tis you, Mrs. Pooley. Morning!"

"Can *I* help?"

"No, 'tis all right, Mrs. Pooley. Just passing. Making sure this young man here was getting enough to eat. . . ."

"Oh, we're looking after him."

"I'm sure you are, Mrs. Pooley. Well, we'll be off." He lowered his voice to a whisper. "Sorry, Cunning. I *thought* it were too soon, but after what you gave our Barbara last night . . . ."

"Was that your sister I met?"

"You made a rare difference to her, Cunning. She was half an hour washing herself this morning—first time she have washed herself in weeks. What was it you gave her, Cunning?"

"Soap," I said. "Medicated soap."

"Oh, aye. Cunning." He grinned like I was teasing him, but he didn't mind. "Be seeing you, Cunning. Morning, Mrs. Pooley."

Father and son walked off hand in hand down the lane.

"Who *was* that?" I said.

"Matthew Fassett, one of Derek's cowmen. He's a nice chap, very attached to that little boy. What did he want?"

"He wanted—" I took a deep breath "—somebody called Paul Podgam."

"Paul Podgam? He wanted Paul *Podgam*? I didn't know anybody still used it."

"But who *is* he?"

"It isn't a he, it's a plant. The polypodium fern, dried and crushed up. It's an old country remedy for practically anything from toothache to rheumatism. Fancy Matthew giving the boy Paul Podgam, and him so proud of his twin-tub washer and color telly. It just goes to show. . . . But why did he want it off *you*?"

I didn't know the answer. But I knew one thing. Whatever plot was being hatched, Susan wasn't in it. She was as far out in the cold as I was.

As soon as I parked my bike by the War Memorial, somebody said, "Morning, Cunning."

Same all down the village street. Kids stared till pulled away by their mums. Gaffers nodded knowledgeably. Couple of yobbos shouted it with loud bravado, and sniggered once I was past. I was famous in Besingtree. Went into a tobacconist's for a box of matches. He gave me three and wouldn't take payment saying, "That's all right, Cunning."

Fled into a bookshop. Amazing how many Suffolk villages have secondhand bookshops, run by elderly gents with posh accents who spend the day reading their own books and ignoring customers. But once you start chatting them up, you find they knew Winston Churchill, or all about the secret sex life of the Royal Family. Very hard to stop, once they start. Ex-dons, failed writers, guys who showed promise in the nineteen-thirties but somehow nothing quite happened. How do they make a living? Their shops are always empty.

This guy had a bald head and horn-rims, a pink shirt and matching tie.

"Got anything on local customs?"

He waved to a shelf of guidebooks. *Tales of Old Dunwich, The History of the Southwold Railway*, etc., etc.

"I was thinking more of folklore," I said.

He indicated another shelf, without pausing in his reading. The supernatural, astrology, I hate that crap. Every second book had the surpassingly ugly mug of Alasteir Crowley, the Beast from Twenty Thousand Fathoms, looking as smug as a village bobby with a parking offense. Anyway, I kept on plowing through the indexes, looking for "Cunning." At last I found the name *Cunning Murrell . . . p74.* Turned to the page and read:

"Few realize that witchcraft in East Anglia survived to such a recent date. Witches were organized in groups under a Master Witch, always a man. A photograph actually exists of the last Master Witch, a farm laborer called George Pickingale, who was the center of occult life in Essex until his death in 1909 at the age of 109. Pickingale was descended from the witches of Canewdon, where legend states that as long as the church tower stands, there will be six witches in the village, 'three in silk and three in cotton.' Pickingale was said to have the power of the evil eye. Hares in the fields would eat out of his hand. He was a 'black' witch, who would put spells on people and crops for money. He was much in demand at the season of annual fruit-and-flower shows.

"Pickingale's main rival was Cunning Murrell, the

cobbler of Hadleigh, who is said to have taken observations of the stars late at night from the ruins of Hadleigh Castle. Murrell was a 'white' or 'blessing' witch, who would remove Pickingale's spells for a small payment. It may be that they worked in conspiracy to defraud the superstitious. Murrell was consulted far and wide, even by the gentry, about casting horoscopes and finding lost or stolen property.

"Dr. Margaret Murray has stated that 'nowhere in Essex was there a village more than ten miles from a known Cunning Man. The countryside was simply covered with practitioners, sometimes several to a town.'

"Opposition to Master Witches was often violent. William Andrews records that as late as 1863, one was drowned in a pond at Hedingham; but it was remarkable that the murderers were townsfolk and shopkeepers, the farm-laborers refusing to join in the killing.

"When Murrell died in 1860 his landlord was so terrified of his possessions that he buried them in the back garden. They were later recovered by Murrell's son Buck, and are now in the Prittlewell Museum, Southend. Among them was Murrell's code book, containing his witches' cipher.

ABC	DEF	GHI
JKL	MNO	PQR
STU	VWX	YZ

The first letter in any box is portrayed by the outline of that box; i.e., A is ⌐ . The second letter by the outline of the box with one dot; i.e., B is ⌐• . The third letter has two dots; i.e., C is •• . To give a small example: the word 'witch' would be written:

⌐• ⌊•• ⌐• •• ⌊•

I reached in my pocket for a little crumpled bit of paper. But I had no real need to look at it. Above the door of my upstairs bedroom at the barn, hacked into the stone with incredible ancient hatred, was the word *witch*.

"Do you intend to *buy* that book, young man? Or merely stand there all day reading it?"

The bookseller was smiling at me. Or was he *laughing* at me? I couldn't see his eyes; the shop windows were reflecting in his spectacles.

"No," I said ambiguously, slammed the book back on the shelf and left.

Kicked the Cub into life and burned the whole length of the village street at eighty. Faces lifted toward me in surprise, from the butcher's and the tobacconist's, and the War Memorial seat. Stuff them; I didn't care what *they* thought. They'd had it, with their rotten little presents of eggs and strangled rabbits. But why had they picked on me? I'm a Civil Engineer. I know bugger-all about blessing and cursing and finding stolen goods. I'm a stranger, just passing by.

Yeah, like the poor sodding fly that the Venus flytrap plant catches and eats. . . . Well, they'd picked the wrong one in me. I had a mum and dad and even a prof who cared what happened to me.

I was burning past Derek's, sod him, when the horrible thought hit me. My mum and dad hadn't a clue where I was. Hadn't written to a soul since I got here. To them, I could be anywhere in England, Scotland or Wales. *The body was never found.* Ten thousand people vanish in England every year. Unless they're under eighteen, the police don't even try to trace them.

Get out, Webster. Fast! Pack your panniers and go with every ounce of burn you've got.

Going up the track to the barn, I was twice airborne over bumps. Left the bike running; she was warm and idling nicely. I plunged into the barn.

"News-News-News!" I'd take her with me. Nobody wanted anything good for *her*, either. Derek wanted to shoot her. Vet wanted to put her down. Bloody farmhands laying snares that could strangle her.

"News-News-News!" No sign of her. I grabbed what was mine from the barn, stuffed it in the pannier, and ran up the outside stairs. The scratchings round the door shouted, "Witch! Witch!"

I thought News would be lying in my sleeping bag. She always did that when I left her by herself. It made her feel less lonely if she could smell me.

But she wasn't there either. And there was a sudden intense silence that terrified me.

Outside in the yard, the Cub's engine had stopped. She *never* stopped once she was warm. Had somebody followed me from Besingtree and cut off the petrol? I should never have burned out of the village like that; I should have ridden out quietly, so they didn't know I was on to their rotten little tricks. I took a deep breath and clenched my fists, and practically flew down the outside stair.

Nobody about. Several sparrows flew away from round the Cub's wheels as I appeared. Nobody had touched the Cub; the petrol and ignition were still switched on. I kicked her and she fired first time. I increased the supply of gas, so she'd idle a little faster and stronger. Then dived back upstairs for my sleeping bag.

The Cub's engine cut out again. Suddenly, I was frantic. The Cub was my only friend in the world. Once I was on her, they couldn't stop me. But if she broke down now, how the hell would I get to Sudbury?

Steady, Webster. You'll get so knackered running up and down stairs you won't be able to think straight. Gather all your stuff in one big bundle, *walk* down to the bike, pack your panniers slowly and sensibly, start her up and go.

I did just that. Even made sure the pannier straps were as tight as they'd go. Faced the bike round, took a deep breath to stop my panting, gave her one kick and . . . she went.

Sat there revving her, feeling safe, feeling powerful. If any sodding farmhands started walking up the track now, I'd ride straight over them.

"News-News-News! News-News-News?" Where *was* she? Perhaps Matthew Fassett, with his bloody hands and smiling face, had caught her? Perhaps he was hiding behind the barn with a few mates, holding her mouth so she couldn't answer me? Perhaps they were laughing their yokel turnip-heads off.

Stay on the bike, Webster. Or they'll only sneak round and stop it again.

"News-News-News?"

95

I gave up, put the bike in first, and shot away. I hated leaving her. She'd come bouncing back looking for me. She'd wait, not knowing I wasn't coming back any more. . . .

Stop being soppy, Webster. 'S only a bloody cat. You've done her a power of good; she can hunt for herself now.

My engine cut out, dead. Wasn't even a dying cough or misfire. One minute she was firing perfectly, next, nothing.

I kicked her over till my leg seized up. Tried bump-starting her.

No go.

I got off and put her on the stand. I was *extremely* calm. I checked there was petrol in the tank, even though I knew it was half-full. Removed the sparkplug and checked for a spark.

Spark was OK.

I checked petrol was reaching the carb. I checked the float bowl, the choke, the ignition timing. Checked the compression. Checked for blocked jets. Just like the motorbike manual tells you.

Everything was perfect. She just wouldn't start.

I think I stayed so calm because the main road was only fifty yards away. Cars kept passing, making me feel safe. If the worst came to the worst, I could hitch to Sudbury and come back with a breakdown truck. Cost a bomb, but at least it would get me out of this hole. And if I was hard-up, I could go and scrouge off the parents for the rest of the vac.

And then, as I was having a last fiddle with the float-chamber, the sky darkened.

Bloody rainclouds, coming straight at me.

Nobody gives you a hitch when it's raining. Nobody

wants a muddy great hitchhiker on their new seatcovers. And I suddenly saw myself trudging round Sudbury in a downpour, trying to get a bed for the night with no luggage and an explanation as long as my arm that no one would believe anyway. And the Cub standing in the rain with those sods mucking about with her.

I turned the Cub round and began pushing her back up the hill to the barn. All four hundred pounds of her.

I don't know what happened next. Maybe I'd left the ignition on; maybe she slipped into gear.

She started, began pulling out of my hands up the track. I jumped aboard, and we went shooting back toward the barn.

Turned her back to the main road. Sudbury for me.

She immediately died again, as I reached the same spot on the track.

You'll have guessed the rest. Every time I turned her for the road, she stopped. Every time I turned her for the barn, she re-started first kick.

You hear funnier things at any bike-club meeting. Maybe it was a loose lead or a blocked feed. Maybe it was the change in slope; facing uphill, then facing down. Maybe it was just the sheer bloody-mindedness of mechanical matter. I never found out, because after that time, she never played me up again. Except once.

I got back to the barn in time to avoid getting soaked. News was there to greet me. I picked her up and she rubbed her cheek against mine. Which is the greatest compliment a cat can pay you; treating you like you were another cat.

I looked into her face close-to. The big yellow eyes, never still, checking every straw that rustled in the rain wind, every cobweb that swayed in the dark roof. Big ears, turning this way and that, checking noises outside that I couldn't even hear. Whisker twitching as she separated and traced a smell among the thousand smells of the barn.

"We're all right, News," I whispered.

As if agreeing, she pushed her cheek against mine again.

14

We waited at the barn together.

The supply of strangled rabbits dried up; likewise the eggs, honey and runner beans. Nobody else came to ask for a love potion, though I did see Barbara in Besingtree. Her face shone with soap and it was obvious from the smirk on it that Jackie had come up to scratch. She was all for coming over, but a massive old dame in curlers, who should have been an Awful Warning to Jackie about his future married life, pulled her away abruptly. Nobody stared at me or called me Cunning. Shopkeepers served me respectfully, pleasantly but distantly. I might have been an ordinary holiday maker. Derek must have "had a word" with a hell of a lot of people.

Instead, it was the week of the strangers. One morning I found a Pickford's van stuck halfway up my lane, and the crew swearing their heads off at the gaffer back in Ipswich for directing them to this God-forsaken hole. They didn't call me "Cunning" either; they called me "mate." Grumbled nonstop, drank endless mugs of tea, and by lunchtime had manhandled a huge antique table up the lane and into the barn.

Funny about a table being just what I needed. News rubbed herself in ecstasy round its bulbous legs, like it was an old friend. It would have sat sixteen people in comfort, and the top was a single slab four inches thick.

Must be worth thousands, even if its rungs *were* worn down into half-moons by people's feet, and somebody had used the top as a choppingblock. I got the giggles, imagining News and I dining in state, her at one end and me at the other.

I hung around the men, helping and asking questions. Their only answer was that the table had been delivered to their Ipswich warehouse by another furniture van. I signed for it, since their orders stated specifically *Webster, Vaser's Barn, Besingtree*. They obviously thought I was nutty like everybody else. They had an awful job backing down to the main road.

I thought of loading the Cub in the furniture van and going with them. But I had a deep conviction that something else would only go wrong; I didn't want the furniture van overturned in the lane. In a rainstorm of course. But more than that, News and I were waiting for something now, and I was half-content to wait. Maybe the endless flybuzzing afternoons of summer Suffolk had something to do with it. I felt relaxed, like before an operation when they've put a tranquilizing jab in your backside.

Other strangers turned up with bits of furniture. When I caught them at it, they were in a hurry to get away. They were just doing a favor for a cousin or "Squire Pooley loaned un to us years ago. You'll have to ask ee about un." I tried to argue but they wouldn't stop to listen. And Squire Pooley never showed his face. Susan turned up twice, admired my dozen milking stools and my battered warming pan, but had nothing to offer but shrugs and sympathy.

Then a builder called Pete arrived and began pulling the boards off the boarded-up windows and replacing them with glass. Slowly the barn looked more and more like a house. A house being got ready. For what? Matthew Fassett's yarb mother? I tried to visualize her, but she always came out as the district nurse who examined us for nits at school, plunging our infant heads into her massive starched bosom.

Pete came every day from Chelmsford in Essex. He had an hour's drive, morning and evening. But he didn't mind; Derek paid his traveling time. It was costing Squire Pooley a bomb to stop me interrogating the locals. I liked Pete; he was a bit hippy, with his long red hair and curling beard. News liked him too. She put on her acrobatic display for him up in the barn's rafters, leaping from tie beam to king post like the daring young man on the flying trapeze. Pete marveled.

"Knows this building, don't she? Like the back of her hand. She born here?"

Just at that moment, News missed her footing, and plunged thirty feet to the floor with a squawk of terror. Luckily I was standing just underneath. Caught her as neatly as a Rugby ball. I take no credit; pure reflex action. I put her down, watched her walk away unharmed and said:

"Not like her, that!"

"No," said Pete, craning his neck to look at the roof, this way and that. "And I'll tell you something even odder. See where she jumped and missed, in that corner? Well, there should be a cross-brace there, but it's fallen out, years ago. You can see the holes where it used to fit. . . ."

Why didn't I see then? A cat that leaped for a cross-brace that vanished years ago. A cat that grew a week, every day I had her. How could I be so blind?

But I was too busy sucking the long scratches that she'd left in my arm.

After Pete left that evening, I sat eating my fried-egg butty on the outside stair. Lovely evening. Clouds high and gold to the west; the valleys and mountains of fairyland. But sad, too, because you knew that even if you could fly, you still couldn't reach them before they vanished. That's what I thought as a little kid, anyway.

It was so still, I could hear the rooks cawing round Derek's church, half a mile down the valley. Skeins of gulls, flying high, headed for fairyland. If they put a spurt on, they might just make it.

News came loping down the track. Stopped and looked at me. Then let out that godawful yowl cats make when they've caught something, or are going to be sick, or when they've been out all night and are coming to your bedroom to tell you how cold and lonely they've been.

I ran to her. She'd caught nothing; she wasn't blooping; and she hadn't been gone from my side five minutes.

Silly little cow! I started back to the steps.

Again she yowled. Leaped onto the wall, her face a blank black mask with pointed ears against the sunset.

She yowled again.

She wanted me to follow her. So I went. Wide awake on a cool evening and not suffering from concussion.

She made no allowances for human frailty. Slipped through rabbit holes in the bottom of hedges; up banks thick with brambles. Barbed-wire fences were nothing to her. A dozen times I nearly turned back, but each time I heard that doleful yowl, and turned to see her poised on some tree branch or wall, waiting for me.

I was soon utterly lost. I'd *have* to stay with her now, just to get home again. As if she knew she had me in her power, she slipped inside the thickest clump of brambles yet.

Inside, because of its very thickness, the clump was dead. A dead hollow, floored with spiky wreckage a foot deep. Bramble stems, thick as my arm and gnarled like trees, wound their way up into a green roof. It was very dark, but there was still a glimmer of sunset beyond the far edge. I wormed my way across and parted the leaves.

I was at the side of a corn field, just reaped. In a dim light, under a pale moon, a long line of reapers swept on toward my right, scythes swinging in a strange scattered unison. All wearing long white shirts outside their trousers, with long white sleeves not rolled up. Behind came women and children in long gray dresses, gathering the cut corn and tying it into sheaves with incredible deftness and speed. Then came a handful of youths, picking up the sheaves and throwing them up to, or rather at, another youth balanced precariously on top of a moving haywain.

He was having a hard time, that youth, trying to keep his balance on the moving wain and trying to build a good load that wouldn't fall off. While all the time the others were bombarding him with sheaves, trying to knock him over and bury him. I could hear him yelping with indignation, and the rest laughing like drains.

Then an older man, leading the horses that drew the wain, shouted at them and they stopped dossing about.

I was . . . entranced. So the cat really could make time jump! Back to an England before the smell of tractor oil, and the wasp-rattle of the combine harvester. Like the old photographs you see in country-life books. I began to break down the brambles, so I could get through to them.

A voice said:

"Sic swuven frum natherly er uysterly?"

I was so startled I fell back onto a particularly sharp patch of dead bramble, and said, "Ow!"

There was a giggle, that went well with the young female voice. "Dowsun come frum the Annointed, ou frum the Grand Moister, ou frum Who Below Is?"

I stared round. Where the gray bramble stems clustered thickest, sitting low to the ground and nearly invisible in her gray dress, was the little girl of the gibbet. Naughty little thing, skulking in here, when all the rest were working their guts out.

She held up a dribbly-looking bottle with a neck that leaned at an angle. Handmade bottle; fetch a bomb in those bottle shops that are sprouting up all over London.

"Wilt gaven inner bothy, for there refreshment is, both breed en drink?" It was a maddening accent, a bit like broad Brummie. I kept nearly getting the meaning, then losing it again. She found that *very* funny. Then she seemed to remember her manners, and in a strangely formal party voice, rather stilted and limping, she said quite clearly, "Do you carry marks or angels?"

"Marks? Angels?"

She dug into a pouch on a belt round her waist. A stringed leather pouch, like the hippies sell at Barsham Fair. She held out two coins, one bigger than the other.

"That is a mark. And that is an angel."

"I carry fivers," I said, and showed her one. Two could play at that game.

She took it, stared at it closely.

"Whose likeness is that?" She really wanted to know.

"The Queen's!"

"That is *not* the Queen. The Queen does have ringlets. I did see her once, poor lady, before she went to France."

She smelled the note like a little animal, holding it

close to her nose and wrinkling up her face. "It does smell strangely. You do smell strangely. You do smell like an apothecary's shop I did once see burning down in Ipswich. You do smell of burning, sir. Are you from Him Who Below Is?"

"Who's that?"

"That is the name we do call the Devil, sir—the Lord of This World."

"I'm from London."

She nodded, satisfied.

"I did go to London, once, to my Aunt Vavasour's in Chancery Lane, over against Lincoln's Inn, two doors from the bakehouse by Justice Ackham's house." She came nearer and sniffed at the sleeve of my bike jacket, and nodded. "You do smell of the sea coal that is burnt in great houses . . . yet it is not quite the same."

She ponged pretty strongly herself, of damp and mildew, lavender and cow dung. And I saw she was not as young as I'd thought. Under her stiff scratchy gray dress, her bosom swelled. And there were lines on her face children don't have. She must be seventeen at least; but small.

For some reason, that panicked me. I began to edge out through the gap in the brambles toward the distant reapers.

"Do not go out there!" She spoke so sharply that I obeyed.

"Why *not?*" I was so edgy I nearly shouted.

She put her finger to her lips, watched the reapers with great intentness, then relaxed. "Because they would hang you for a witch."

"*What?*"

She put all her fingers across my lips. "Do you speak quieter. If you did go out there, they would see you are a stranger. Then they would mark your mantle of strange weave." She fingered the oily nylon wonderingly. "Then they would mark the strange devices on your mantle." She touched the badges saying BSA and NORTON. "Then they would smell you, and then tie your thumbs to your big toes, and throw you in the duck's pond. And if you did not float you would drown. And if you did float they would hang you for a witch."

"Oh, *tripe*." I stared at the reapers, who were throwing loose straw over each other, having just finished a wainload of corn.

"Did you not see the poor man on the gibbet? He did only steal a sheep, because his children cried for hunger."

"I must be going bonkers," I said out loud.

"Bonkers?"

"Mad."

"I do not think you are a Tom o' Bedlam, sir, for your hosen and shoon too fine seem. Are you a gentleman? Though gentlemen do wear gold buckles, not silver." She played with the triple chrome buckles on my bike boots.

"I'm at University."

"You are a *scholar!*" She said it with a curious finality, as if that settled what I was forever. "Are you of Oxford or Cambridge? Master Cromwell did go to Cambridge; but Oxford did sell their gold plate to buy cannon for the Kings."

"I'm at London."

"You do *jest* with me, sir. I did never hear there was a university at London. What is your name?"

"John Webster."

"Then I shall call you Master Webster. Or does your father still live? Then I shall call you Master Jack. Master Jack Webster. It is a *pleasant* name."

I was hardly listening. I was staring at the reapers. They were lounging about, now the laden haywain was making its creaking way down the field. Drinking from dark bottles. It looked idyllic . . . till I remembered the smell from the gibbet.

"They do take their midnight rest. They will work all night, till the dew does fall. They must gather the corn quickly, before the rain does come to blacken it."

"Midnight? Don't be daft. It's only sunset!"

But down in the valley, the clock struck twelve.

"That is our new clock," said the girl proudly. "Sir William Pooley did buy it for the church, in memory of his wife."

It was the same clock that chimed every day. Derek had told me it was four hundred years old. I put my face in my hands, wanting everything to go away. I was suffering my second spell of what I came to call time-poisoning: the utter strangeness that saps your energy, your confidence, your will to act.

"If they do call for me," said the girl, "I shall not go. I shall stay here with you. My name is Mistress Johanna Vavasour, but you may call me Mistress Johanna. Those are my father's tenants." She put a cold hand on my arm. "Do not fret—I am your friend, Master Jack. *Poor* Master Jack. I shall take care of you." The smell of her came again; mildew and lavender. "Shall we play riddles? What is it that creeps and twines her arms about you, and you shall die of her embraces?"

"Dunno," I said, watching the reapers through cracks between my fingers.

"The answer is *ivy*—or Mistress Villiers—or Mistress Coxswin."

"Yeah." I was watching two of the reapers, a man and

woman somewhat apart from the rest and in the cover of a large heap of cut corn. They were starting to make love. There was a flash of white petticoats and bare legs. It seemed indecent, somehow. Or like a painting by Breughel.

Breughel was sixteenth-century.

"Master Jack! You must pay heed. Listen to this riddle. What shall fall upon you from the sky to be a decoration, and yet shall not stay on you?"

"A snowflake," I said, almost without thinking.

She clapped her hands. "That is very good. Now you shall ask me a riddle."

"What animal goes on four legs in youth, and on two in its middle age, and on three legs in old age?"

"A *man*. For in old age he does have a stick." She laughed scornfully. "Your tutor did teach you *that* one. My tutor did teach *me* that one. It is the only riddle that tutors do know. Why are you staring at that man and that woman, Master Jack? What they are doing is lawful —they are man and wife. Do men not deal thus with their wives in *your* time?"

"What do you mean—*my* time?"

"The time that you do come from—oh. . . ." She put her hand to her mouth, as if to block out the words.

A wet nose touched my hand. I looked down. News climbed onto my lap, pounding away with her front paws enthusiastically.

When I looked up again, Johanna had gone. So had all the reapers. There was still a sunset glow beyond the brambles—showing, where the corn field had been, a field of turnips. By the edge of the turnips, clicking as it cooled, was one of Derek's tractors. It smelled vilely of paraffin.

"What did you want to spoil it for?" I yelled at News. "It was just starting to get really interesting!"

I'm not mad; lots of people talk to their cats.

Trouble is, the cats never answer back.

She only *prooked*, to tell me it was suppertime. And showed me the way home.

We were only two fields from Vaser's Barn. Or rather, Vavasour's House.

15

When I wakened up next morning, News was sitting watching me. As soon as she saw I was watching her, she gave a dubious little chirrup and fell to washing her shoulder vigorously.

"I should bloody think so, too!" I said to her. "Master Jack Webster and his wonderful time-cat. We should be on the bloody telly, you and me." She just kept on washing herself. Maybe she could hear the bitterness in my voice. I was starting to get on the wavelength of the lady who saw the ghost of Louis XVI at Versailles. And the lady who wrote down the latest works of Chopin and Mozart. Nobody would believe *me* either.

After breakfast, I went back and lay down in the middle of the bramble patch again. The tractor was gone, but it had left a lovely pool of oil so I knew it was the right place. I lay a long time, thinking that the patch probably hadn't changed a bit in the last four hundred years. What's four hundred years to a bramble patch? They live quiet lives.

I lay a *very* long time. I got very stiff. Then I finally realized I was missing one item: the wonderful time-cat.

I went back and tried to fetch her. She didn't want to come. When I tried to make her, she nearly clawed my eyes out. You can never *make* a cat do anything.

I'd just started to check the Cub's tappets to soothe my nerves when I heard her give that mournful yowl again.

Nearly jumped out of my skin, but she was just coming out of the dark slit onto the outside stair, carrying something dead in her mouth.

I chased her off it; for once she didn't put up much of a fight. I picked the thing up by the tail. It was about the size of a small rat, but not like any rat I'd ever seen before. Glossy black, huge ears and a tail as long as its body. It had a sleek, slim look, like it was built for speed. Its lips were drawn back over its sharp yellow teeth in a grimace of agony. Or like it had tried to bite News before she finished it. A nasty-looking piece of work altogether.

Stood there swinging it by the tail, wondering if Susan would like it. It would give me a chance to go to Derek's place, see what he was up to. I put the rat into an empty bean tin, shoved it into my top-box and lit out for the farm.

The moment I stopped the Cub's engine, I heard them quarreling. When my parents quarrel, they go into another room and fight in hoarse whispers. But like a lot of upper-middles, whether fighting or celebrating, or just discussing the day over a pint in the pub, Derek and Susan let it all hang out.

I walked round the corner of the house. Susan was hanging out of her bedroom window, clad in a fetching lace nightie and damn-all else. I didn't mind; with her face flushed and her hair hanging below her shoulders, she looked a proper treat.

Derek was standing on the lawn with his back to me, shoulders bursting the seam of his check sport jacket as usual. He had a soily spade in his hand.

"I'm going to do it *now*," he bawled.

"You *can't*, Derek. It'll frighten half the neighborhood to death."

"Do 'em good. Slugabeds."

"It'll upset the cows."

"Instant milk shakes. Do the milk yield a power of good."

"I'll have to open all the windows. Warn people. There isn't supposed to be anyone within a hundred yards."

"Do it then. Give you ten minutes."

"Oh, God!" Susan retired hurriedly, clutching her hair back with one hand and her splendid bosom with the other.

Derek turned and saw me. "Hah. Come and give me a hand—show you something worth seeing!" He led the way to a new brick outhouse, with a handbag-size padlock. He unlocked it; gave it to me to hold. It weighed a ton.

He switched on a light. The interior was windowless, except for two ventilators high up. The walls were whitewashed and very thick, and lined with shelves. The right-hand shelves were laden with large fireworks.

"Do a display—Bonfire Night—local Rotary Club—good chaps—make pounds for charity—keeps fireworks out of kids' hands—very dangerous—shouldn't be allowed—damned government won't put their foot down."

On the left-hand shelves was a row of green metal boxes, about as big as petty-cash boxes you see in offices. Derek selected one, weighed it with his hand, tossed it up and down thoughtfully and announced, "That'll do." He opened it. Inside was another, cardboard, box. And inside that again, wrapped in greaseproof paper, was something that looked like putty, only too dark a gray.

"Ever seen that before—hah?"

"Waterproof putty?"

"Urf, urf, urf!" Derek convulsed until he had to support himself with his spare hand against the whitewashed wall. "Put windows in with that, lad, and you won't keep the draft out long. Here, poke your finger in it."

I dutifully poked.

"Plastic explosive," said Derek, still tossing it up and down. "Used a lot in Korea—blowing up bridges. Only do tree stumps now though. Put that lot in the right place, blow a stump clean out of the ground without even splitting it. Good to make a bang now and again—clears out your system—perks you up. Here, hold it. No, safe as houses—unless you've got a detonator. Drop it—hit it with a hammer—put a match to it—nothing happens."

I held it gingerly. Derek delved into another box; handed me four things like slim silver cigarettes.

"Detonators. Hold 'em by the *open* end. Hold the other end—they'll take your hand off!"

He reached down some coils of white cord, a bit like light-flex. "Delaying fuse—various sorts. This stuff burns through two foot a minute—we'll take twenty feet." He hung it round my neck, like I was a hat stand. "Not scared—are you?"

"No," I lied.

"Right—quick march—can't hang about all morning—vet coming at ten—funny man—can't stand bangs—was at Dunkirk, too—think he'd have got used to them."

We quick-marched across the lawn, to where the victim lay, felled years ago, but with roots still spreading across the lawn.

"Old oak—got to go—can't use the mower for it. Here's the spot."

Under the stump was a place where a demented badger seemed to have been trying to dig a new semi-detached.

"Put four charges under there—one in each corner—and

it'll lift the stump out whole—no mess." He set to work, vigorously rolling the gray putty into large unappetizing sausages, and sticking silver cigarettes into them, like cocktail sticks. "Pliers—where's the pliers?" He dug them from a bulging pocket, shoved the end of the fuse into the open end of a silver cigarette, and crimped the end tight with a grimace. He did all four, holding the pliers in his mouth betweentimes like an enthusiastic retriever.

Then he reached deep inside the hole and shoved them into invisible crannies, face working with concentration. Finally, only four ends of fuse protruded.

"All same length—should go off together—do you smoke?"

While I still goggled at the non sequitur, he lit up a Silk Cut Kingsize, puffed on it like a steam engine until the end glowed nearly white-hot, and suddenly applied the end to the fuses.

"Out-out-out!" We ran across the lawn, and crouched behind a row of garden urns, like gunfighters in a Western.

"Come out clean as a whistle—promise you," said Derek.

There was no flame—just a jet of yellow smoke from under the stump, and a crack that pressed like two fingers against my eardrums. Then a shower of rotten wood, bouncing off the urns in all directions. There was a tinkle of glass from the house behind us, and a wail of "Oh, *Derek!*" And a great clatter of milk pails and a frantic mooing from the milking parlors down the farmyard. The church rooks wheeled and circled overhead in an angry demo, and I could see starlings and wood pigeons and clouds of chaffinches going up into the air all the way to Vaser's Barn. Then the echo of the crack coming back from every tree and slope in the valley, like a salvo. Whole sylvan scene in bloody uproar.

"Oh, dear—miscalculation," said Derek gleefully, walking out on the lawn and staring round. It was obvious the stump had not come out whole. A finely graded selection of firewood covered lawn, house roof and everything else in sight. "Still, it's out," he added.

No doubt of that. There was a crater two feet deep and ten feet across.

"Come and have coffee." Susan met us on our way in, still in her nightdress, dustpan and brush in hand, and a *look* on her face.

"*Men!*" she said venomously, looking at Derek and me impartially.

Hastily I remembered my peace offering, and reached the bean tin out of my jacket pocket.

"What's this rubbish?" she said, prising up the lid that was still thick with bean juice. The rat slithered out onto the clean Formica table. It too had acquired a coating of bean-juice on its journey. Not a sight to delight the housewife. For a second she seemed about to explode worse than the tree stump. Then her face softened with nature-lover's wonder, till it was like a child's.

"It's a black rat. Derek, it's a *black rat!*"

"News caught it," I said modestly. "Thought you'd like it."

She took it to the sink, and washed it carefully. "Look at that tail—and those ears. You know what it is, don't you, John? It's the Plague Rat—the rat that caused the Great Plague of London in 1665. It came all the way from China in trading ships. Then later, the brown rat —the rat we have today—came and wiped the black rat out, because the brown rat was bigger and fiercer and ate up all the black rat's food. That's why we don't have the plague any more. There can't have been a black rat round here for three hundred years. But if they're coming back, it means the plague could come back. I must write to *Nature*—send them the evidence. I'll put it in the fridge to keep fresh. We'll have scientists down—investigation teams. . . ." Her face was suffused with joy.

"Rubbish!" said Derek, his huge hand closing over the small black body. "It's a pet rat—from a pet shop. Somebody's kept it as a pet, then it's got loose. Like the blasted mink and the blasted coypu. I wish if people must keep kinky pets—they'd keep 'em safe—'stead of letting 'em lose—overrunning the countryside."

"Derek, it's *not* a pet rat. It's a black rat—*Rattus rattus*," wailed Susan.

"Plenty of black rats in Britain—seaports."

"Only small colonies in Yarmouth and the Isle of Dogs —and they're both fifty miles from here. If they're migrating, people ought to know. . . ."

"*Nobody* is going to know!" roared Derek. "Don't want a lot of snoopers round here." He moved across to the Aga cooker in the corner.

"*Derek*!" Susan was practically screaming now, trying desperately to get to the little black body, while Derek held her at arm's length with ease. "Derek, it's important. I know it's important. It could mean life or death. You can't destroy scientific evidence. Nobody'll believe me, if I can't show them the body."

"Exactly," said Derek. He lifted the hinged lid of the Aga. A red glow lit the kitchen ceiling. A wave of heat hit me in the face.

"DEREK. FOR GOD'S SAKE. . . ." Her scream echoed round the kitchen.

Derek dropped the rat into the Aga. There was a brief puff of black smoke, and a foul burning smell. Then Derek closed the lid.

"Oh, Christ," said Susan. "You rotten, stinking sod. I'll never forgive you for that. Never, never, NEVER!" She ran out in a storm of weeping.

I was horrified. I'd seen them row often enough, but this was for real. I looked at Derek, and he looked at me.

"Stuff and nonsense—she's at—tricky age—sorry about that." But it was a poor effort at bluster, even for Derek, and I was suddenly as mad as hell.

"That was a Plague Rat, wasn't it?"

"How should I know?"

"Why did you have to burn it, if it was only a pet rat?"

He shrugged, staring out of the window. But he was very upset.

"If that was a Plague Rat," I said, with cruel gentleness, "it was either in the wrong place, or out of the wrong time."

"What the hell are you talking about?" But he'd gone as white as a sheet.

"I'm waiting for an answer." I knew I had him over a barrel in some way; I just couldn't quite see how to follow it up. But if I just went on standing there, he'd have to say something, and in the present state of the game, *anything* would be valuable.

He thought a long time; being Derek, he found thought difficult. He heaved and sighed, then said finally:

"Funny place, this." In some way, he had given in.

"How?" I pressed.

"This house—used to be the village inn—old coaching inn. Opposite the church—always find inns opposite the church in a village."

"Village? *What* village?"

"This is Old Besingtree—that's New Besingtree, down the road. That track—up to your place—is the old village street. Those hawthorn hedges—old cottage garden hedges —gone wild. The cottages are still behind 'em—all the way up to your place. Your place was the manor house—in the old days. Show you if you like—just fetch my gun— might get a rabbit—good place for rabbits."

I accepted his offer; I wanted to be out of the house before Susan came back.

He carried his shotgun like a gent, under one arm. Not like young cowboys carry them these days, upside-down over one shoulder.

He found a weak place in the hedge on the left of my lane, and pushed his way through. Beyond was a sea of stinging nettles, but the drought of summer had hit them hard. In big patches, they had died and dried; rectangular patches, the shape of houses.

"See the mounds?" He kicked away the dead nettles, and revealed low lines of brick rubble. "Foundations. And there was a doorway there—doorstep." He kicked again, and the thin layer of earth and root yielded, and there was a sandstone doorstep, good as the one at home. "And here's a well!" Under his foot the sods fell in, splashing into hidden stagnant water, leaving a jagged black hole.

We went from house to house, locating doors and windows, and the place where stables had been. *Kick, kick, kick* went his welly. Turning up a mass of blue-black shells.

"Mussel shells. People practically lived on fish in those days."

118

Then there was a mass of black cinders, under a broken pantile.

"Fireplace."

"This is fantastic," I said. "Do the archaeologists know about it?"

"Nothing out of the ordinary," said Derek. "Know how many abandoned villages there are in Engand and Wales? Over a thousand—archaeologists are busy chaps —can't investigate them all—nothing special about this one."

His voice had gone shifty again.

"Where did all the people go? And why? Was it the plague?"

He shrugged. "Could've been. Plague was bad in Cambridge—1662—refugees fleeing from London—brought it with them. Cambridge closed the city gates—people died off like flies in the villages around—buried them by the pitfull in Great Eversden. Plague wasn't just 1665—that was just the worst year."

"So this whole village could've died of plague?"

"Not necessarily—could be one of a dozen reasons— lack of work when the wool trade faltered. Maybe the local landlord knocked down their houses to improve the view—lot of that in the eighteenth century. Maybe they moved to New Besingtree to get the benefits of tapped water. Any number of reasons for abandoning a village— no point to gettin' hysterical about it."

Quite a long speech for Derek, that. Shifty again, too. It brought back the memory of Susan's ouburst to both of us.

"No point to making a fuss over a black rat. Lots of cellars—under these ruins—half fallen-in—dangerous—lucky the kids don't know about this place. Lots of things live in the cellars—rabbits mainly—like the dry shelter—live down here—browse up the hill there—stupid things—easiest thing in the world to pot a few—walk quiet a bit!"

Easier said than done, with the waist-high nettles, and the bricks hidden beneath that turned your ankle when you trod on them. But we gained a hundred yards, across the endless succession of low mounds. I sounded as quiet as a baby elephant.

Then Derek broke his gun, took two shotgun shells from his pocket, and pushed them up the twin dark barrels. "Stand behind me—then clap your hands—loud."

I clapped my hands, feeling ridiculous.

Nothing happened for a second; then the hillside above us was alive with small frantic brown bodies, charging down from the fringes of a small wood, smack into the barrels of Derek's gun.

I stepped forward in helpless horror.

"Stand *back*," roared Derek, reinforcing the command with a violent sweep of his right arm. Then he put the gun to his shoulder and fired both barrels, swinging the gun between shots.

The main force of rabbits reached the nettles and vanished. But about ten bundles of frenzied vitality remained on the hillside, kicking and wriggling in crazy circles like defective toys, and getting nowhere.

"Come on, man!" Derek put down his gun among the nettles and ran among the rabbits. I followed reluctantly, my hands clenched tight.

Derek picked up the first struggling bundle by the hind legs. It whiplashed wildly in his hand. He did something small and intimate to its head and it stopped moving. He dropped it, and ran to another, and beat its head against the ground. Three, four, five, six, seven. Another seemed almost to recover normality as he reached for it.

With both front legs and one back leg working, it made straight for me. I stepped aside and let it slide desperately past. It vanished in a clump of nettles.

"Damn, lost him," said Derek. "Bit squeamish, aren't you?" He began picking up all the blessedly still little bodies.

"I can't stand hurting animals!" I shouted.

Derek nodded grimly to the clump of nettles where the rabbit had vanished. "You've done *that* one a bad turn. Could've been out of his misery by now. Thanks to you, he'll spend a week in his burrow—dying by inches."

I knew he was right, and I hated him for it.

"Like to have a go?" he asked, breaking the gun. The two empty shells leaped out, red and gold and marked *Eley-Kynoch*. He slipped two news shells in, past a thin trail of blue smoke.

"Here!" He passed me the shotgun. "You'll have to grow up sometime."

"I won't grow up by murdering innocent animals." I stepped back, leaving him holding the gun stupidly outstretched.

"Killing for the pot's not *murder*." He gave that incredulous snigger that types like him are so good at.

"You?" I said. "Killing for the pot? With a deep-freeze at home so full you can't get the lid shut? You don't kill for the pot—you just like *killing*."

"You're gutless."

"Put that gun down and I'll show you who's gutless. You won't eat rabbit for a month. You won't have any teeth left to eat rabbit *with*."

"You're a funny sod," he said. "You'd beat me to a pulp; then cry over a dead mouse. Can't you bear to kill *anything*?"

"Yeah. Murdering sods who go round torturing innocent creatures for a laugh. I could stand killing a lot of *them*."

He studied me a long time; not scared, just weighing me up. "I really think you would, John. You'll do; you'll do." The thought really seemed to cheer him up. Then he said, "Just do me one favor. Let me show you how this gun works. You might need it sometime. . . ."

"For what?"

He smiled. "Killing sods who torture innocent creatures, perhaps?"

I let him show me how to load and unload the gun. How the safety catch worked. I liked that; I enjoy any kind of machinery. I wondered whether he was still trying to coax me round into shooting rabbits. But when he'd finished showing me the gun, he picked up his little victims and strolled off smoking his pipe, leaving me in the middle of my deserted village.

I was squire of Old Besingtree.

It was enough to make a cat laugh.

But why did Derek, as he walked away, have the look of a man who's done a good morning's work?

16

The next time News yowled in that doom-laden way, I made her wait while I dressed the part. Old cotton tennis shirt with ragged collar. Pair of brown corduroy trousers my mother had bought in a sale and a fit of misplaced enthusiasm. They had sixteen-inch bottoms. Every time I wore them, people called me Paddy, and asked when the M1 was going to be opened.

On top, I wore an old sheepskin bomber jacket that I'd cut the sleeves out of for summer riding. Then I jammed my old felt hat on my head; the one I wore at the Battle of Hammer's Field. With my bike boots, I must look a right yokel, ancient or modern.

I slipped my biggest monkey wrench in my pocket. It would bend a few skulls before anyone tied my thumbs to my big toes. . . .

News took me another different route; a little way up the path to the ring of trees, then left into a potato field. She began to dig a hole, well inside the field, about the tenth furrow. Made the soil really fly. I could see the pale flanks of new potatoes starting to show through.

I politely looked the other way. God help the guy who bought *that* bag of potatoes in the supermarket. But as my dad says, what the eye doesn't see, the heart doesn't grieve. . . .

But she gave another yowl, low, urgent. She was deep inside her hole now; only her scrabbling hind legs showing, like a rabbit's. Thinking nutty thoughts about buried treasure, I went across to her. The loose soil smelled damp and good.

As I stepped down into the furrow beside her, my foot dropped farther than I expected, and onto harder ground. It gave my knee a nasty jar.

When I looked up from making sure I hadn't injured myself for life, the potato field was nowhere in sight. I was among thin scrub, on the very fringe of the great hoof-marked road. And something was clopping and jingling and creaking up that road from the right.

And good old News had vanished, which I didn't like at all. Since she was my return ticket home. I wriggled deeper into the scrub and took the monkey wrench out of my pocket. The main point in dealing with nightmares is to get something in your hand quick to clobber the bogeymen with. I was a lot bothered by the devil in my childhood dreams; till I invented a fire engine with a hosepipe full of holy water.

The creaking and jingling stopped right in front of me. Something big and piebald blocked the light. I moved my head to get a better view and nearly whistled aloud.

It was a trooper of Cromwell's New Model Army. I thought for a second he might be one of the Sealed Knot yobs, but he wasn't show-off enough. He wasn't poncing round wearing his helmet; he had it tied behind his saddle with a bit of old string for comfort. And his buff-coat and thigh-boots were scuffed and greasy, like he lived in them. The piebald horse was in shocking nick, caked with clay up to its belly. Any little Home-Counties-gymkhana-girl would have had the RSPCA out to him.

I could see the butt of a pistol sticking out of his saddle holster, and one of those bandolier-things over his

124

shoulder, with the little round pouches dangling, each full of powder and shot. His cropped hair was gray and he had a very ordinary sort of face: the kind of middle-aged face that sits down next to you on the beach, and then within five minutes starts ordering you to turn your transistor radio off.

He dismounted, grumbling, and tried to lift the horse's front hoof, with a lot of, "Ho, Bessie-lass, whoa, Bessie-lass, *stand*, you Malignant bitch!"

Then he looked round furtively, as if afraid someone might be listening. I was, but he didn't see me. But either the mare knew I was there, or she didn't fancy the guy mucking around with her hoof. She rolled her eye and backed off vigorously, pulling him about ten yards back the way he'd come.

Then I heard a female voice say:

"Good-day, Trooper Collins. You do dance a fine dance with a strange lady."

"Good-day, Mistress Johanna." He had a cringing voice, with a bit of bully in it.

"I shall *thank* you to call me Mistress *Vavasour*, sir, for my mother is dead! What is the matter with your horse?"

"I had her after Naseby, mistress, and I swear to this day she is for the King and cannot bear the hand of Parliament."

"If the Scripture did allow me to swear, sir, which it does *not*, I would swear she does look for a gentle rider, whether he support King or Parliament. Let me see the hoof, sir. Look, here is a small stone that did fret her."

"It does fret *me*, mistress, to see you walking here alone. Where is your servant? What is in your basket?"

"Bread, Trooper Collins, and drink."

"Who for?"

"Would you put me to the test, sir, here on my own father's land? When I do but as the Scripture commands, keeping myself pure in all things, and tending to the widows and orphans? As the Lord did tend the Five Thousand, by the Sea of Galilee?"

"There are Malignants about, mistress."

"If I believed all that you did prate, Trooper Collins, then I should believe there were Malignants on the very benches of the Parliament. Aye, and in Colonel Cromwell's privy. Let me pass, sir. What *saint* did ever hamper the Lord's work?"

The word "saint" came out very sarky.

Collins' voice was wheedling now. "We must take care for the King and Parliament, mistress. . . ."

"Mayhap we must take care for the poor King. I do think the Parliament will very well take care of itself."

Collins mounted and went off, grumbling about the monstrous regiment of women. Johanna called out, very low, her voice bubbling over with mischief, "Come out, Master Jack!"

I parted the bushes and she burst into a fit of giggles.

"I see you did put your best finery on for me today, Master Jack. And that is a fine staff you have in your hand. Are you going to give me a great buffet?"

"I am trying to look less like a witch!"

"Oh, you have *succeeded*, Master Jack. You do look like a Common Cur, who has robbed an old-clothes booth." Her giggles renewed.

I took her small cool hand, and drew her deep into the bushes.

"Nay, Master Jack. You must not handle me like a strumpet from a stew. What would good Trooper Collins say?"

126

I made her sit down. "Now look, Johanna. . . ."

"*Mistress* Johanna . . . or I shall make you call me Mistress Vavasour, like poor Trooper Collins."

"Look, this may be a great joke to you, but it's not to me. Am I dreaming, or what?" Even at the time, it seemed pretty stupid, to ask a person in your dream if you were dreaming or not.

But she stopped laughing, and took my hand. Then she deliberately dug her nails into my palm. I yelped, and pulled my hand away. There, in the palm, were four bright-red half-moons, deep, and two oozing blood.

"You are not dreaming, Master Jack. For if you awaken a dozen times, those marks will still be there."

"But what is this place? How did I get here?"

"You are full of riddles today, Master Jack. Let me ask you one. What is it that shall come upon you mightily at a time that you did not seek it, and the more you shall behold it, the less you shall see of it?"

I thought about that one. Seemed pretty relevant to the fix I was in.

"Don't know the answer."

"The answer is *mist*, Master Jack."

How right she was. I was in a mist, getting more lost and feeling odder by the minute. How did I get out of here?

"Do you wish to return to your own time now, Master Jack?"

I gasped. Was she a mind-reader or something?

"No, I don't want to go back—yet."

"Then you must follow behind me, and carry my basket. So that I shall have a servant . . . as good Trooper Collins wished."

"Where are we going?"

"To see Goody Hooper and tend her."

"But . . . ." I indicated my clothes.

"Do not fret. She is old, and talks much nonsense. Even if she did gossip about you, no one would believe her. We are quite safe. If we do meet someone on the road, stand behind me with your eyes lowered, and I shall say you are some poor Tom o' Bedlam, but a good servant and faithful to his mistress. Then they will not clap you in the stocks."

"Oh, go on!"

"Do you ask Trooper Collins. He is a great fellow for putting poor people in the stocks."

The smell hit us, and I thought: pigs.

The smell got worse. We turned off the road and there was a large mound in the corner of a field, with a low stone wall round the bottom and broom and furze flowering all golden on top.

We went round the far side, and there was a low hole in the mound and I thought: why do they keep their pigs in there? They'd flourish better in an open field.

Johanna bent and entered the hole. I heard murmuring; something about a taper. Then Johanna put her head out and said, "Come, Master Jack." She wasn't giggling now.

I bent double and went in, and the smell was horrific. I kept trying not to throw up, and managing. But the acid of vomit was in my throat every time I belched. I was just standing hunched in the dark, trying not to throw up. Then I noticed a candle burning, and the silhouette of Johanna holding the hand of someone lying on straw. The somebody moved and the straw rustled.

"Goody," said Johanna softly, gently. "Goody, I have brought a gentleman to see you. Master Jack Webster."

A head turned toward me. Tangled gray hair—and along every gray strand a row of shining dots. I knew what they were, because my dad once brought a boy home from school who had the same.

The old woman's hair was full of lice.

She had a bit of ragged blanket over her legs and another bit over her shoulders, but she hadn't much else on, except a bit of white and ginger fur across bare wringled breasts. I'd never seen breasts so wrinkled. They were like . . . .

The bit of white and ginger fur moved, and two green eyes stared at me with lordly indifference. It was a cat. After a long minute it turned away and thrust its nose back between the wrinkled breasts. Then I saw there was another cat, a gray tatty thing, lying under the blanket that lay across the woman's legs. Just its head and ears showing. God, there were cats all over, staring from corners.

"This is a fine young man," said Goody Hooper. "A very fine young gentleman." She held a hand to my mouth, and I had to kiss it. The skin was thin over the bone, and the knuckles were too big; the whole hand stiff somehow.

"He is a *kind* young man," said Goody Hooper. "I shall sing you a song, kind young gentleman."

She started, and the sound was like the puffing of a pair of old leather bellows. But there was a tune to it; the tune we now call "Scarborough Fair." I'll never forget the words, because I had to strain to hear every one of them.

> *"Will you make me a fine cambric shirt*
> *Parley with Red Mary in time*
> *Remember me to one who rides by*
> *She was once a true love of mine.*

First there was one and then there were two
Three and six and then there were nine
The Devil make you a fine cambric shirt
Mary was once a true love of mine.

Off with her gown and off with her shoon
Off with her kirtle all made of green
Off with her skin and break up the bones
Now she's gone, she's no love of mine."

The old woman laughed. "Do you know what I have just sung, young man? It is a song to be sung for casting off the spell of venery. Cast upon you by a witch who is also your paramour." She laughed with ancient sexy knowingness; I had no need to ask what venery was.

"Do not talk like that, Goody!" said Johanna sharply. "Hobekinus is coming."

The old woman was silent for a moment, like a crushed child. Then she flared up. "What do *I* care for Hobekinus? I shall be dead before Hobekinus comes. He will not dig me out of my grave." Then she turned to me. "Give me a kiss, young gentleman. Give a kiss to a poor old woman who has lost her leg."

She drew back her ragged blanket with a gesture like a strip-tease dancer, and there was one scrawny bare leg, and another cut short at the knee and rounded off like a stick.

"Kiss me. You shall not be the first. The Devill has come to me every night these last eight years. A fine black man, in black velvet with a lace collar. He says, 'Meg, I must lie with thee,' and he has his way with me till morning. But he is cold, cold as clay. I do fancy you would be warmer, young gentleman. Be kind to Mistress Johanna, as she is kind to us all. Is *he* the one, Mistress?"

But Johanna was busy with her basket. "Now I have brought you bread and milk, Goody, and you must eat and drink both, and not give all to these *wicked* cats. . . ."

"He has not kissed me!" wailed Goody Hooper. "The young gentleman . . . ."

I fled.

I was still throwing up into the hedge when Johanna joined me.

"Thanks very much," I said savagely. "Did you have to do that? Your idea of a joke or something?"

"I do go and see her every day. She is a child of God. If I did not take her food she would starve."

"She's a . . . a *witch*!"

"She is not. She is just old—more than *forty* years old. No man will go near her, since her husband did die, and then her son."

"But all those cats . . . ."

"How can she keep them out, unless she does shut her door, and then she will have no light? The cats do steal all her food, but they do keep her warm and they do keep her company."

"But all that stuff about the Devil . . . ?"

She shrugged. "There are many Common Curs who do come to widows in the night, and *say* they are the Devill, to make sport with them. But they do only come to *young* widows. Perhaps they did come to Goody Hooper once, before she did lose her leg. Now she does but dream it."

"But why, for God's sake?"

"When you do lie in your bed and cannot sleep, Master Jack, do *you* not imagine that young women come to you? Comely naked young women? Ah, you do blush, Master Jack!"

"But why does she have to make it the Devil?"

"Who else would want her now?"

"But isn't it dangerous, her talking like that to complete strangers?"

Johanna nodded sadly. "Very dangerous. But I do not think she cares if she be hanged or not, she is so old. I do think she would like to be dead. And sometimes, if she does talk like that, people give her things to eat, out of fear or wonder. It does help her in her begging, if the farmers do think she is a witch and could put a spell on their cow."

We walked back down the road. It was all so strange, my head felt it was bursting. I kept drawing it down between my shoulders, like I was a tortoise or something. Kept on staring about me wildly, as if anything could jump out at me from anywhere. A muscle was twitching in my left cheek, and another in my bicep, and there was an ache in all my bones.

"Master Jack . . . did you ever—in your time—hear tell of a man called Hobekinus? He is a man of the law who lives by Manningtree. They do say he does not buy his shoes at the booths like other men. He does have them made specially, so that he can walk silently, and hear what men say before they know he is come. Men do pay him to hang witches, and I have heard he is coming here."

"No . . . no." I was trying to listen, but it was all going round and round inside my head.

She shook me, small hands very urgent. "Will you find out about Hobekinus, Master Jack? Will you *promise* on the Scriptures? Many will die. . . ."

"I promise," I mumbled.

She put a hand on my forehead; cool. "You have had too much fret, Master Jack. Sleep now . . . find Hobekinus."

I think her lips brushed my cheek.

I came round lying face down in the field of potatoes. my mouth full of soil and my shirt-front stinking of vomit. There were the marks of four fingernails in the palm of my hand. Far too small for my fingernails, but they'd taken some of my skin with them.

17

I was at the end of my lane, waiting to turn left, when Susan drove past in the Land-Rover.

I waved.

She looked the other way. Quite deliberately she set her mouth and looked the other way; up the hill, the way she was going. Like I was a bloody stranger. Or someone she no longer wanted to know.

I panicked and went after her. I was panicking pretty easily by that time. She put her foot down hard, but it didn't do her any good. A Cub can burn off a Land-Rover any day. Caught her before the top of the hill. But she went on driving, right in the middle of the road, so I couldn't get past her. Sounded my airhorns, enough to waken the dead, but she never gave a sign she heard. I could see her dark head through the rear window, staring straight ahead.

We went through Besingtree at eighty, an accident waiting for a place to happen. Lucky there were no cops or kids about, because she was driving wild, going over the white line at every corner. In the end I cut the speed, scared. She slowed down too. But not enough for me to pass her.

Villages went past like a nightmare; never even noticed their names. Kept on wishing the Cub was some Jap-crap, like a Honda 400 Four. There were straight bits of road where I could've taken her, on a 400 Four. The Cub just hadn't got the punch.

Then, suddenly, she pulled up. Nearly went into the back of her. I cranked over just in time, then had to crank the other way to avoid an amazed GPO van. Ended up tangled with a large road sign, welcoming me to Clacton, Queen of the East Anglian Coast.

The postman got out to give me his views on my driving. He had me by the lapels of my jacket for ten minutes, but he was too small to hit. By the time I'd persuaded him people were posting early for Christmas, I expected Susan to be gone.

But she was still sitting, a hundred yards back, hands on the steering wheel, face a pale blur through the windscreen.

I walked back, legs shaking. "What the hell . . . ?"

Then I saw the suitcases on the back seat.

"I'm going away," she said.

"Where?"

"I don't know."

"When you coming back?"

"Never." She was dragging on a fag like it was a blast furnace, and the ashtray was full of fag-ends, one still smoking. Her hands were shaking, and I don't think it was my near-crash with the GPO van.

"What about Derek?" I asked feebly.

"We had a row."

"About the rat?"

"That's how it started."

"Did he tell you anything?"

She stared silently down the road; wherever she was headed for.

"Did he *tell* you anything?"

"Everything."

"Well?"

"I had to promise not to tell you. Before he would tell me *anything*."

"For God's sake—you owe me something. You *promised*." My voice was starting to sound hysterical.

"I owe Derek something too; I love him."

"Which is why you're leaving him?"

"Yes, if you like. I'm not staying round to watch while . . . ."

"Yes?"

She chewed her lip in a way that must have hurt her. Then looked at me like somebody tortured and said, "See where we are?"

"Yeah, Clacton. Civilization. I'd forgotten what it looked like."

"You're *safe* here, John. Why don't you just keep on going? Go home to your parents. . . ."

"My gear's back in the barn."

"Give me your home address and I'll send it on to you. Promise!"

"How can you send it on, if you're going away?"

"If you go away, I can go back. I'll *have* to go back. . . ."

"This is *mad!*"

"It's the truth."

"Please tell me what's going on." I held out my hands to her, imploringly.

She took hold of my wrist; stared at the marks of the fingernails in my hand. "Who did *that*?" Her mouth quirked up in . . . disgust?

"Nobody that matters."

"Go now, John. Or you'll never go."

"What about you?"

"I'm not important. It doesn't matter if I *go* back or not.

"I'm not going away. I've made a promise and I'm going to keep it. I believe in keeping *my* promises."

"Oh, my God," she said, and began to cry.

"Stuff you!" I shouted, and went back and disentangled the Cub. As I passed Susan she was still sitting with her hands on the steering wheel. Still crying and not bothering to wipe the tears off her face.

I rode back to Besingtree feeling one hell of a hero. *Greater love hath no man* and all that crap.

The Besingtree Bookshop, Prop J. Manning Fielding, was open. J. Manning himself, resplendent in bright red shirt and oatmeal tie, was finishing a crafty Gauloise in the doorway. Analyzing the lamp-post habits of the local hound, before once again immersing himself in the navel-fluffing rituals of eighteenth-century Persian blacksmiths.

I ran up to him and blurted like a schoolkid, "Ever heard of a guy called Hobekinus?"

Anybody else would have made some smart crack about wasn't Hobekinus playing outside-left for Borussia this season? But old J. Manning simply retired to his desk and began tapping an ivory paper-knife against his lips, whisling a tuneless tune.

"Hobekinus . . . dog-Latin. Somebody trying to make himself sound important sometime in the seventeenth century. That rings a bell. Hobekinus . . . Hopequins . . . Hopkins. . . . Our old friend Matthew Hopkins . . . yeeeesss." There was a dry charitable regret in his voice. Rather as if Hopkins had been a promising pupil, sent down for getting the Vice-chancellor's daughter pregnant.

He turned to his occult shelf, went straight to a fat gray book, consulted the index and said, "Pages 201–214. That'll be one pound to you, sir." He held the book out tantalizingly. He was a better businessman than I'd thought. Or *was* he? Did any bookseller know his shelves *that* well? Or had he had the book waiting for me, all the time? I stared at him; but the light of the windows was reflecting in his spectacles again.

I coughed up my quid, carried the book out to the saddle of the Cub and read:

"Matthew Hopkins alias Hopequins alias Hobekinus. Self-styled Witchfinder General. Seventeenth-century man of mystery, date of birth unknown. Death recorded in burial registers of Mistley-cum-Manningtree 12th August, 1647. 'Nobodie in the localite was present at hys burial, outside the precinctes of the church in the dark of night when no one else was about his business.' It is thought the vicar of the parish forbade his burial in holy ground. For centuries after his death, he was so hated, that the name of 'Hopkins' was taboo in the area.

"Fourth son of James Hopkins, Puritan minister of Wenham Magna. Whole family ultra-Puritan. Mother, Marie, coming from the Low Countries, had suffered much at the hands of Spanish Papists. Hopkins was sent back to his mother's country to complete his education. Studied maritime law in Amsterdam. Gained knowedge of French which enabled him, on his return, to get work as a shipowner's clerk in Mistley. Also learned Latin, which enabled him to read deeply into the law of witchcraft trials. Unlike England, these were rife on the continent at the time. Four hundred witches were burned in one day at Toulouse. Hopkins may have realized during his time in Holland that the discovery and execution of witches was an excellent money-making profession.

"His claim to be a lawyer has been proved fraudulent by consulting the contemporary rolls of the Inns of Court. Nevertheless, he knew much more of the laws of witchcraft, as set out in King James' book *Daemonologie* than the country magistrates with whom he dealt.

"He instigated witch-hunts in 1665, when the fabric of law and order in England was crumbling under the impact of the Civil War. The first witch-hunt was carefully stage-managed in his home town of Mistley. He owned the Thorn Inn where the trials were held. The magistrates were friends of the Hopkins family.

"The victims were carefully chosen; women of the poorest class, usually widows and spinsters without menfolk to support them. Such women, forced to make their living by begging, were a nuisance to the surrounding Puritan farmers.

"Hopkins claimed he had met and got the better of the Devil, and won from him the notorious 'Devil's List' in which every witch in England had signed away her soul in her own blood. In truth, he had set up his own spy network of Puritan committees, who would send for him when the mood of their district seemed suitable for a witch-hunt.

"Having hanged the Mistley witches, Hopkins was summoned to conduct larger witch-hunts in Suffolk, Norfolk, Rutland, Cambridge and the Isle of Ely. He made a fortune from his work; he was paid £6 at Aldeburgh, £15 at King's Lynn and £23 at Stowmarket. The Stowmarket money alone would be worth £3500 today.

"However, even during the Civil War and among

Puritans, opposition swiftly gathered, mobilized by the Roundhead broad sheet *The Moderate Intelligencer*. Worse, drunk on his success, Hopkins went so far as to suspect Oliver Cromwell himself of being a witch, because of his belief in the lucky number, three. Even worse, he tried to start a witch-hunt in Great Staughton (Hunts) the parish of a famous Puritan divine called John Gaule. Gaule not only repulsed Hopkins, but led a campaign against Hopkins throughout East Anglia, on the impeccable Puritan grounds that *Hopkins was doing it for profit.* Hopkins' later witch-hunts, ever wider-ranging and for diminishing returns, are thought to have been frantic attempts to keep one step ahead of the Gaule faction.

"Nevertheless, in spite of Gaule, and a Parliamentary Commission sent to curb his 'swimming' of witches, Hopkins caused the death by hanging of five hundred women, and amassed a personal fortune of £60,000 in today's terms.

"He was aided in his work by a team of witchfinders; the bigoted but sincere ranter John Stearne, and the notorious ex-midwife Mary 'Goody' Philips, who stripped and searched the accused women for the so-called 'Devil's teats' at which the Lord of Darkness was supposed to suck nourishment. The team was known sarcastically as the 'three spotless lambs of the Lord.'

"Unlike Stearne, there is no evidence that Hopkins was a man of any religious fervor, or particular Puritan piety. It must be concluded that he did the work purely for profit."

Great guy, our Hopkins, then. Himmler's sweetheart. Perfect penfriend for Jack the Ripper. All neatly packaged up long ago, in the slick language of the color supplements. But the next bit wasn't so neatly packaged Lists of Hopkins' victims.

"Boones, Joyce. St. Osyth. Hanged.
"Cock, Susan. St. Osyth. Died in jail.
"Moone, Margaret. Widow. Died on her way to execution.
"Moone, Judith. Daughter of Margaret. Dealt with as an informer. Died in prison.
"Lakeland, Mary. Widow of John Lakeland, who she murdered. Burned.
"Blackburn, Mary. For entertaining evil spirits. Hanged."

The lists went on and on, page after page. Like those graveyards full of crosses you see in France, during telly programs on the First World War.

"Hooper, Meg (known as Goody Hooper). Besingtree. For having intercourse with the Devill. Hanged. April 1647."

Goody Hooper; Goody Hooper. The name rang in my mind. Goody Hooper, lice in her hair. Naked but for cats and ragged blankets. Only one leg. Give me a kiss, fine gentleman.

Hobekinus had come, for Goody Hooper.

A sudden panic hit me; the brisk main street of Besingtree became faint, and the noise of passing weekend traffic faded away. My eye ran on down that awful list, as frantically as if it had been my own exam results.

"Vavasour, Johanna. Besingtree. For leading a coven of witches. For having the Devill in her house. For keeping a familiar spirit, in the form of a cat. Hanged?"

There was no comfort in the question mark. All the names after Goody Hooper's had *Hanged?* after them with question marks. Probably some nerkish clerk to the court who hadn't kept his records clean, dry and legible.

I stared around me wildly. But there was no one in the world who could answer my questions. Not even J. Manning Fielding.

I rode up my track in the most glorious sunset. Why does the weather always mock your feelings?

As I killed my engine, News came out of the slit by the outside stair. She had nothing in her mouth. But I had the curious conviction that, inside the slit, there was a light on in the lost room.

I was half-nuts by that time, so I went across to look.

There was a light of sorts. As the sun dipped toward the western horizon, its light was streaming in the western slits of the lost room. Why had I never noticed before?

I put my eye to the slit by the outside stair. Couldn't see much, because the slit was only three inches wide, and the wall was two feet thick.

I thought I could make out the back of a knobbly chair, and perhaps the top of a table. But I couldn't be sure because everything was smothered in dead brown autumn leaves. Blown through the slits in how many autumns?

Then the sun went down and I couldn't see a bloody thing.

There wasn't much point in going to bed that night. I quarreled with my sack worse than Derek with his Land-Rover. Then all the beans in my stomach began telling each other funny stories.

I usually slept with the door open, but the moonlight was too bright. So bright I could see all the way down the valley to Derek's and all the way up to the ring of trees. I could see the hawthorn hedges of my lane, that used to be the cottage hedges of Besingtree. Where people used to live; where Hobekinus hanged Goody Hooper. Who had called me a fine young man and sung me a song.

Funny, I could remember the song; every word of it. I started to sing it, then didn't like the sound of my own voice in the silence. If you sing, somebody might be listening.

I tried shutting the door, but that made the inside seem small and stuffy as a prison. And the moonlight still came in through the window, lighting every corner. The room was pretty empty, since I'd chucked out the oil drums and nesting boxes. Just me in my pit, and my clothes lying in a heap like a corpse, and a milking stool with my watch on it where I could reach it. And the bloody great mangel-wurzelers in the corner, eight feet high with its cast-iron wheel and big wooden funnel on top. Still, I was grateful for one thing; in no kind of light could the wurzeler have borne any resemblance to someone standing watching me in the corner. Not unless the someone had a head as big as a barrel. . . .

Every time I put my head down, I seemed to hear a

143

noise coming up to me through the floor, from the lost room. A noise like little feet walking on the mass of dead leaves down there. Up and down; up and down. Like someone restless, trying to make up their mind about something, and not quite managing it.

But every time I raised my head, the noise vanished.

Mind you, I knew what the noise was really. I'd had a bit of catarrh over the last few days. Catarrh does funny things to your ears. Once, when I was a kid, I had a cold, and all through one night I seemed to hear railway engines puffing past on the London line, nonstop. Which was crazy, because the previous week British Rail had changed over to diesel. Next morning, my dad told me that, with my eardrum blocked with catarrh, what I was hearing was the sound of my own blood whizzing through my veins.

Catarrh was as good an explanation of the footsteps as any. Except the puffer trains had gone at the same speed all night, nonstop, whereas these footsteps slowed, quickened, stopped and started. I even thought I could tell in which part of the room down there the little person was. I wasn't scared; just worried about the little person who was so upset. Except the little person was really inside my head and did that make me insane? But everyone is insane in their dreams, so I was OK really.

I *must* have dozed off; because suddenly I shot bolt upright inside my sleeping bag. I had the distinct impression that somebody had knocked on my door, four times. Not loudly, or threateningly. Quietly and discreetly, as if to say, "Let me in, on the sly."

Was it Susan, come back? She'd have been welcome to share my sleeping bag, that night. I went to the door, but there was nobody there; just the moonlight, still flooding the fields with white. You could have seen anything that moved, for miles. But nothing was moving.

I seemed to hear the knocks several times. And something that could have been a cat scratching to be let in. But I wasn't letting myself be fooled again. I just gathered the rags of sleep around me and slept on. Like Goody Hooper had gathered her cats and rags of blanket. . . .

The cat-scratching noise got louder. Only this time, thank God, there was a real live meow with it. A very cross meow. News. Glad of real—I almost said human—company, I went to the door to let her in. Now we could snuggle up.

But the damned cat would not settle. Walked all over me, like she was wearing hobnailed boots. Walked from corner to corner of the room, scratching at the floor and making little cat-grumbling noises to herself. Like she was determined to keep me awake.

Then—and I admit I was fully awake this time—four clear, quiet, discreet knocks came again. Not from the door; from the mangel-wurzeler.

I giggled hysterically. Perhaps it was a *mouse* with hobnailed boots. Or a Plague Rat using a two-pound hammer. . . . Oh, you're a real bundle of fun, Webster.

But old News walked over the wurzeler, tail upright and quivering. Uttered that ghastly yowl. Scratched frantically at the tall wooden machine, as if there really was something in there.

Knock, knock, knock, knock.

Then, in the moonlight, the whole height of the wurzeler began to sway. Just a little bit at first, then more and more. Like the dance-hall pillars in that movie about the San Francisco earthquake.

News gave one more doleful yell, and the whole thing fell onto its side with a godawful smash. News leaped for safety just in time, digging her claws into my jugular vein as she landed. I don't blame her; the thing missed her by inches and must have weighed a ton.

Then it was lying across the floor to my very feet, all planks of wood and iron cogwheels, shattered beyond repair.

Suddenly, everything became clear. The floorboards must have given way, after years of bearing the wurzeler's colossal weight. What I'd thought were knocks had just been nails giving way, or floorplanks splitting as they gave up the ghost.

But no. When I walked over, every plank of the floor was intact and in place.

Only, where the wurzeler had stood, there was a trapdoor in the floor. The entrance to the lost room, finally revealed. Why hadn't I thought of a trapdoor?

Knock, knock, knock, knock. Loud, now, under my very feet. And the cat in my arms called in answer, a glad mournful sound.

Knock, knock, knock, knock.

In a burst of rage and terror I pulled the trapdoor open. It was that or run away screaming.

I saw a flight of narrow steps. The kind it's best to walk down backward. But I walked down forward.

A wave of warmth met me, and a gold glow of candles. Only the candles were short and fat and gave off the smell of roasting meat, instead of the usual waxy smell.

There was a wooden table; dark oak and well-polished. There was an armchair with crossed legs and sagging leather for a seat. Leather books on the table, and a strange crisscross pattern of rushes on the floor. Norfolk reeds, like they use for thatching today.

And by the window slit (how funny to see it from the inside for a change) was a small figure in gray, with white collar and cuffs. Peering out of the slit, with one arm held out toward me, and the hand on the end of that arm waggling up and down, cautioning silence.

"Horses," she said in a whisper. "Horses coming from Sudbury. Four horses. *Gentlemen's* horses."

I couldn't hear a damned thing; only after straining a long time could I hear the sound of hoofs.

"The horses are tired," said Johanna. "They have come a long way. Two are carrying men, and two, women."

The cobbled yard was full of the sound of hoofs now.

"Hallo the house!" called a loutish voice. "Hallo in the Lord's Name!"

A female voice answered him, from the kitchen next door.

"*Which* Lord? The Lord of This World? Him Who Below Is? That is the lord that Common Curs do cry to, in the middle of the night."

"Tell your master that the Witchfinder has come, to find witches."

"Tell *your* master that no witches here are. Only broomsticks to sweep garbage from our kitchen, so he had best not enter it."

"Is this a *Malignant* house?"

"Nay. My master is Major Vavasour, who is with Colonel Cromwell at London. And his daughter, my mistress, is Colonel Cromwell's goddaughter. This is a house that fears God and Parliament. Get you down the village, to the cott by the pump, for there Bate the Constable is. The same that summoned you, God rot him."

"Do you curse the Constable, madam?" It was a new voice. Still a man's but only just. Soft and lisping.

"Nay, Hopkins, I do not curse the Constable. But I know he will rot in Hell for this day's work, by God's

147

Providence. As Cain does rot, who slew his brother. As the wolf does rot, that came in sheep's clothing. Do you not fear God's Providence burning against *you*, Master Hopkins?"

There was a muttering in the yard, in which a querulous female voice complained her bones did ache.

"Fret not, Goody Philips," lisped Hopkins. "We shall return to this house. Then you may seek for what you will find."

The sound of hoofs straggled off down the lane.

Johanna left the window, and sat down across the table from me. Her eyes were huge; full of the shadows of thoughts and points of candlelight.

"What have you learned of this Hobekinus, Master Jack?"

Have you ever seen a man eating winkles with a pin? Poking them out of their shells, as they still do in the East End? That was what Johanna's brain did to my brain that night. In the end I grew weary and dazed, watching fascinated as her little hand spidered thick black lettering across thick brown curling paper. Noting most carefully every fact I told her. I supposed I must have dozed off, because I suddenly heard her say, "Farewell, Master Jack!"

I opened my eyes too late to see her. All I got was a dreamlike vision of autumn leaves pouring in through the slits of windows, billowing in the air like brown snow, like brittle feathers. Settling on the table, on the floor, on me. I pushed back the chair and tried to get to my feet, but instead collapsed painlessly into the sea of leaves and slept.

18

I wakened in semidarkness. Heavy boots were clumping on the floorboards overhead. Got in a panic, thinking Hopkins' lot were coming for *me*. But it was only Derek.

"Hallo, John? Hallo? Hallo? Hallo?" He sounded worried; bloody worried.

I called out from the mass of dead leaves in which I was reclining so gracefully.

Derek came belting down the trapdoor stair. The rope handrail came apart in his hands.

"Hah—there you are—had a wild night? Right old mess—dangerous junk—should have been cleared away —years ago. Could've broken your neck—upsy-daisy." He hauled me upstairs by sheer brute force. Two farmhands were already carrying the remains of the mangel-wurzeler out to a tractor and trailer that stood in the yard. They had the silent respectful efficiency of undertaker's men.

"Brought you a bed," said Derek. "Can't have you sleeping rough forever. Must clear up that room downstair first though—frightful—can't have been seen to in years. Nip down the village—get a breakfast—here's two quid—treat yourself."

I went to the local transport cafe. Had a slap-up breakfast—cereal, bacon, sausage, eggs, toast and coffee. Ate till I could hardly move. Just as well. It was the last good meal I had for some while.

When I got back to the barn, everybody had gone. So had the leaves from the lost room. The farmhands had shoveled them into black polythene bags and left them by the barn door, where they lay like the decently covered victims of some air disaster.

The bed had been duly installed in the upstairs room. I could see why Derek had treated me to a breakfast. Had I seen it before they installed it, I wouldn't have given it house room. It was a four-poster in black fat knobbly oak, and hung with thick dull brown curtains. It was only about five feet long and four feet wide, and when I got inside and drew the curtains, it felt like a cage with a sagging brown roof. It had a feather mattress, and the quills stuck through the mattress cover and into my hands. It smelled of damp and mildew, cowdung and lavender. And it was full of ghosts whispering and making love, and screaming in childbirth and poisoning and dying. That's how it felt to me, anyway. Middle-aged people go on and on about how dangerous motorbikes are; they should've tried that bed. A hundred people die in bed for every one that dies on a bike, and at least a bike's a *clean* death and quick. . . . I moved my gear and sleeping bag back to the main barn. The straw and mouse-droppings felt like heaven.

Then I had a nosy down into the lost room. It was a room to crack your brain—oak panels on the ceiling as well as the walls. Settles, cupboards, chests, tables, chairs —just like a museum. All marvelously preserved—no dry rot or anything. Still, I could tell why that was. It was cool but bone-dry. Kept so by the little breezes that played constantly from one unglazed window slit to another. The walls were too thick for the rain to get in. And rats and mice hadn't managed to get in either—the window slits were too high up the walls.

But I couldn't bear to stay down there long. The thin light coming through the slits only made the darkness worse. And the silence—you couldn't hear a thing that was happening outside. I picked a book off the table, and took it out into the sunshine to read.

It was John Gerard's *Herball*—the sixteenth-century first edition, calf-bound. I was holding several thousand quid in my hand, like it was *Playboy*. But I no longer thought about it. Familiarity breeds contempt. On the flyleaf was written *Joh. Vavasour, her boke.*

I opened a page at random.

"MANDRAKE. There hath been ridiculous tales of this plante. That it hath rootes that resemble the legges of a man. That it is seldom found growing naturally but under a gallows, where the matter that hath fallen from the dead body hath given it the shape of a man. That if a man do pull it up he will surely die a short space after. Therefore he must tie a dog thereunto, and tempt it with rost meate, that in going after the meate it pulleth it up. The mandrake will give a greate shreeke. Strange effects are supposed to bee in mandrakes, to cause women to bee fruitful and beare children if they carry the same neer their bodies. With many other such doltish dreames. But the fruit of the wombe are the inheritance that cometh from the Lord (Psalm 127)."

Beside the print, in a tiny hand, Johanna had written, *What doe* men *know, Master Gerard?*

I turned to another page.

"SPURGE. Walking along the seacoast with a gentleman called Mr. Rich I took but one drop of spurge in my mouth; which did so swell and inflame my throte that I did hardly escape with my life. In like case the other gentleman, which caused us to take for our horses and post for our lives unto the next farmhouse to drinke some milke to quell the extremity of our heat."

I looked up from the book. Little puffy white clouds were sailing overhead; the wind was moving all the leaves in the tree, just enough to make that pleasant hissing that sometimes sounds like rain, and sometimes like the waves of the sea. It would be pleasant to spend all day out here, reading a seventeenth-century book of herbs.

But the slit by the outside stair watched me blackly; and News, sitting in the doorway of what had been my bedroom, watched me blackly too, and opened her mouth in a silent pink triangle of demand. There was something I had to do.

I went down into the black silence of the lost room, and waited. News waited with me, very still and quiet, not licking or scratching.

I kept on glancing up, at the light coming through the open trapdoor. I could just see one of my bike panniers, where I'd left it in a corner of the bedroom. It was a comfort.

But after I'd waited a long time in vain, it came to me that I was *clinging* to the light of the trapdoor, the sight of the pannier. To the present day and sanity, motorbikes and the Welfare State.

No guts, I said to myself. And reached up and closed the trapdoor.

When I turned, there were candles flickering, and Johanna was sitting at her table, her head in her hands in a way that frightened me.

Then she looked up, and there were great shadows under her eyes, and her face was wet with tears.

"They have hanged Goody Hooper," she said, too calmly. "They did take her the first morning. Bate did lead them straight to where she did live. And she did confess she was a witch and had the Devill in her bed; and did sing them her songs. Then they brought her to the court and gave her meat and drink and she was happy to have the attention of so many fine gentlemen. But when she had said all she did have to say, they did press her further, to tell who her fellow witches were. And she did say there were none. But they did keep her awake, both day and night, without sup, and threatened her with burning if she would not tell who her fellow witches were. But if she did tell they would spare her.

"On the third day, to make an end of their badgering, she did name one, and then another. But they were not satisfied till she did name nine. Then they did write all down, and got her to make her mark. Then they did say they would spare her from burning but not from hanging, and they did take her out and hang her, and burnt her body after."

"But . . . why?"

"A witch's dying testament hath greater virtue than a living witch, who might recant when she did see the damage she had done. Today they do try the nine. And more are taken and pressed—honest women. I have walked all night, hearing their children crying. I must go to the trial."

I wanted to call out to her not to go. I wanted to warn her that she would be accused herself . . . and hanged. But it wouldn't have made any difference. Her little face was set and stony.

"But what good can *you* do, even if you go?"

"Hopkins does have it all his own way, because honest folk do turn their backs and will not go. But if honest folk were there . . . . Only, will you come with me, Master Jack? I must not go without a manservant to guard me, and my father did take all our men when he joined Master Cromwell. I will keep you safe, Master Jack."

I thought wildly. Half a mo, I thought. I'll just nip back for my Colt 45. Or Starsky and Hutch. Kojak. The Brigade of Guards.

But when I'd stopped thinking, there was only me there. And where was I going to get a Colt 45?

"Will you come, Master Jack?"

"Yeah," I said, my legs starting to tremble, and my guts threatening to drop down between them like a newborn calf.

She came close, sniffed at me and said briskly, "You do smell right now. You do not smell like an apothecary's shop."

I almost grinned. Hadn't been riding the Cub much recently, and hadn't had a bath for a fortnight.

"I have brought clothes. Do you put them on."

A loose woolen shirt, so short I could hardly tuck it into the coarse scratchy trousers. Square-toed boots; both the same shape so I could have worn each on either foot. When I tried walking, it felt like I was wearing a pair of leather buckets. She showed me myself in a dark steel mirror, no bigger than a bike mirror. My hair was dirty and came down on my shoulders. I hadn't shaved for a week. I looked a right scruff. Horribly like somebody who somebody else might burn for a witch in a fit of abstraction. I felt naked without my bike gear. Oh, this was all no more real than a nightmare. No worse

154

than fighting the Japs or Dracula. I'd find some way of waking up before Hopkins and his mob got their hands on me. . . .

"Come, Master Jack. Put this in your pocket. If you keep it safe, it will keep you safe."

She passed me a scrap of stiff brown paper. On it she had written, "Thys man is God-fearing and no Common Cur. Hee is dumbe from hys Mother's wombe, but a goode Hodge who will work an honest daie for hys supper. At times hee doth wander abroad for many daies on end. Yf any man of goodewill do read thys note, give hym a daies worke and hys supper and do you point hym out ye true road to Diss, wheer hee ys my faithefull servaunt.

Kill-sin Kendall, ye servaunt of
God atte Diss in Norfolke"

I was still deciphering the spidery words when Johanna said, sharply, "Drink this!" and put a little cup in my hand.

I drank it without even looking at it.

Next second I was reeling about, falling over benches and banging into the walls of the room. My throat felt like I'd drained a battery of acid. My eyes were so full of tears I could see nothing. Then firm little hands directed me to a chair, and she actually laughed.

"I do not poison you, Master Jack. It is but the spurge. Do you drink this milk, after the fashion of Master Gerard."

She put a pitcher in my hands, big as a pint-pot, and I drank it to the bottom, not caring if it was pee or prussic acid. But it was milk, though I could scarcely taste it. After that my throat only felt like the worst sore throat you ever had. I opened my mouth to say, "What the hell did you do that for?" Not a sound came out, but a croak.

"*Croak*," I said again. "*Croak, croak, croak.*" I couldn't even manage "Nevermore" like Edgar Allan Poe's bloody raven.

"It is to keep you safe, Master Jack!"

"Thanks," I said, only it came out croak.

"It was the only way, Master Jack."

She led me upstairs, and down into the yard; there was an apple-cheeked little woman standing there in a dark blue dress that stretched to her feet. At least she would have been apple-cheeked, if she had not been white as a sheet. Johanna said it was Mistress Podmore, and she was coming too. The woman said something sharp, and I recognized the voice that had given Hopkins the rough time that other night. So we set off, Johanna and Mistress Podmore walking in front, and me trailing behind.

There were a pair of stone pillars with balls on top, at the entrance to the yard, where there was only a dirty big gap in my day, and then we were walking down the village street of Old Besingtree.

I suppose you want to know what it was like? Well you can forget Merrie England, with black-and-white half timber and roses round the door. These houses straggled down a mud track, and they not only had no telly aerials on the chimneys—most of them had no chimneys, just sort of stubby towers of stones and mud with smoke coming out. The thatch looked old, black and moldy, the half timber was sagging and rotten, and people seemed to have filled holes in their walls with straw and stones and bits of old basket and cowdung— any crap that came to hand. No glass in the windows —some had sodden bits of paper flapping over them, and some had Sweet Fanny Adams—just holes in the wall with dirty faces peering out. It made the barn look like Buckingham Palace.

But I didn't notice all that much, because everybody was staring at me. I thought I'd been rumbled; till I realized they were all bloody midgets—they made me feel as big as King Kong. What they were staring at wasn't a suspected witch, but a strange giant.

We went down down the hill. Derek's house and the church seemed a million miles away, but we got there in the end. And the nearer we got to them, the more folk were out of doors, standing in little knots, like people do before a wedding or after a road accident. They were all staring at Derek's house. Which looked much the same, except it had no garden in front; just a big space of cobbles and one or two horses tied to posts.

Nobody said a blessed thing, but they were all looking at Johanna, and you could tell they worshiped the ground she stood on. She really was some sort of bigwig; I could tell that.

She didn't make straight for the front door of Derek's house; she went up the side, where a ring of people were standing silent in a cobbled stable yard. A stable yard that isn't there any more.

Johanna pushed her way through the ring of people, and Mistress Podmore and I followed.

"They do test the witch, Mistress Vavasour," said a man. "They have walked her all night, and now they do wait for the Devill to come to her."

In the middle of the cobbled yard, quite alone, a plump old lady sat on a high stool. She was naked, apart from a dirty vest-thing that didn't cover her at all below the waist. Her old hand kept trying to pull the vest down, to cover herself decently. But she couldn't manage; it was far too short. And all the time she was rocking on the stool, backward and forward, sort of crooning to herself with grief. Her eyes stared at nothing and nobody.

The man said, in an awed whisper, "She has called upon her familiar spirit. It is a black pullet called Nan. We are waiting for it to come and suck sustenance from her Devill's teats."

Johanna turned on him in a fury. "A black pullet called Nan? Do *you* not have six black pullets at home, Master Dacon? That do lay you fine eggs?"

"Aye, mistress," The man gave back before her fury.

"And did not Goody Finch here buy a black pullet from you? That same pullet she does call Nan?"

"Aye, Mistress Vavasour."

"Are not all *your* pullets familiar spirits, then? For you do call them by name; Bess and Mab, Mary and Marjorie."

"No, Mistress Vavasour. Yes, Mistress Vavasour. I do mean . . . ."

"I do not think you know *what* you mean. Mayhap the Devill has taken your wits also, Master Dacon?"

The man turned pale. "I am no witch, mistress!"

"Then neither is Goody Finch here." Johanna swept forward and put her arm round the old lady, who came awake and seemed to recognize her, and gave her an odd, faraway little smile.

But a stout woman in brown had pushed her way into the ring. She faced up to Johanna, with a kind of crude authority.

"Do not touch the witch. Or are *you* her familiar, mistress, that seek to bring her comfort?"

"Oh, I am familiar. I am familiar with you and your works, Goody Philips. I did hear you were the worst midwife in Manningtree, till Master Hopkins took you

158

from the ginnel, and put you on a fine horse—when the magistrates did want to put you in the stocks for ridding women of unwanted babes."

The shot went home. The woman bit her lip and then said slyly, "Who did tell you my name? No man knows me in this place."

"Oh," said Johanna, turning to the crowd so they could get the full benefit of her words, "it does not need the Devill to tell me that, Goody Philips. My friends at Bury do tell me of your work, and my friends at Norwich and my friends at Ely. You are *famed* for your works, Goody Philips. I do read of them in the broadsheets, and they are spoken of even in the benches of the Parliament."

Every shot went home. The coarse woman kept looking toward the house, as if hoping someone might come out and help her. She didn't seem all that bright. And Johanna kept up her attack remorselessly.

"Who does say that Goody Finch is a witch?" She looked inquiringly at the crowd. People began shaking their heads, denying that *they* had said Goody Finch was a witch. The crowd's mood was swinging. They were jumpy and uncertain; ready to follow anybody who was firm.

"Goody Hooper did say that Goody Finch was a witch," said the coarse woman, stubbornly. But she was sweating now. "Goody Hooper did say that Goody Finch did send her black pullet Nan to blight Master Alderman's cows and dry up their milk."

"Master Alderman's *cows!*" cried Johanna incredulously. "But Master Alderman did only ever have *one* cow, and she was barren from birth. You prate of things of which you know nothing. Let this woman go. Where are her clothes?"

"She does carry the Devill's teats," shouted Goody Philips. "Where her impes do suck at her."

"Where? Show me!"

Two white-bonneted heads bent over the old lady's bare legs.

"Hemorrhoids!" shouted Johanna. "That all women do have, once they have borne children."

"They are the Devill's teats!"

"You have a wrett on *your* face, Goody Philips. Doth the Devill kiss you there? And have you no hemorrhoids? I will show you what is under my skirts, if you do show me what is under yours."

"You are but a maid. . . ." But Goody Philips' protest was lost in the great shout of insulting laughter that went up from the crowd. The kind of laughter that is half a jeer. People were approaching the old lady on the stool with garments and half-kind expressions, as if they were ashamed.

"Look!" shrieked Goody Philips. She pointed dramatically up in the air, and the crowd fell back, suddenly silent. "Look, Satan comes!"

I glanced round, like the rest, not knowing what to expect.

A butterfly was dancing in the sunlit air above the yard; a normal cabbage-white.

"The impe comes," bawled Goody Philips.

The butterfly flew here and there, almost seeming to settle, then changing its mind. But it was hovering nearer and nearer to the old lady, who continued to rock and stare into space.

"If it do settle on her . . . ," whispered Goody Philips, dramatically, "it is proof she is a witch."

"And if it settle on *you*, Goody Philips?" asked Johanna.

160

"Or on me? Or on John Godbear there? Or on yon gate-post? Pray tell me, mistress, what will *that* mean? Is every flea and cockroach an impe?" But her voice was desperate, for the butterfly came ever nearer to the old woman.

Then, as always, the butterfly changed its mind, and soared upward, and clean over the roof of the house.

"I do think the impe hath smelt a better cabbage somewhere else!" shouted Johanna. "Get you back to Mistley to discover witches, Goody."

"There are no witches left in Mistley," shouted Goody Philips.

"That is because Master Hopkins hath put them on fine horses, to ride hither and thither to pester honest folk!"

Goody Philips shouted and shouted, until she was red in the face. But not a sound could be heard coming out of her mouth, for the yell the crowd was putting up. People began pushing her away from the old lady, and stamping on her feet. You could tell they really hated her guts.

Then the old cow burst into tears and ran into the house. For a second, the crowd looked frightened. People began to back away from the house door, as if they were expecting Hopkins to come out with the devil riding on him bareback. Then Johanna yelled, "Let us go and see God's justice done!" and made for the door herself.

As one man, the crowd swept in after her, parting me from her.

19

A long low room, with a row of beer barrels on trestles at the far end. The windows were small, but daylight showed through chinks between the woodwork of the walls. Ceiling and beams black with soot, and a poor smoky fire burning to the right. There was sawdust on stone slabs of the floor.

I remembered Derek had said his house used to be the inn; this must be the taproom.

I pushed in among everyone else, and sat on the sawdust of the floor. There were benches, but they'd been arranged in blocks at the far end, one on the left and one on the right.

On the right, the accused witches sat. I hardly looked at them. Nobody seemed to look at them. They seemed the least important people in the room; just a mass of blue and brown and gray, head bowed and faces hidden by those funny bonnets that came down onto both cheeks. They only raised their heads sometimes when someone mentioned them by name. Otherwise they stared at their clasped hands, and writhed on the hard benches to ease their stiffness, and coughed and belched continually, as if to let out their fear. They had the look of flowers in a vase, just before your mother throws them in the dustbin.

The lot on the other benches were livelier. A back row of soldiers, lounging against the wall with their helmets off, and their sword belts and bandoliers tossed down on the floor among the sawdust. There were six, and I think they must have been on leave, because two had bandaged hands. Certainly they were in crap-order for soldiers. They kept on wandering across to the barrels and helping themselves to a refill, every time there was a lull in the business. You could tell they thought a lot of themselves. Trooper Collins was among them.

The bench in front of them was filled with shop-keepers; men with leather aprons and sour expressions; like they'd been cheated by one customer too many and were wondering where next week's rent was coming from. One of them was constantly leaping to his feet and they were calling him Bate the Constable. He had a sleeveless leather jerkin, a potbelly and little yellow whiskers all over his chin.

Towering above them all, sitting astride a beer barrel, was a broad red-haired man with a bristling mustache and fierce blue eyes. He looked so ridiculously like Derek, I almost called out to him. Then he looked at me, and his eyes were a little crazier than Derek's; and a lot cockier. Like he owned the earth and *knew* it. He was certainly a Pooley, if only from the way he called for order, hammering his boot-heels against the barrel he was sitting on. I remembered Susan talking about the Pooley family portraits.

The mob fell silent. All but one silly nerk who couldn't find a place to sit. Pooley gave him a *look*, and he decided to go on standing up.

Then the fierce blue eyes turned on Johanna.

"What do you do here, Mistress Vavasour?"

"I did hear you were doing the Lord's work here, Sir William Pooley."

"That is so."

"Then the Lord's servants must see to the Lord's work, lest they be linked to the foolish virgins who did have no oil for their lamps."

They stared at each other; knife cut knife.

"This is no place for a well-born lady."

"I do come as my father's heir. Would not my father be sitting at your side, if he were not about Colonel Cromwell's business?"

Sir William nodded after a minute, like she had a point there. "A chair for Mistress Vavasour. How *is* your father, mistress?"

"Well enough, sir. He does hope to be home for Christmas, if Colonel Cromwell can spare him."

"What commander could ever spare his sumpter? Who would feed the Army? And your brother, mistress?"

"Still with Fairfax's Horse, sir. He is recovered the wound he did get at Naseby, and is captain now."

"No more than his deserts." Sir William smiled at her, and the rest of the court might as well not have existed. So they had an old-boy network in those days too. . . .

Which didn't suit the character who now got to his feet, and plucked at Sir William's buff-coat with a white languid hand. He muttered something in Sir William's ear, looking sideways at the mob as he did so. That's the way I'll always remember Hopkins; the plucking hand at somebody's coat or shoulder or elbow; the swarthy olive face glancing sideways, weighing up the situation. A great watcher, Hopkins, Didn't miss a trick.

Even among all those semidwarfs he was little; slender as a girl, with a high forehead and beaky nose, and large brilliant eyes. Wore his hair long and yukky with oil. Thin little mustache, and a beard no bigger than the handle of a cup, that he played with while he was watching people. He wore a high hat with a brim, even indoors, and the heels of his boots were twice as high as anybody else's. To make him look bigger. Carried a staff taller than himself; never put it down; used it to tap on the floor when he was making a point, or to jab in people's faces, or to poke the witches and stir them awake, like they were bloody cattle.

His fingernails were long and shapely and polished, and he was the only guy in the whole court wearing a clean shirt. I could have broken him in half with one hand; I *would* have broken him in half, in modern life, even if he'd only asked me what time it was, with his rotten creepy little hand on my sleeve.

He *felt* me hating him, and turned to look at me. I had to get my eyes down quick and do my harmless-yokel act.

"Ah-erm," rumbled Sir William. "Master Hopkins—has asked leave—to address the court—since . . . ." He even sounded like Derek.

Hopkins threw back his short black bum-freezing cloak, and tapped his staff for silence. He waited till you could have heard a pin drop.

"Many common folk have come into the court. I did never see so many in any court where I did sit. That is not good. For when common folk do come to a trial of witches, they do look at women who have been their neighbors for years, and they do say, 'That is but Thomazine, who did nought but charm my wart; and that is but Anne who gave me a spider wrapped in cobweb as a pill to cure the Old Johnny.' And so, in familiarity, God's case against the Prince of this World is lost.

"The trial of a witch is a fit place only for persons who do know of witches. I—do—know—of—witches." He emphasized every word with a tap of his staff.

"I have known of witches since I was a child, when I did first see an apparition of the Devill. One night, a black thing, proportioned like a cat, only three times the size, did sit in a strawberry bed and fix his eyes upon this Informant. When I went toward it, it leaped over the pale but ran quite through the yard. Our greyhound did go after it, but returned to this Informant, trembling exceedingly. That made a very great impression on me of the diverse tricks of the Devill. For he is a spirit and Prince of the Air, and may appear in any shape whatsoever. Which shape is made by him through the joining of condensed thickened air together.

"As when he came once in the shape of a familiar called Vinegar Tom, a greyhound with a head like an ox, a long tail and broad eyes. Who, when this Informant spoke to him, and bade him go to the place provided for him and his angels, immediately transformed himself into the shape of a child of four years without a head, gave a dozen turns round the house, and vanished at the door."

Oh, yeah, I thought. About as likely as my Aunt Fanny keeping her eyeballs in the deep-freeze overnight.

But the crowd around me had settled into that quivering silence that accompanies the telling of a good ghost story.

Hopkins had been dropping his voice lower and lower. But now he shouted, "May it please your worships to understand that witches and sorcerers are marvelously increased within this realm, within these last few years. Our brothers pine away to death; their color fadeth, their flesh rotteth, their speech is benumbed, their senses bereft.

"Many persons of both sexes, straying from the Faith and unmindful of their own salvation, have abandoned themselves to devills, incubi and succubi. And by their spells, conjurations and other horrid offenses have slain infants yet in their mother's womb. Also the offspring of cattle. . . .

"Witches have blasted the produce of the earth. They hinder men from performing the sexual act, and women from conceiving. Whence husbands cannot know their wives, nor wives receive their husbands.

"Witches have raised tempetuous winds and thunderstorms, to the overthowing of houses, stables, barns. . . .

"The land is full of witches; they abound in all places. I have hanged five hundred of them. There is no man can speak more of them than myself. Few of them would confess. But they do have on their bodies divers strange marks at which—for some have confessed—the Devill sucks their blood. For they have forsaken God.

"And it is *your* fault; the fault of all here present. The bulk of our people are wicked, and their hearts not yet prepared for the yoke of the Lord. They are unreformed themselves, and it is no wonder they are so opposed to the work of the Lord's thoroughgoing reformation. This sty of pestilential filth hath even infected the state and government of this Commonwealth."

Hopkins paused, and looked pointedly at Johanna. Everyone else turned to stare at her as well. But she took it very cool.

"I am much interested, sir, in what you do say about the government of this Commonwealth. Is it true what men say of you, that you do hold my godfather, Colonel Cromwell, to be a witch also?"

She said it so innocently, so expectantly. The crowd gasped in horror, then were silent. In the silence, Goody Philips screeched, "You prating fool, Hopkins. I did warn you of her. She will have us all hanged."

But Hopkins was bent double, over a white lace hand-

kerchief, pretending to cough his guts up. At least I
thought he was pretending, till I saw the blood on the
lace. Yet he recovered quickly enough.

"There is only One, mistress, who could put such a
slander in your mind."

"Indeed there was one who put that thought in my
mind, sir."

"Then his Name is Satan!"

"Indeed it is not, sir."

"Then name me his name!"

"His name is . . . ." Johanna let the silence grow; she
was better at this game than Hopkins. "His name is
. . . John Gaule, and he is vicar of Great Staughton
in Huntingdon."

It was like a bomb. Goody Philips made a bolt for the
door. Hopkins caught her with a cruel hand round her
wrist, and forced her to sit down again, smiling calmly at
her the whole time. All the miserable shopkeepers began
demanding to know who John Gaule was. Then another
guy leaped to his feet.

A guy I'd been watching some time; big fat guy in
greasy leathers who couldn't leave himself alone. Kept
picking at his nose; and the huge and ancient spots on his
face, and tearing at his gray greasy hair. His fingers were
never still, and he turned and chafed on his bench like
he had the worst piles you ever saw. Hopkins had kept a
firm eye on him till now; but now Hopkins was up to his
eyes in irate shopkeepers.

Anyway, this guy flexed his lungs like he was going to
throw a discus, and gave vent to a bawl that filled the
court.

"I smell the stink of the Devill's agents! This woman is
a Malignant witch, a Royal sorceress, a harlot of Prince

168

Rupert's sent hither to hamper the work of the Lord!"

He said a lot more, but that's all I can remember; that, and Hopkins' little white hand trying vainly to pull the fat guy back to his seat.

When the guy finally finished, there was a shocked angry silence. Then someone said, "Doth he speak of Mistress *Vavasour*?"

"Mistress Vavasour did feed my children all last winter, when our cow died."

"She is a gentlewoman, of godly and religious life. . . ."

Sir William thumped on his barrel for order, then slowly turned frosty blue eyes on Hopkins.

"What is the name of that man who sits by you, Master Hopkins?"

"I did tell your honor," said Hopkins, his voice low and smooth. But the hand that held the handkerchief was shaking. "His name is John Stearne, and he is an earnest laborer for the Lord."

"He is a bag of wind," said Sir William with dangerous calm. "He is a noisome barrel of lard. He is an offense to this court. Do you bridle his mouth or I will put him in my stocks."

"He does mean no harm, sir. It is but his zeal against witches. . . ."

"If he does open his mouth in my court again, he will feel my zeal against his arse!"

Then, suddenly, they all froze. Because Johanna had risen from her chair, and was walking across to the benches where the witches sat. She bent over them; said something. Slowly, dazedly, they parted to leave a space in their midst.

Johanna sat down among them. There was a horrified gasp from everyone in the room.

"What do you there, mistress?" asked Sir William, leaning forward anxiously. "Have the witches bewitched you?"

"Nay, Sir William. But I have been accused. That man does say I am a witch and sorceress. And I do think that this is the place in the court where the accused do sit."

Hopkins was on his feet instantly. "There is no charge of witchcraft, sir, against this good gentlewoman. My friend did speak in heat; it is nonsense. . . ."

"Aye, Master Hopkins," said Johanna. "It is nonsense. As *all* you have done in this court is nonsense. How do you *know* I am not a witch, Master Hopkins? How are you so sure? Because I am a *gentlewoman*? And a friend of Sir William? And godchild to Colonel Cromwell? But suppose I was poor, Master Hopkins, old and ugly with a hairy lip, gobber tooth, squint eye or squeaking voice? Without money or friends or a son to speak for me? Would I be a witch then? How say you, Master Hopkins?"

"Gaule hath put you up to this," whispered Hopkins. "Is he come?" He had to hold on to Stearne's greasy shoulder to stay upright.

"Master Gaule did say he *might* look this way, Master Hopkins." There was a sly little smile on Johanna's face. "But *I* am here. And I do tell you, I am as much a witch as any of these poor women."

Hope flared in Hopkins' face. "Do you admit you are a witch?"

"Nay, I did not say that. I did say I am as much a witch as any of these women. And I do say that all your charges are a nonsense and they are no more witches than I. Now, either prove me a witch and hang us all, or I will prove you a great liar, and the servant of the Master of Lies—and then the magistrate will know how to deal with *you!*"

There was an ugly noise from the mob. I got a feeling they were going to kill somebody by the end of the day. So did Hopkins.

"May I request the court be adjourned a while, Sir William? All this is new, and I have a ruggedness of the throat and jaws that doth quickly tire me."

"You may have a *short* rest, Master Hopkins. Then we shall proceed with this trial, in proper order."

Hopkins held a huddled conference. I watched their bent backs and heads close together. They were starting to quarrel and blame each other, like a team losing twenty-nil at halftime. But Hopkins kept his grip; sent Bate the Constable and Trooper Collins belting off somewhere, like all the imps in Hell were after them. Trooper Collins even put on his helmet and picked up his pistol from the sawdust of the floor.

And all the time he was talking, Hopkins' eyes were roaming the court. Kept noticing me, for some reason. Every time he tried to catch my eye, I had to turn away quickly. But it didn't matter. Nobody else would look at him either.

"Pray continue, Master Hopkins. Where you left off . . . ," said Sir William, with a cruel little smile at the Witchfinder's expense.

Hopkins had to clear his throat, several times.

"Evidence against Goody Mercer, by Thomas Applewick, farmer. Item. That early one morning, about four o'clock, he did pass by Goody Mercer's door. It being a moonlit night, he did perceive the door to be open. He did look into the house, and presently there came four things in the shape of black rabbits, leaping and skipping about him. Having a good stick in his hand, he struck at them, thinking to kill them, but could not.

"But at last he caught one, by the body of it, and did beat its head against the ground, intending to beat the brains of it. But when he could not, he took the body in one hand and the head in the other, and endeavored to pull off its head. But the head stretched and slipped through his hands like a lock of wool.

"Yet he would not give over his intended purpose, but knowing a pool to be nearby, he went to drown it. But as he went he fell down and could not go, except crawling on his hands and knees, till he came to the water. When, holding the thing fast in his hand, he did plunge his hand down into the water up to his elbow. After a good space, he conceived it was drowned and let go. Upon which it sprang from the pool high into the air, and so vanished away."

Somewhere, far off, thunder rolled: the room was suddenly dark, the air sweaty. There was a half-impressed silence. Then Johanna asked innocently, "Why does Farmer Applewick not give his own testament? Is he bewitched or bereft of sense?"

"He is in Colchester Gaol," snapped Sir William, not pleased.

"Upon what charge, sir?"

"Being drunk and raving, and assaulting the Watch."

There was an audible snigger in the court.

"Did he tell the Watch he had met the Man in the Moon," inquired Johanna, "and received of him a pound of good green cheese? Or did he tell them he was King Turnip and all the turnips in the world were his loyal subjects?"

The snigger grew louder.

"And when Farmer Applewick did rave at the Watch, was it early one morning, about four o'clock?"

Sir William had to thump on the barrel for order, be-

172

cause people in court were stamping and bellowing with laughter.

"Charge dismissed!" roared Sir William. "Next charge?"

"I pray you, let me conduct my case in my own way, Sir William," snapped Hopkins pettishly. "This is no matter for laughing. Four in the morning is a vital time. Witches are most active near dawn. Once they did send a bear all of twenty-five miles, at that time, to kill me as I walked in my garden."

"I do not know about the bear in your garden," roared Sir William, "but I will not have you make a bear garden of my court, Master Hopkins!"

It hung, then, on the verge of ridicule. People simply could not stop laughing. Every time Hopkins made a gesture to get their attention, they burst out laughing afresh. Someone threw something from the back of the room. It hit Stearne and splattered Hopkins with yellow substance. "That egg was bewitched, Master Hopkins," bawled a broad Suffolk voice. "See, it did leap from my hand of its own accord!"

Sir William called again for order, but tears of laughter were running down his face. Johanna was so near to winning . . . .

Then the courtroom door burst open. Bate the Constable staggered in holding his belly and screaming. Trooper Collins followed, his helmet battered nearly flat and blood streaming from his nose, making all his chin a scarlet beard.

The court fell silent, listening to Bate having hysterics. It was a horrible, unbelievable noise. Like when a kid I know came off his bike at seventy and broke his pelvis and both legs, and had to lie half an hour in the road waiting for an ambulance.

When the worst was over, and there was just endless

sobbing, Trooper Collins said in a shaking voice, "We did go to Mistress Vavasour's house, sir. To search for imps and poppets, as Master Hopkins commanded. As we did reach the house, there was a little storm of thunder. Only above the house, for in all other parts it was blue sky. Bate did say to me it was the Devill's weather, that comes when witches are abroad.

"We did go within, sir. There was a thing in the shape of a black kitten. Bate did try to kill it with a billhook, to fetch its body to the court. And I did guard the door, for it flew hither and thither with a great screeching.

"And then . . . the Devill did come, sir. And his boots were black, and his hosen and mantle were the color of flame. And his head had no shape, nor ears nor hair, but was yellow as butter. And he had no face, save darkness.

"Bate made the Papist sign of the Cross, but it availed him nothing. For the Devill smote Bate, and Bate cried out and fell down in a swoon. Then the Devill did come at me, sir, and I did fire my pistol and blew off the Devill's head. But he grew another head, as of a young man with a beard. And the Devill did take me in hands like black leather and beat my head against the wall and so left me for dead.

"When I did return to my senses, sir, the Devill was gone, and the thing like a black kitten also. But we did find pieces of the Devill's head, sir, that he did have at first."

And, while we all shuddered and craned our necks, Collins produced an old sack and shook it upside down.

Onto the floor, among the sawdust, fell the shattered remains of a motorbike safety helmet.

The crowd drew back, with a shuddering breath, leaving a wide circle round the yellow fragments. Only Sir William leaped from the top of his barrel, knelt down and poked at the pieces.

"They are not metal," he said slowly. "Neither wood nor clay pot. They bear no mark of hammer or file. They were not made by the hand of man. . . ." He went on staring at them, pushing them around pointlessly, as if dazed.

"I smell the stink . . . ," bawled Stearne, but Hopkins' hand caught him round the arm like a vice, and stopped him in mid-breath.

Then Hopkins said softly, "Here we have proof, your honor. Proof incontrovertible that the woman Vavasour is a witch. I demand that she be charged and swum and searched for the Devill's marks. . . . Sir William? *Sir William?*"

Sir William nodded dumbly, not raising his head, still staring at the fragments.

"Take the witch away," said Hopkins, triumphant.

"Wait!" said Johanna. "The first to touch me shall die, whether I hang or not." She was as pale as wax, but her eyes were huge and touched men like swords. No one moved toward her.

Then her eyes went gentler. "Sir William," she called. "Sir William, pay heed."

And he looked up from where he knelt on the floor; looked up like a little child.

"Sir William, I do solemnly charge you, for the love you do bear my family, to keep our house and chattels safe, till a Vavasour shall come again to claim them. Do this, and your family shall prosper. Fail and your fruit shall wither. Do you swear it?"

"I do swear." The great red head drooped toward the floor again.

Then Johanna turned and looked at me. She was

biting her lip with the fear of what awaited her. But from the look in her eyes I could tell she was still thinking of me, wondering whether I would be safe.

It was then that I went berserk. Tried to tear my way through the mob of dirty narrow-minded midgets. I plowed through the great mass of them, smashing them from hell to breakfast, trampling them underfoot with about ten of them hanging on my back. I nearly reached her; I nearly reached Hopkins to smash his wincing mincing girlish face in. . . .

Then something exploded against the back of my head and the world went black.

I came to, with a groan. Except it was a croak.

"*Croak*," I said, "*croak, croak, croak.*"

I was lying in front of Derek's house, on the cobbles that shouldn't be there. There were still horses tied up. People were standing in a ring, looking at me.

"Poor afflicted man."

"The witch did bewitch him."

"He did foam at the mouth."

"I never did see such frenzy."

"The spell hath left him now—he doth wonder where he is."

"What shall we do?"

"As the note doth say—set him on the road to Diss—to his master, good Kill-sin Kendall."

"Will he not be required for a witness?"

"How can the dumb be witness?"

"There is evidence enough to hang the witch already."

"Who would have thought . . . Mistress Vavasour!"

"The Good Book doth say . . . wickedness in high places. They will hang them all, at six in the morning."

"Where?"

176

"By the gibbet, up the Sudbury road. Sir William has decreed it."

"Did you hear how the witch did charge him—to keep her house safe till she return? Else she would blight him and his seed hereafter?"

"She will need no house where she doth go—saving tar and a little cage."

"Do they gibbet her, then?"

"Aye. Burn the bodies of the others, but gibbet hers. For a warning to the county."

"Aye—a timely warning. Give me a hand with this poor soul, to set him on his way. How do men get to Diss—know you?"

"By way of Hadleigh and Stowmarket."

They heaved me to my feet, matey enough. They almost had to carry me. There was a colossal bump on the back of my skull, where some crafty midget had used a pistol butt. And I could only see what lay to my right; to my left, all was gray fuzz. Concussion again.

They saw me through the village, and onto a clear track through the trees. Told me, as if I was some child or dog, to go straight home to my master and it would take me four days. Then they left me, with shaking heads and pitying looks. I walked about half a mile, then sat down in a ditch, groaning aloud and not with my bruises either.

What were they *doing* to her now? Goody Philips' foul hands, searching her young body? Making her sit half-naked on a high stool, in front of a hundred staring, suddenly-hating eyes? Perhaps she would drown when they swam her. I hoped so; that would be the best way. Only that book had said "hanged."

I started walking again, to stop myself thinking. Couldn't have cared less about myself—it was all her, her,

her. *I* could just curl up in some ditch and die—they let you get away with that in the seventeenth century.

I don't know how far I'd walked when I heard, from some bushes on the left, a commanding meow. I dived into the foliage, and there she was, purring softly. I nearly hugged her to death, pushing my face into her warm furry body to shut out the other things.

She led me cross-country, stealthily, cautiously, for nearly the whole afternoon. The sun was just touching the rim of the valley when we came to the barn—or rather, the house.

It was a terrible shambles—doors swinging in the wind, sheets and blankets trampled in puddles, a dead dog and three bloodstained bodies of sheep. It might have started as a search for incriminating evidence, but it looked as if it had ended up as pure looting and massacre.

I crept in round the back, and into the lost room. That had not been touched. Fear of the Devil had overcome greed. I laughed to myself at that very ironical thought. Anyway, my own trousers were still there, and my bike boots and the old floppy hat from Hammer's Field. I put them on and threw away the other rubbish and felt better—a bit better, anyway.

As I finished, the light coming through the window slits suddenly changed, and the cat gave a triumphant *prook*. It might only be a cloud passing overhead, but . . . .

I pushed open the trapdoor, so full of hope I scarcely dared breathe.

And saw my motorbike pannier standing in the corner.

And heard a tractor revving, in the next field.

I was home. I was back in the twentieth century, and Johanna had already been dead three hundred years.

But that last thought didn't make me feel any better at all.

I opened a tin of beef, ate a mouthful, and threw the rest away. It hit the cobbles of the yard and splattered in a dark red fan. News pounced on it and began to eat greedily. There was nothing wrong with *her* appetite.

A soft rain began to fall; no more than a mist, really. Down the valley, the church clock chimed one. It was very quiet; not even the sound of the tractor—Derek must have gone home for lunch. The quietness was like a blanket to me; but the blanket wasn't thick enough. Memory was too strong. Where News was eating the corned beef, a dead sheep still seemed to lie.

Johanna had kept her promise; had kept me safe. But what did *that* matter? Somewhere, she was suffering God knows what hideosities. No, not somewhere. Sometime. And it was all my fault. If I hadn't beaten up those two Puritan yobs in the barn . . . .

The wrongness of it was not to be borne. It put me in mind of what my dad once said. When he was still a kid my age, he was a rear-gunner in the last air raids on Germany. I used to ask him how he put up with it, all the flak and that, and nightfighters coming out of nowhere, trying to blow off his head with their bloody great cannon. But he'd never talk about it. All he would ever say was, "We couldn't live in the same world as Hitler."

Well, I couldn't live in the same world as Hopkins. I

wanted to go back in time and blow off his head with a submachine gun.

Kid's stuff! Where would *I* get a submachine gun? A plastic one from Woolworth's? I wouldn't ever get a submachine gun.

But Derek had a shotgun. He'd shown me how to use it. He'd offered to let me have a go. Maybe he would lend it to me.

Suddenly shaking with excitement, I hopped on the Cub and went down to his house.

"I've changed my mind," I said. "I want to have a pot at those rabbits."

"Can't come today," he said. "Going to a sale—fat cattle —I winter a few—quick money—handy for Christmas presents."

"You needn't come," I coaxed. "You've shown me how it works."

"All right," he said, reaching to where the gun stood in the corner of the kitchen. "You're a sensible lad. Just be careful not to fire into dense woodland, or over the crest of the hill—anywhere where you can't see the ground is clear behind. And don't point it at anybody, whether it's loaded or not—unless you want to kill them, of course." He gave his short laugh, which stopped like somebody had switched a radio off.

"You'll need some ammo." He reached into his pocket for shotgun shells, and produced two. "That won't get you many bunnies—come along—I keep more in the magazine."

Once more I stood with that massive padlock in my hands, and looked inside the little brick hut, with its whitewashed walls and shelves lined with fireworks and plastic explosive.

"Here's a box of shells," said Derek. "Bring back what you don't use. No—on second thoughts—put the shells straight back in here—safest place. And the gun. I'll leave you the key to the magazine—if I'm not home—pop the key through my letter box when you've finished. Good shooting."

He locked the padlock, gave me the key, and stalked away.

I had to tie the shotgun along the length of my bike, with binder twine I found lying about. Farms like Derek's just *live* on binder twine. They'd grind to a halt without.

The gun bumped against my petrol tank all the way home, and took a bit of the enamel off, but I wasn't bothered. Just struck me that a full-size shotgun is a rotten weapon for a motorcyclist.

News sniffed the barrel of the gun enthusiastically, like it was a buttercup. I walked up to my old bedroom, and down into the lost room, with her all round my feet. Trod on her tail in the dark and she gave a godawful squawk, which made me jump a yard in the air. Lucky the gun wasn't loaded. But I had the shells in the big pocket of my bike coat.

I took one last look at my pannier, and closed the trapdoor.

"Now, you wonderful time-cat," I said, "get us to the right *time*."

I opened the trapdoor again.

The pannier was gone. I crept up the stairs and to the outside door like I was John Wayne in Indian Country.

It was darkish; dawn or dusk. I looked out cautiously. There was the faintest red flush in the east. Dawn, then. The dead dog and the dead sheep still lay in the yard. A few black birds, that had gathered round them, flew off as I opened the door. I looked down the valley. Everything was still.

Then the church clock chimed six.

There were men in black stirring at the door of the inn. As I watched they formed into a tight group and began to walk up the hill toward me. A string of other people followed, walking in single file. Women. Women in white bonnets with their heads down.

I knew it was the time I wanted. News had hit it spot-on. I suddenly felt a need to go to the lav. But I stayed where I was.

The people came nearer. I could see Hopkins with his staff, and the bulk of Stearne, and the potbelly of Bate the Constable, and about five others. Stearne had a pistol thrust in his belt importantly. It stuck in his wobbly gut with every step he took. But nobody else was armed.

It was a cinch. They'd walk right past my gateposts. I only had to wait behind one of those gateposts, and give them both barrels, one after the other. Perhaps Hopkins would scrabble about frantically, like those rabbits Derek had shot. That was OK by me. Hopkins was no longer a member of the human race. Nor were any of the others, come to that. I suppose those clever guys in gold-rimmed spectacles back at U.C. would say that Hopkins was a child of his time; a psycho, a paranoid or something. Ought to have treatment. Well, I didn't have a yellow van handy. Only a shotgun.

But life's never that simple.

Before Hopkins had got halfway up the hill, a mob of soldiers came out of the inn's stable yard on horseback. They threw a lot of leather beer mugs at a barmaid in a white apron, who began doing her nut.

Then they put their horses into a gallop, and passed first the witches, and then Hopkins' mob in fine style, shouting and laughing their heads off, like it was August Bank Holiday. Then they settled at the front of the column, and came on at a walk up the hill. Trooper Collins was in front, telling everybody what to do.

I could tell they were a rabble. Not alert, or keeping any kind of lookout. Mainly guys on leave, come to see the fun. But there were twenty of them, and they were wearing helmets, breastplates and weapons.

I suddenly knew it was no good; I might knock over a few, and then that would be that. I was willing to risk getting killed; but not getting killed pointlessly.

They were so near now, I could see Hopkins coughing into his hanky. Stearne was assaulting a massive bleeding spot on his neck, leaning his head sideways so he could get at it. Then I saw Johanna. She was walking first in the line of witches and limping badly. Staring at nothing. But at least she held her head up straight, not bowed like the other women. Her wrists were tied behind her with rope, and the rope dipped, then bound the wrists of the next woman . . . Mistress Podmore. So they'd got her too.

They were near, now. Fifty yards. What should I do? Knock off Hopkins? Kill Johanna, to put her out of her misery? Jump down and blaze away blindly, to put an end to thinking?

Thirty yards. They would have seen me hovering in the doorway, if they'd looked up. But they were all busy with their own thoughts.

I just stood there, paralyzed. Time and life were too heavy for me to alter. And somehow I knew that if I let them pass the gate, I would be consenting in Johanna's death. Even with my time-cat, I would be too late to save her.

Then the cat meowed, direly, warningly. I turned and ran down into the lost room, and shut the trapdoor, without thinking.

When I reopened it (and I stood quite a while down there, shaking in the dark) the pannier was back, and I was again in the twentieth century.

But I did not want to be in the twentieth century. I wanted to be back with her. The lost room drew me, like an aching tooth draws your tongue.

So I took the cat back into the dark and closed the trapdoor again. Again, the pannier vanished, and I stood looking out at the dawn through the bedroom door. Again the clock struck six, and there was a stir of people in black at the inn door. Again the column began to ascend the hill. And the soldiers came and galloped past the line of witches. Like an action replay of a World Cup goal on telly.

I gasped. It seemed the cat had made me master of time itself. I tried it again and again, like a kid.

Then I began to use my brains.

I had the advantage. Hopkins was the prisoner of time. I could make him perform the same action a hundred times, always the same. But *I* was free; I could do whatever I liked.

I could go away for days, and come back, and Hopkins would still be climbing that hill. I could go away and get a tank, or a company of Royal Marine Commandos. . . .

Go on, Webster—you haven't *got* a tank. And if you talked to a company of Commandos, they'd just send for their M.O.

There's just *you*, Webster boy. All on your own.

You haven't got a tank; but you have got a motorbike. You haven't got any Commandos. But you've got Derek's magazine, full of plastic explosive. . . .

And you've got *time*, Webster. You've got *time*!

I sat on the Cub inside the barn. I kicked her over; she started first time. I cut the engine.

I flicked a switch, and the whole end wall blazed as bright as day from my twin quartz-iodide headlamps. I'd bought them in Ipswich, and they'd cost me twenty-five quid. I'd had hell of a job fixing the wiring, and wedging the twelve-volt battery they needed inside my top-box. But it was worth it. Quartz-iodides can blind you even in daylight, if you look at them too directly and too close. When Trooper Collins saw them heading straight at him in the dim light of dawn, at eighty miles an hour, on something that roared like all the devils in hell . . . .

Mind you, the whole jerry-built contraption wouldn't last very long—ten minutes of bumping on that track. But this job wouldn't take very long. Win or lose in ten minutes. In ten minutes either Trooper Collins or I would be dead.

I switched off the headlamps; didn't want to waste the juice. I felt to see that my left pannier was strapped securely. It was full of fireworks and fuses. My right pannier was full of plastic. And something that jutted out comfortably, just where my hand could reach it quick. The butt of the shotgun. It fitted in the pannier snugly, now I'd sawed off both barrels to an eight-inch length. It had been a hell of a job with Derek's rusty hacksaw. Shotgun barrels are made to last. I had blisters all over my right hand.

A sawed-off shotgun is a weapon no person on earth is

licensed to carry. Not even police. A sawed-off shotgun is a lunatic's weapon. You can't miss. It sprays lead like a hose. You can get two years in the nick just for being in possession of one. God knew what Derek would say; if I ever saw him again. I patted the pockets of my bike jacket. The brass ends of the shotgun shells clinked cheerfully.

I was wearing black boots, and my hosen and mantle were the color of flame, and I was wearing my crash helmet yellow as butter, and I had no shape or ears or hair to my head, and I had no face, only dark.

Matthew Hopkins had summoned up the Devil, and the Devil was coming to Besingtree.

One last thing remained. Could the cat force the whole mass of gear over the time gap, out here in the open barn, without benefit of trapdoor?

There was a cheery chirrup in the dark.

"News-News-News!" She leaped up onto my lap in the dark. Thrust her face inside my open visor and licked my nose.

"Let's go, girl! And I want five hours to work before Hopkins comes."

Subtly, the quality of the darkness changed. The barn door, open to the deep blue night, grew smaller and square, instead of round-topped.

We'd made it.

I kicked the bike over, and revved her very softly. Maybe it was a daft risk to take, but I had to know it would still work, in 1647.

It did. And nobody came to see what was happening. Which was just as well for them.

I sneaked out through the door. The dead sheep were still in the yard; warm and not yet stiff. The church clock

186

chimed one. I had five hours to do what I had to do.

There was a gap of a hundred yards between the barn and the first house of the old village. Nothing in the gap, save the hedge each side of the road and a few huge dead trees growing out of the hedges.

I stuck the shotgun in my belt, took a pannier on each shoulder, and slid behind the right-hand hedge. Came to the first dead tree, opened the first box of plastic, and began to climb. It wasn't easy, working by the light of a pencil torch bought in Ipswich. But Derek had been a good teacher, and plastic's notably easy stuff to use under awkward conditions. That's why the Army chose it. I rammed a half-pound sausage into the crown of the tree, where it was cracked and rotten, shoved in an aluminum cigarette and crimped the fuse. As I descended, I trailed the fuse down the back of the tree, where it wouldn't show easily in the dawn. Somewhere, in the hedge, all the fuses would meet. Ten-minute fuses, because I'd timed old Hopkins up the hill on one of his action-replay journeys. And in ten minutes he would just be reaching this tree.

When I had fixed five trees, I began burying plastic in the soil of the field. Ran more fuses to clumps of fireworks farther up the hill. Why shouldn't the Devil have all the good bangs?

I stood back, pleased with my handiwork. Somewhere, down in the village, an alert dog barked at me, and soon every dog in the village was howling.

They could howl on; it would be a brave fool who came up to the barn that night, with the Devil abroad.

Astride the Cub, half-hidden by the gatepost, I waited.

The clock struck six. Black figures showed by the inn

door. Began walking up the hill. I knew it all off by heart, now. Just like Dad knew the John Wayne westerns he watched on telly. No chance of Lady Chance taking a hand . . . .

I'd lit the fuses. They'd burned all right, withering and blackening slowly, with a tiny haze of smoke. I'd run back to the bike and got my breath. I was sweating a bit, that's all. Except, God, I was so bloody *tired*. How long since I'd slept? In my time? In their time? I'd never know. Well, in ten minutes I'd either be dead or I could sleep for a week.

When they reached the dead tree, it would explode. Before they knew what hit them, there'd be trees exploding everywhere. Lo the Devil comes! At eighty miles an hour, straight at them, on a beast whose eyes would blind, and whose voice would deafen. . . .

The troopers wouldn't know what had hit them, but I reckoned their horses would bolt in all directions. I'd wham straight through, give Hopkins' mob both barrels, grab Johanna, cut her rope, shove her on the bike behind me and straight into the village. Turn in a wide space, straight back through them again, into the barn and onward through time. I wouldn't even have to abandon the Cub.

The troopers were nearly up to the tree. In fact, one of them had come awake, and was leaning sideways in his saddle, trying to see what the funny yellow object was behind the gatepost. . . .

The first tree exploded. Matchwood showered round me. The soldiers crouched in hunched paralysis, until the second tree exploded behind them. Then a column of earth shot up behind the hedge.

Now!

I kicked the Cub.

She wouldn't start.

I kicked and kicked. Nothing. Now the fireworks were crackling off behind the hedge. And Hopkins' tradesmen friends were running like hell, back to the village, as fast as their rotten little midget legs would carry them.

It was now or never. I despaired of the Cub. And the soldiers hadn't scattered. They were having a hell of a job holding their horses, but they weren't panicking. I'd forgotten; they would *know* about explosions; they'd have had a bellyfull of them, in their Civil War.

I grabbed the shotgun, and began to run toward them, throwing off the safety catch as I went. Maybe there was still a chance. . . .

They must see me in a minute. Then the musket balls would start flying. They might be terrified of the Devil, but they'd still shoot at him.

But they weren't looking at me. Trooper Collins was pointing right, up the hillside toward the little wood.

"It is the Malignants!" he shouted. "Rupert comes, to rescue the Royal Witch. They have a field-piece."

Another column of earth shot up, behind the hedge. More fireworks went off, and yes, it did seem like a battle. And to crown it all, a couple of guys poked their heads out of the very part of the wood where Prince Rupert was supposed to be. They were probably poachers or something—old guys from the next village, wondering what all the noise was about.

But it was enough for Trooper Collins.

"For the Parliament, *chaaaaaaaarge!*" He thrust his horse through a gap in the hedge, and in a second, every trooper was following him. Even Stearne ran puffing, far to the rear, waving his pisol. Nobody even noticed the Devil on the road.

It was ridiculous; it was magnificent. They lifted into

sight again, beyond the hedge, pounding up the rabbit-warrened slope, slipping and sliding, shouting encouragement to each other.

"Remember Marston!"

"Let God arise; let his enemies be scattered!"

"Oliver, Oliver!"

Broken-down serving-men and tapsters they might have been; Oliver would still have been proud of them. *They* didn't know there was nobody up there; *they* weren't to know there wasn't a whole Royalist regiment up there. Muddleheaded, bigoted, they were still Englishmen.

And I was left standing in the road, with Johanna and her line of witches. She grinned at me, wriggled, and the rope fell off her wrists. I might have expected that; she had small, determined, nimble hands.

I was just about to push up my visor, and yell at her to come on, we hadn't got all day, when she shook her head and tapped her lips in a warning way. Then she looked right.

I looked where she was looking. Someone was lying against the hedge. He looked very small, lying there, with his tall hat off and road dirt in his oiled hair and beard. But he had raised himself on his elbows, and his eyes roved: hooded, crafty, still dangerous.

I walked toward him, and I knew how it must have felt to be Dracula or Jack the Ripper, for his eyes settled on my non-face and never left it. I had every last morsel of his attention; he was all *mine*.

I had the shotgun trained on him, loaded. One little squeeze on the trigger, and he would be just a nasty mess on the road. Like a spider I once squashed into a dirty mark.

But I hadn't wanted to kill that spider; I like spiders. Unfortunately, it had been on a window frame I was painting for Dad, and my paint-loaded brush had caught it before I saw it. Half its body was paint, and half its legs, and there was no hope for it. You can't clean a spider like an oiled seagull. But it was still very much alive; it was a life. It was a long time before I squashed it into a dirty mark.

Hopkins was a life, too. It would have been different if he'd been on his feet, with his rotten midgets round him, trying to kill me. . . .

Johanna took the decision out of my hands. She laid her own hand on my right arm, and pushed the shotgun down.

"Master Hopkins," she said gently, almost lovingly. "This is *my* Master, who you did call the Prince of Air. It is the Lord of This World, in whom you did never believe. Did you, Master Hopkins? No more than you did believe in the Lord God in Heaven?"

Hopkins tried to say something, but it wouldn't come out. Instead, he nodded dumbly.

"My Master is not pleased, Master Hopkins. That you should hang His servants for money, yet not believe in Him Who Below Is. Do you believe in Him now? Do you wish to serve Him? There is *much* money in it."

Again Hopkins nodded, his eyes never leaving my visor.

"Then kiss His foot, and become His man."

The man crawled to my foot, and pressed his mouth to it. When I pulled it away in disgust, there was a wet mark in the dust of the toe.

"Watch and wait, Master Hopkins, watch and wait and my Master will come to fetch you. You will know Him

by the color of his jerkin. It is fine red, is it not? Anything of this color doth come from my Master. Watch
and wait, Master Hopkins. . . . Now avert your eyes—it
is not becoming . . . ."

Instantly, Hopkins dropped his face into his hands.
Johanna turned to the old women, who were still standing in line, tied together, humble and vacant-eyed as
cows.

"Come, Goody Finch, Goody Marton. Rest is at hand."

We hurried them along the road to the barn. I glanced
up at the hillside; Trooper Collins and his men were still
having a ball, racing in and out of the wood, hallooing
like huntsmen.

We had reached the barn door, and the old women had
already passed inside, when I remembered the Cub.

21

As I ran back to fetch it, I got a feeling things were changing. Up on the hill, the joy had gone out of the troopers' shouts. They were angry now, baffled. And as I crossed the yard, several of them saw me and began spurring down toward the barn.

Being so close to success, to escape, panicked me. The Cub was hard to get off the stand, and when I tried to turn her, the dead sheep got in the way. I could hear the hoofs coming now, thudding softly on the turf of the hill. But I wasn't going to leave the Cub; the sods would burn her. I made a mad, head-down push for the door. I was panting and the visor of my helmet was misting up. The brake levers and panniers were grating on the limestone doorway.

"Hurry, Master Jack, *hurry!*" Even through the polycarb of my helmet, I could hear fear in Johanna's voice, for the very first time ever. "Close the door, Master Jack! *Quick!*"

I grabbed the door handle and pulled.

The edge of the door just caught the corner of my right pannier. I was beyond thinking. I hammered the door against the pannier like a fool. Wood splinters flew; the bike rocked and gave a little.

Then Stearne burst into the yard, holding his heaving gut and waving his pistol. He saw me, hesitated, then decided his hour of glory had come. He might not be able to kill the Devil; but he could certainly blow his head off, just as Trooper Collins had done. And pick up the pieces afterward and keep them to show his grandchildren. . . .

I raised my shotgun again.

He advanced with comic slowness across the yard, trying to cock his pistol, and sticking his tongue out of the corner of his mouth with the effort. Like a child doing something *very* difficult; a fat, ugly, wrinkled, gray-haired child.

"Yield, Satan!" he bawled, and pointed the pistol straight at my face. It was shaking wildly, and he had his eyes screwed tight shut.

I could have blown him away, no sweat. But it would have been like killing a child. I could only stand there between him and the poor old women.

But he had no such qualms; he was saving the world, by assaulting the Devil.

The hammer of his pistol clicked. There was a fizz of powder. The black hole of the barrel pointed straight at my nose. So this is how it ends, I thought.

Then Johanna cried one word. It sounded like "Itaka," but I can't be sure now.

A weight landed lightly on my shoulder, and leaped again. A dark shadow, straight at Stearne. It landed on the pistol and drove it back into his face. There was a bang, like a big ill-made firework. Something dark and furry thumped into my visor. Then Johanna pulled me inside and slammed the door.

Through it, I could hear Stearne shouting, calling on God and yelling that he had been blinded by a stroke of Satan. He was clawing and thumping at the door, but he

194

wasn't trying to get in. It was a disorganized, agonized thumping.

But the yard was full of the sound of horsemen.

And News was outside. And there was blood running down my visor, and it wasn't my blood, or Stearne's.

"News-News-News!" I called.

But there was only a thunderous hammering on the door for answer. My time-cat was dead. I was trapped in 1647.

Have you ever read a story in which the writer talked about cool desperation? I thought it was a rotten cliché, till then. But it's not. I got the women back into a corner of the barn in a trice. Then I knelt down at one side of the door, pointed the gun and waited. When they burst in, they wouldn't expect me to be kneeling down; they'd have to look for me, in the dark. They wouldn't look long; they'd get both barrels. Then I'd run over the bodies, loading as I went, and give the guys outside two more, left and right. Maybe with luck I could keep them on the run till I'd killed the lot. . . . That was our only chance, to kill the lot. And then most of the villagers— the men, anyway. And then . . . .

Otherwise, they'd stand off and set the barn on fire and drive us out. . . .

"Master Jack! Master *Jack*! It is *over*. We are *safe*." How long had she been talking to me, soothing, gentle? I had an idea it must have been a long long time. Once again, she pushed down my arm, and the shotgun it held. "*Listen*, Master Jack."

I listened. There was no sound of hammering on the door; no sound of horses in the yard. Only the sighing of the wind through the stone slabs of the roof.

And a spider had spun a web across the handle of the door. It wasn't even a new web; it was broken and dirty. Cobwebs.

"But . . . we lost the cat. How . . . ?"

"Did you think traveling in time was just cat?" Her giggle was like a stream running in darkness.

I leaned against the wall. My legs gave way, and I hit the floor with a bump that jarred the whole length of my spine. Sliding down the wall like that mustn't have done the waterproofing of my bike jacket any good. I closed my eyes and kept them closed, and listened to the blessed silence. Outside my head and inside.

Then Johanna speaking.

"Goodwives, my Master hath wrought a miracle for you, to save your lives. He hath brought you through time itself, making many years pass. Hopkins is dead. Good Colonel Cromwell is dead. The King's son has returned and rules the land well. No man doth hang witches. You are safe.

"You have been delivered, as Moses did deliver the Children of Israel out of the hand of Pharaoh. Therefore, goodwives, be like unto the Children of Israel and serve the Lord all your days. Do not beg. Or if you must beg, and any man refuse you, depart from him with a blessing and do not curse him, nor even say one angry word to him. Do you be charitable to one another, and do not gossip spitefully of one another. Obey the word of Mistress Podmore, whom I shall send with you to guard you in all things. She hath money for your need, which I have given her. Seek some quiet place, which no man doth covet, and live by labor and growing good herbs. . . ."

She went on and on, like a bloody sermon, but I didn't listen much more. My head was muzzy and I was very tired.

But I got up to see the old women go. They went out into the light of day, blinking and timid. Almost afraid to take a step, lest Hopkins be waiting with the troopers.

Then they saw the changes in the yard. The dead sheep were just scatters of white bones. Grass grew between the cobbles, thin but high. The roof of the stable wing had fallen in. Nobody had been back; nobody had touched a thing.

They went out through the gate, the old ladies. I watched them go down the village street. The street was narrower than I remembered; had more green on it. And I had the feeling that most of the houses of the village were empty; lots of bare rafters poking through wind-stripped thatch. Old Besingtree was dying.

"Come, Master Jack. Our work is done." Johanna laughed and took my hand, and dragged me back toward the barn. But at the doorstep, I stopped.

There were two things on the doorstep. One was a thin rusty object, lying in a dried pool of rust. I picked it up. It was still recognizable as one of my combination spanners. I must have dropped it in the dark, while I was fixing the quartz-iodides, the night I played the Devil.

The other thing was worse; a little skull, delicate and fine, clean and white like something in a museum showcase.

A cat's skull. I know a cat's skull when I see it. That's why I started bawling my eyes out.

"Do not grieve, Master Jack. Her work is done also. She was only a cat."

"I loved that sodding cat. She used to walk on me when I was asleep and rub my cheek and push her nose into my ear."

Johanna giggled and snuggled up close. Pushed her own nose into my ear. Her nose was small and cold.

"Did you think that was just cat?"

It was an invitation; a very sexy invitation. My arms tightened round her. My hands began to rove across her thin shoulder blades and down the small of her back. . . .

And then the smell of her came up to me, strong. The smell of lavender and cow dung, wood smoke and mildew. The smell that led back to Goody Hooper, with lice in her hair and cats at her wrinkled breasts. It froze me cold, to the marrow of my bones.

I broke away, pretending to be baffled. "What the hell do you mean, did I think it was just cat?"

She was not fooled; she knew I had rejected her. But she just smiled, and said, "Thou shall have cat again, Master Jack. But it will not be the same. Still, she will do to catch mice. . . ."

For some reason, I shivered violently. And didn't ask any more questions.

22

Early next morning, I heard the barn door handle turn stealthily. Small quiet feet crossed the barn. I wasn't worried. It was a friendly stealthiness, the sort that doesn't want to wake a sleeper.

And I didn't want to wake up, yet. I was still tired, with a deep satisfying sort of tiredness; pleased with myself for once. I had rescued our heroine from the jaws of death, and all that crap. Even if our heroine had ended up rescuing me . . . at least I hadn't run away.

Trouble was, once rescued, our heroine had turned into a female I now had to cope with. Never lived with a woman, except my mother, and she could be difficult enough at times. I reckoned a seventeenth-century woman wouldn't be any easier. I wanted time to listen to her, get to know the way she did things, when she didn't know she was being watched.

She did things briskly. A scraping of metal on stone, bit like a Stone-Age cigarette-lighter, then a vigorous puffing of cheeks and a crackle of flame from the fire. A pouring of water; a splashing and gasping. Then a muttered complaint about the lack of a broom; all men did live like pigs. I was no better than her brother John, who walked in his boots on the best carpet, and had dogs in his bedroom. In fact, if one did not put one's foot down, John would have a *horse* in his bedroom. But there was no real anger in the muttering; just the eternal female complaint that men were babies to be cleaned, fed and scolded from cradle to grave.

She began moving the furniture round, with stealthy but vigorous shoves of hips and bottom. *Everything* was in the wrong place, nothing dusted or polished . . . *men!* Boots and clothes tossed everywhere. There would be some changes made.

She got among my food supplies. She put her hand in a packet of cornflakes; suspicious sniffing. Tins blooping as they were vigorously shaken. Fancy having pictures of food on tins! Raspberries recognized. Amazement at fine white bread, fit for our lord the King. Amazement at butter cut square and wrapped in silver. Rage at water jugs being used for milk and milk jugs for water. Then an unusual smell of cooking.

"Master Jack? I have made you a breakfast and it is eleven of the clock. Do you intend to lie in bed all the day, sir?"

I gave a realistic waking-up groan. "How can I get dressed with *you* here? Did gentlemen dress in front of ladies in *your* day, mistress?"

"Gentlemen did sleep in *bedrooms*, in my day, sir. Only the Curs did sleep in kitchens, and the master of the house did throw them out at cock-crow with the dogs. I will turn my back—I have plenty to do!"

I dressed and came to the table. She plonked a pewter plate in front of me; boiled cornflakes with bits of hot dog floating in it. Hot dogs I'd left in an open tin two days ago; hot dogs even News had turned up her nose at . . . I flinched away from remembering News, and forced the stuff down me. She sat across from me, pulling faces at her own plate.

"Are you so poor, sir, you cannot afford a good breakfast?"

"Like bacon and eggs?"

She pulled an even worse face. "You do jest. Who does eat *eggs* for breakfast? No, I do mean good cold beef, or a dish of fine chops, or an Irish stew."

"I hate stews!"

"I thought *all* young gentlemen did like a fine stew."

From the arch way she said it, one eyebrow cocked, I knew there was another seventeenth-century joke in the offing.

"Now I shall tell you how to make a *fine* stew." She had put on a sort of lecturing voice. "Take several fine ladies of the court, and a discreet-hit house near the Vauxhall Gardens, and some malmsey and fine sack, and players on the lute and viol . . . ."

I *had* to laugh. "I'll nip into Besingtree this morning," I said, "and get a *couple* of fine chops for tonight. . . ." But I was worried. I'd started off the vac pretty flush, but the quartz-iodides and other stuff for the attack on Hopkins had flattened my grant pretty badly.

"Do not fret, Master Jack. I do not come without a dowry." Again the arch smile, the uplifted eyebrow. She produced two coins from the pouch at her belt. "Here is a mark and an angel." The pouch was bulging, clinked heavily.

I took the coins. Gold, in mint condition; the dead king's head clear and shining. What would they fetch? Thirty pounds, fifty? I knew gold sovereigns fetched twenty-five, in mint condition. "I'll have to go into Ipswich to change these."

"Have a care, at the booths, Master Jack." Her sudden look of intense wariness reminded me of the wolf's teeth that had been snapping at her heels, only a night ago; it was a look you never see on a modern person's face.

"I'll manage," I said, cheerfully. "I'll try and get you some gear as well."

"Gear?"

"Hosen and shoon."

"But I have brought my wardrobe with me also. What did you think was in that great chest? I even do have my fine red velvet and my *bridal* gown. I could go with you to your Queen's Court and not shame you, dear Master Jack."

I was suddenly excruciatingly embarrassed. "You can't go about looking like *that*! People wear short dresses now . . . tights."

"Will they hang me, or put me in the stocks for not wearing . . . tights? Even the Puritans did not do that. You did tell me you came from a time when men were *free*. . . ."

"Ooooh. . . ." I knew I was being unreasonable. I was muddled. Of course she could get away with what she was wearing. Hippies got away with worse. But . . . .

"You can't come for a ride on my bike in a long dress."

"May I come with you on your . . . ?" She gestured toward the Cub with such plain delight that my heart softened. "Shall we go very fast? Faster than a galloping horse?"

I should have been warned then. How did she know what a bike was for? But she said, "Very well, you may buy me *gear*. And I will ride on your bike faster than the wind, and hold you very tight round the waist and *sing*!"

And in her joy, the moment passed.

"I'd better get going," I said.

"I pray you do shave before you go, Master Jack, or

they will throw you from the booths. I will fetch water. And do you buy potatoes of Virginia, and turnips and cabbage and then I shall make you . . . a fine stew!"

There went that smile again.

I went to the poshest antique shop in Ipswich. No point in selling to guys who don't know what they're buying. For some reason—perhaps that look on Johanna's face—I cautiously parked the Cub round the corner.

The only thing that interested the antique dealer was my oily boots on his wall-to-wall carpeting. He moved up on me quickly, before I could shove a grandfather clock in my top pocket.

"Yes, sir, how can I help you?" Meaning how can I help you out of my shop with the toe of my highly polished winkle-picker?

I showed him the coins.

"We don't buy modern reproductions."

"Try biting them," I suggested, putting them into his hand so he could feel their weight. After that he couldn't get his little eyeglass out fast enough. When he'd had a really good look, he said casually, "Quite nice. I *might* be interested. . . . What price were you thinking of?"

"Hundred quid," I said coolly.

"How did you . . . come by them?

"My grandfather left them to me."

"Collector, was he?"

I almost said no, a deep-sea diver with an insatiable lust for mermaids.

"Do you mind if I consult my partner for a moment? A hundred pounds is a . . . considerable outlay."

He was trying to control his breathing, but he still sounded like he had just finished a race. Sweating, too.

And that look in his eyes that accompanies doing a *very* nasty trick in a *very* moral cause.

I reached out to stop him; but he was gone upstairs in a flash. Then he made his *big* mistake. As he picked up the upstairs extension, the phone in the shop gave a faint *ting.*

He didn't talk to the police long. Hurried back downstairs to make sure I hadn't run away. Unfortunately for him, he still had the coins in his hand.

I asked him for them back, nicely.

He said his partner wouldn't be a moment, if I didn't mind waiting?

I cocked my ear for the approaching panda car, and gave his wrist the same treatment I'd given the young vet's, so long ago.

I got my coins back, and scarpered.

He didn't seem inclined to follow. As I went round the corner, I whipped off my orange bike jacket, revealing a dark blue jersey underneath, and calmly rode away. Met the panda on the corner, but he was looking for a guy in an orange jacket.

Had a good laugh, but it didn't last long. Drawing your last twenty pounds out of the Post Office is a lowering experience. But I bought two fine chops, and a pair of boy's jeans in a sale, and a green sloppy-Joe sweater and even a cheap skid-lid in a back-street shop. Going cheap 'cause it was the chinless sort that's now illegal to sell, though not to wear. I wore it on the way home, to augment my anti-panda disguise. Mind you, I couldn't get myself to worry too much about modern cops. They can't burn you or even hang you, can they?

I met Derek and Susan, just coming out of the end of my lane. Derek pulled down the Land-Rover window, and I reluctantly tracked across.

"Er . . . the shotgun . . . ?"

"Don't mention it," said Derek hurriedly, blinking like a Morse-code lamp. "I've got it—in the back here—better dispose of it—served its purpose—nasty things to have around—drop it down the nearest well—no names, no packdrill."

"Erm . . . the plastic . . . and the fireworks . . . ?"

"All taken care of, old lad—don't bother your head—just go ahead—enjoy life." His smile had regained the authenticity of a toothpaste ad.

All this time, Susan had been very busy ignoring me. Wouldn't look at me. Just stared straight forward through the windscreen.

"Aren't you going to say hallo?" I said, roughly.

"Hallo," she said in a low voice, and shivered, hunching her head down inside her coat collar, even though it was a lovely day.

"I see you came back then?" I persisted. "Got it all sorted out, have you?" I know it was rude, but I was getting really mad with the way she'd gone on.

Then she did turn and look at me, and she looked terrible; much worse than when I'd seen her last on the outskirts of Clacton. Guilty, like she'd murdered somebody and the police hadn't found the body yet.

"Don't worry," I said, "it's all over. I won."

"*Is* it?" she whispered. "*Did* you?"

"Look," I said, "I'm still in one piece. . . ."

"See you around," said Derek, abruptly. "Have a good time." And thrashed off in a shower of stones from the Land-Rover 's wheels. Still, he looked like a man with a load off his back. Whose back was it on now? I went up the lane slowly, feeling oddly depressed. Johanna came running to meet me, just like News used to.

Still, she admired the chops, and was very intrigued by

the skid-lid. I had to explain what a skid was, and then what a lid was, and that not only pans had lids, and how could a skid have a lid? Seventeenth-century teasing's a bit long-winded. I suppose they had nothing better to do on the long winter evenings.

Then I produced the jeans. She pulled a face. "I did only once wear breeches. When I did go riding horses bareback with my brother John. It is very fine riding horses bareback by moonlight. I shall take you one night, Master Jack." Then she returned to the jeans thoughtfully. "But to wear breeches by daylight, when curs might see all your woman's shape; it is most improper. Even Mistress Villers would not do it; nor Mistress Coxswin! But I suppose you do live in lewd times, Master Jack, for even a staid dame like Mistress Pooley does wear breeches. . . ."

"Has Mistress Pooley been *here*?"

"Yes," said Johanna airily. "She is well enough, but a spiritless dame who was not pleased to see me. But Master Pooley . . . is he not like the great Sir William? I did think I was to be hanged all over again. . . . But he has given me these pictures of your Queen, so you need not fret about money any more, good Master Jack."

She handed me a great wad of fivers.

"How long will that last us, Master Jack?"

"Two months—three maybe."

"And he will give us more when that has gone . . . much more."

I stared at her in horror.

"Nay, nay, Master Jack. I did not threaten him with witchcraft. He has fully discharged Sir William's pledge, and his family are free from harm forever now. No, I did give him my marks and angels. He do know a fellow in the City of London who can find a ready use for them and give a good fair price."

I handed back my own mark and angel. "Better have these too. . . ."

"Nay, Master Jack. Do you keep them as a love gift."

I stared at the ground, feeling angry as hell. Why? My narrow squeak with the panda? No. It wasn't that. I somehow felt I'd been sent on a fool's errand, like a child got out of the way while the adults transacted the important business. For the first time, I felt smaller and weaker than Johanna; like putty in her hands.

"Do not be cross with me, Master Jack." She pouted. "Do you show me what other fine thing you have brought me."

She opened the bag and took out the sloppy-Joe sweater, and burst into tears.

It took a lot of hugging and soft talk, before I got her to dry up. Even after that, I was ages getting her to tell me what was wrong.

"I would rather not have that tunic, sir, for it is *green*."

"Green?"

"Green is the color the ladies of the court do wear, when they seek a new paramour. Green is the color of *whores*, sir. I do wish to *be* to you, sir, but not in the fashion of an *harlot*."

Her eyes were huge, warm, beseeching and close. But their only effect was to throw me into a rage. "All *right!*" I shouted. I pulled off my blue jumper and gave that to her, and struggled into the green one. "*I* shall be the harlot!"

"That is a poor jest, sir. Green is for lewd fellows, and I do not think you are a lewd fellow." She was nearly in tears again.

"Oh, *stuff* it!" I shouted, taking it off and throwing it down. "I'll use it to clean my bike with."

"Do not even do that. Green is ill luck. Green is the color of death."

I kicked the jumper into a ditch and left it.

It was our first real quarrel; and nothing was ever quite the same again.

Mind you, there were marvelous times; especially on our walks. Once she saw a tractor plowing stubble, two fields away, and went tearing off after it, thinking it was a genuine fire-breathing dragon.

Another time she vanished behind the hedge. I walked on, and came back with a cluster of kingcups for her, for she was crazy about plants.

She sniffed it, eyes shut. "You did find it growing in a damp place by a stream, where cows do come to drink, and frogs are, and the slow-worm does come to hunt frogs. And nearby are rotting trees clad in ivy; and close by is foxglove, that Master Gerard doth call digitalis. That strengtheneth the heart, taken boiled; but not in excess, for then it is deadly poison. . . ."

"How do you know all that?" I asked, laughing, for she had described the spot I found the kingcups exactly. "Did you follow me?"

"Nay. I was busy about my busy-ness. I did tell all from the smell of it. Can *you* not smell it all?"

All it smelled of to me was kingcup.

Other times weren't so funny. Out on a bike ride, I risked taking her into a roadside cafe. There were a man and woman opposite, sitting drinking tea.

"That man is going to die soon," whispered Johanna. "His wife does hate him and all that he does. She doth spend her time thinking of ways to make him feel small.

And she has just thought of a great good new way, and soon she will tell him, and his heart shall break of it and he shall die."

I stared at the man, horrified. Certainly he was elderly, and had those nasty red marks in his cheeks. He wouldn't make old bones, but . . . .

"Tripe!" I said.

Just then, the woman leaned forward with a smile and said something to her husband. He choked over a scone, went very gray and hurried from the room. His wife followed him.

"Now we shall never know," I said triumphantly.

Johanna smiled, and bit into a chocolate biscuit.

When she had finished the biscuit, there was a commotion outside in the lobby. People hurried past the outside window. Someone was using the phone, urgently. Five minutes later, while I was still pooh-poohing, we heard a siren approaching. I ran to the window.

In the cafe carpark, an ambulance was drawing alongside a green Rover. A body was lifted from the car, still breathing. At least the blanket wasn't over his face. The wife we had seen followed the body into the ambulance.

I sat down abruptly. "How the hell . . . ?"

She said nothing, just ate another chocolate biscuit.

A motorbike passed on the road, invisible.

"Is that the same bike as you do have, Master Jack?"

"Hell, no," I said. "That's Jap-crap. Yamaha RD 250. Twin-cylinder two-stroke. Kid who's riding it's an idiot. He's thrashing it—*and* he's got the wrong type sparkplug in. Burn a hole in his piston in another hundred miles. And he's got a baffle loose in his exhaust. More money than sense. Rich daddy bought it, I expect."

"How can you know all that—you did not even *see* him?"

"I'm interested in bikes. I just *know*."

"And *I* am interested in people. That is how I did know about that man and his wife. . . ."

But it is her singing that haunts me still; she had a sharp sweet voice, and sang more than anyone I've ever known. Brightly and cheerfully round the kitchen in the morning; faint and sad from her bedroom after she'd retired for the night.

> *"Sweet, stay awhile,*
> *Why do you rise?*
> *The light you see comes from your eyes.*
> *The day breaks not,*
> *It is my heart*
> *To think that you and I must part.*
> *Oh stay, or else my joys must die*
> *And perish in their infancy. . . ."*

She sang as if to keep up her spirits in a sad and lonely time, and often I wanted to run upstairs and cheer her up. But then I thought of that bed, with its brown dusty curtains, and I couldn't. Instead, I would wait for her to sing her final song, always "Come Away, Death." All her songs were strange to my modern ear, full of flourishes and curlicues, with meandering tunes that never seemed to come to a definite end.

Only once I recognized some words.

> *"Blow, blow thou winter wind,*
> *Thou art not so unkind*
> *As man's ingratitude*
> *As man's ingratitude.*
> *Thy tooth is not so keen*
> *Because thou art not seen. . . ."*

210

"I *know* that," I yelled, and sang her the modern version.

She picked up the tune quickly and sang it straight through. Then she looked at me darkly, and said, "I can sing it *your way*, Master Jack, but you cannot sing it *mine*." Her eyes were very sad, and full of wanting me.

"All right, teach me your way," I said, willfully misunderstanding her. So she taught me her meandering tune, and I finally mastered it.

"Now I can sing it your way!"

"Nay," she said quietly. "You have mastered the notes, but you still will not sing it *my* way."

I went off then and fiddled with the Cub. But ever after, the tune of *her* way was a reproach to me. Especially floating down from her bed at night. Especially the second verse about "benefits forgot."

Nevertheless, I stuck firmly to my sleeping bag in the barn.

One evening, I found a long lock of dark hair on my sleeping bag pillow; tied with red ribbon. In the morning, I tried to make a joke of it.

"You want to be careful, leaving hair around like that. People here think I'm a witch; they call me Cunning Webster. I might use that hair to cast a spell on you. . . ."

"If you did try, Master Jack, you would not find it difficult." She caressed the line of her jaw with the knuckle of her forefinger, gently, over and over. I'd never seen a girl use that trick before, and I've seen plenty. A seventeenth-century trick, maybe, but bloody come-hitherish just the same.

I looked away, and went on looking away.

After a moment she said angrily, "What would you have me leave for a sign—a lace handkerchief, like a common whore?" Then she banged out of the barn.

She had me torn in half. Daily she grew lovelier. She ate as heartily as News had done; in her time *nothing* must have got enough to eat. She filled out bewitchingly, as the twentieth-century vitamins hit her; all but her tiny waist. She even seemed to grow taller. She fell in love with shampoos, and washed her hair every day. Released from her bonnet, it hung to her waist, fine and glistening like black cobwebs. To look into her eyes was to look into infinity.

I was careful never to look too long.

And she spoiled me; Lord how she spoiled me. Meals always waiting when I got home. She even took my boots off for me; not like a servant, but like a mistress. Never asked me to do a spot of housework, except fetch wood and water, which were men's jobs. She had a genius for stroking the male ego; what did I think she ought to wear? Did I like her new way of dressing her hair, pulled back from her face with a red ribbon? She made me feel ten feet tall. If any other man had so much as looked at her, I'd have killed him.

I told her my every thought; kissed her often. I knew I could have her for the asking, providing I asked nicely.

But every time I got to the brink, something held me back.

Was it the way she stood, when she thought someone was coming? Shoulders bowed, head down, hands together as if praying, eyes slanting sideways, watchful under dark hair. It made her look like Laurence Olivier playing the part of the hunchback Richard III. A relic of a crueler, slyer age.

Or was it her smell? She bathed every day—far more than me—yet, the moment I held her close, that old smell would come back: lavender and cow dung, wood smoke and mildrew . . . but that's oversimplifying it. The warm dusty smell of a healthy cat; dew on grass in the early morning; the silent breath of a forest. But underneath, the smell of moss and stagnant pool, churchyard yew and . . . Goody Hooper.

Even now I'm not being totally honest. Try again. . . .

I've known girls you could make love to and part good friends, and you'd see them in the forecourt of U.C. next day, and they'd grin and lower their eyelids appreciatively, and you'd know they might again, or on the other hand they might not and it wouldn't matter.

Johanna was the exact opposite. Making love to her would have been like a plant putting down a root. Maybe the plant would live a thousand years, and grow into the biggest tree ever seen.

But the one thing no tree can ever do is to pull up its roots and walk away. . . .

If I'd made love to her, I knew I'd be part of everything forever, rooted in the stones and bones of dead men.

And that turned me stone dead. Every time.

23

One morning she announced, "Today, I would like to go and see the sea. I did never see the sea but once."

"You'll have to wear trousers," I said. She pulled a face.

But she loved the bike now, clinging on close behind, giving little wriggles of glee and shouting, "Faster, *faster*, Master Jack!"

"Better than a broomstick?"

"You do *jest*! I did tell you witches did never ride broomsticks. Except old women in their beds. . . ."

I let the rest get lost in the rush of air and the roar of the engine. Mentioning broomsticks always got her narked; pay her back for being so funny about the skid-lid, or skid-bonnet as she insisted on calling it.

We were just passing a place called the Walls, between Mistley and Manningtree, when we hit a minor traffic jam. Being caused by a huge blue shooting-brake with U.S.A.F. number plates. An old guy in a flat cap and gray belted raincoat was gesturing at the driver through its open window. I thought at first there must have been an accident, but as car after car slipped past in front of me, I could see there were no injuries or damage. I was just about to slip past myself when the Cub's engine cut dead.

"Off!" I said to Johanna, and tried kicking the bike over. Dead as a flaming doornail. Tried three more times then gave her a rest. No point in flooding the carb.

I was just unscrewing the spark-plug when the American family got out of their car: Dad, big, tolerant and crew-cut; Mum, sexy behind sunglasses; kids in savagely colored beach shirts. The old guy led them to the roadside wall and they all peered over. I noticed Johanna drifting across to join them and followed quickly. I didn't want her making any bright seventeenth-century remarks to total strangers.

The old guy was pointing out a patch of grass just beyond the wall. It was about six foot by three, long and darkly discolored. There were cows in the field; they'd cropped the rest of the grass pretty close, so the soil showed through in places. But for some reason they hadn't touched the long dark stuff.

"What do you think that might be, sir?" said the little old guy to the Yank.

"Fairy ring?" asked the Yank good-humoredly. "We saw fairy rings in Shropshire, didn't we, Dolores? But *they* were round."

Dolores held up a cine-camera, with an air of weary duty, and gave the patch of grass a regulation ten-second burst.

"That's no fairy ring, sir. Come on, sir, *think* about it. Six feet long . . . ."

"Dunghill?" asked the Yank, dutifully. "Turnip clamp?"

"It is a *grave!*" said Johanna, in a voice that brooked no argument. "For when a body is buried, the humors thereof, rising, do give virtue to the plants that grow thereon. That is why we did always bury the bodies of fresh-drowned kittens in our herb garden. . . ."

Every American mouth was agape. The old guy looked furious at someone stealing his thunder, but went on fiercely, "Quite correct, madam. But do you know whose grave it is?"

I saw Johanna's mouth open again, and grabbed her

hand so hard she squeaked. "No, we don't know," I said. "We're just tourists passing through."

"It is the grave of Matthew Hopkins, the notorious Witchfinder. He was on the television only last month, played by Vincent Price. They shot the whole film in Lavenham village, just up the road from here."

"You remember, Pop," said Junior. "We stay up to watch. The Roundhead captain gouged Hopkins' eyes out. Wham!"

The old man made another desperate attempt to control his audience. "That is *not* how he died. His death was far stranger. . . ."

That silenced us; we all love strange deaths.

"Now Hopkins was Cromwell's Witchfinder-General, and he tried and burnt his first witches in these parts."

"They did not *burn* witches," said Johanna. "They did *hang* witches."

He silenced her with a glare. He had a rat-trap jaw and little deep-set eyes. Not the kind of old-age pensioner you feel sorry for.

"When he'd burnt up all the witches round here, he went up into Suffolk an' burnt hundreds. Then he went up into Norfolk an' burnt hundreds more. Then he went off into the Fen Country. . . .

"Each time he came back he were richer. When he came back from Suffolk he bought a farm. When he came back from Norfolk, he built a big house on it. But when he came back from the Fens, he wouldn't speak to no one, but shut himself up in his big house wi' his old housekeeper. Only came out on Sundays, to go to church. Then he sang the psalms an' prayed louder nor anybody else. But he was always looking at the door, as if he was afeared somebody might come through it.

216

"One day, his housekeeper bought him some oranges at Colchester market; to cheer him up, he seemed so down. But he flew into a rage, an' said they were the Devil's fruit, an' threw them in Mistley Pond. Then the new magistrate's wife came to church, an' she had red hair, an' he attacked her, saying she was a witch. People began saying the Devil had turned his brain, to revenge the burning of all those witches. Specially one night, when there was a big red sunset, an' Hopkins ran all round the fields, shouting on God to put out the sun, as the Devil was coming.

"He was seen out walking late; seen out walking all night. Anybody he saw, he pleaded with them to tell him where he might find a witch, an' where they held their Sabbaths. But no one could tell him, because they knew the witches were all burnt-up.

"An' he was always hiding in a place called Mistley Hollows. Now you might think, sir, that Hollows is only a name, meaning some holes in the ground. But a gentleman from Cambridge, who was interested in this Hopkins, told me that the name isn't really Hollows, but Hallows, meaning a place sacred to the Old Religion, which is the Devil. And no one went there after dark, save witches. . . .

"Anyway, a Mistley man, who was courting a Manningtree girl, took a shortcut through the Hollows one night, an' he reckoned he saw Hopkins there, sobbing an' crying an' praying to the Devil to come to him. An' folk reckoned Hopkins *was* mad, 'cause he still went to church more an' more as well. Sometimes the parson would leave him praying after one service, an' come back for the next service an' find him *still* praying.

"Then the bairns took to playing pranks on Hopkins. Following him around, calling that they would take him to a witch for a penny. An' many a penny he gave them, if you can believe the tale. But they just took his pennies an' ran away. An' they would wear any old orange-colored thing they could lay their hands on, an' lie in wait for Hopkins behind a bush, an' leap out shouting they were Old Nick. Then he'd burst out crying, an' they'd pelt stones at him, an' hit him wi' sticks from behind, an' shout they were Beelzebub, an' he must fall down an' worship them.

"Then one day he hit a child—nigh half-murdered it. An' it went home an' had a bad dream, an' called out in its sleep that it saw Master Hopkins coming to take its soul away. Then the child's father vowed to swim Hopkins, to see if he was a witch.

"An' there were a lot of villagers went to help him, for a lot had it in for Hopkins. On account of the fact that they'd helped him find his witches, an' he'd grown fat an' famous, and they'd only had a shilling off him for their pains. And they wanted a share of the Devil's gold, that folks said Hopkins' house was full of. And others said Hopkins had the Devil's book, which was proof he was in league with him.

"They took Hopkins an' swum him in Mistley Pond, which is just yonder, sir. With his thumbs tied to his big toes, an' him stark-naked, madam. An' he swam and floated like a witch, an' reached the shore alive. But they left him lying on the bank, an' ran to his house to get the Devil's gold. Only the children stayed to watch him. He lay there two days an' coughed his life away, and no one would go nigh. On the third morning they found him stark, wi' blood on the grass, an' the crows had picked his eyes out.

"No one would touch him to bury him. The parson wouldn't have him in the graveyard. At last they got a passing stranger to bury him, for the money in his pockets. An' there he do lie, sir; but he don't like quiet.

"One night in the Thorn Inn the landlord's daughter saw him get out of an armchair in the attic an' walk away. An' a lady called Mrs. Bennet, who runs the Spiritualists, she held a seance in the Red Lion an' *she* saw him. Wearing dark clothing, no hat, holding a cane, dank oily hair an' glittering eyes. . . . She only realized who it must have been, afterward.

"An' many have seen him on this very spot, sir, running to and fro across the road. So folk in cars think they've knocked somebody down. Then they see him get over the wall, but when they look over the wall, all they can see is what you see now, sir."

The Americans gave a satisfied shudder. There was the crackle of a pound note.

"Thank'ee very much, sir."

"Do you know," asked Dolores, "is there a picture-postcard of the grave? Can you buy one in the town? Grandma is *so* keen on the supernatural . . . she'll go *wild*."

They got back into their car, with slammed doors and big good-byes.

The old guy gave Johanna and me a look, decided we weren't worth a bean, and made a beeline for another car that had just drawn up, farther down the Wall. Matthew Hopkins was obviously a flourishing feature of the tourist trade.

I went back to the Cub, got her off the stand, and gave her a kick. She started first time.

"C'mon," I called to Johanna. But she was nowhere to be seen. She could only be on the other side of the wall. I went back, a bit cross.

She was kneeling beside the discolored grass, smiling. And it wasn't a nice sort of smile. She said something to herself. Or was it to the thing buried under the ground?

She was crooning away to the thing under the ground.

She put out a little white hand, delicately, and patted the ends of the long, discolored grass. Just like a cat, when it's playing with a live mouse. . . .

Have you ever seen a cat playing with a mouse? They so enjoy it; they're really fed up when the mouse dies. It's the only time I can't *stand* cats.

Suddenly, I got blindingly angry. "C'mon!" I yelled. "C'mon or I'll go off and leave you."

I had to shout at her three times before she even looked my way. Then she looked at me, like a cat looks at you when you take the mouse away from it.

Then she shook her head slightly, as if to clear something from her mind. When she looked at me again, the old Johanna was back.

She came to me, still smiling.

24

That night, the barn was really like a kitchen. Derek's logs roaring up the chimney, and just enough September frost in the air to make me appreciate them. Three oil lamps burning (Derek had brought us two more).

Only trouble was, I had nothing to read. The last of my motorbike mag had gone for fire-lighting, and I know my Cub maintenance manual off by heart.

"Hey, Joh, seen that witchcraft book of mine?"

"No." That was all; just "no." Which was funny, because she was normally fantastic at finding lost spanners and things.

I groaned resentfully, and got to my feet. One thing, the barn wasn't a difficult place to search, and there was no other room in the house the book could be. I did a quick tour of milking stools, table, dresser. Looked under the settle. No sign. I realized I hadn't seen the book for some time. Yet it was enormous.

"*Bloody* funny. *I* haven't moved it." For some reason I went on crashing around, pushing things about, making a thorough nuisance of myself. Finally Joh said, "Wait!" in a tight little voice, and went out. I heard her feet climbing the outside stair and returning. Then she came and put the book in my lap, lips pressed tight together in disapproval.

"Thought you didn't know where it was. Where was it?"

"Under my bed."

"Why?"

"Do you think I do like being reminded of Matthew Hopkins and the things he did do to me?" She went back to the table and began beating hell out of a mixing bowl.

Perversely, I still opened the book. At the only existing portrait of Matthew Hopkins. A crude, stiff little engraving of him in his high hat, carrying his staff. But a good likeness. The artist had caught the big dark eyes and beaky nose, and the smug expression of a guy who *knows* he's right. I looked at him and was glad he was dead. I was also glad it wasn't me that killed him.

Further down the engraving, two witches were sitting in hard chairs. The artist had caught that awful passive look that witches on trial have; like they're assisting in their own downfall. In this case they were telling the names of their familiars, in bubbles coming from their mouths like in a strip-cartoon. And the familiars were bouncing round the bottom of the picture, having a ball. Good old Vinegar Tom, the greyhound with the calf's head. One called Grizzle Greedigut. And a cat leaping.

Called Newes.

"Hey, Joh. Here's a picture of old News."

"I do *know* that." Her voice was more disapproving than ever.

"Hey, was she really a familiar?"

She did not answer for a long time. Then she answered with another question.

"Are you happy, Master Jack? Here, now, in this kitchen tonight?"

Unthinking, I said, "Yeah."

"Then do not ask questions, for if you do I must tell you the truth."

222

"It's just that I miss that cat. . . ."

"I have told you. You shall have cat; but it will not be the same."

"How can I have her? I've got her skull here. And my crash helmet was all blood. . . ."

"You do ask more questions than Matthew Hopkins. It did bring him little comfort in the end."

"Yeah, but . . . whose familiar *was* News?"

"First mine, and then yours. I did send her to you, through Time."

I thought of the little cold nose in my ear, of the soft fur against my cheek, and I shuddered.

But I wasn't going to let her see how scared I was. "Hey," I said. "I don't get this time thing. I mean, it's crazy. You remember when you were being tried by Hopkins?"

"Do you think I shall ever forget it?"

"Well, I was sitting in court watching you."

"Yes."

"Then Trooper Collins rushed in and said the Devil had beaten him up at your house. . . ."

"Yes."

"Well, how could I be sitting in court *and* beating him up at your house? I couldn't be in two places at once."

She smiled; always the same smile, looking inward into her own mind and pleased at what she saw. Then she pointed down to the bread dough she was making. She pinched a little of it up into a hump between finger and thumb. Suddenly it had arms and a head.

"There are *you*, Master Jack." Then she folded the dough over swiftly, several times. "First you were on the outside, Master Jack. Now you are on the inside. Inside a fold. But *which* fold? Can you find yourself again? Not

in a thousand years. But you are still *there* somewhere
. . . and," she pinched the dough again, "here you are
on the outside again."

Her quick fingers went on folding the dough, fold
upon fold upon fold, while I watched, hypnotized, and
wondered where both of me was now.

"You did need time, Master Jack. But a fine witch can
knead Time. . . . I could show you how."

"But I'm not a bloody witch!"

"Do you cross your fingers for luck? Do you touch
wood?"

"Yeah, but . . . ."

"Do you throw salt over your shoulder when you spill
it?"

"Used to, when I was a kid."

"Do you consult the stars about your fate?"

"No." Then I thought of the *Daily Mirror* horoscope,
grinned and said, "Yes."

"Then you are a witch."

"But I don't take it *seriously*!"

"Then you are not a *serious* witch."

Up till then, we were both still half-teasing. But then
she said, "You did know News had unnatural powers.
And you did use them. Master Hopkins did have the right
to hang you, under the Law."

"But I was only trying to help you."

"Anyone who does aid a witch *is* a witch. Master Hopkins did say so."

"But you're not *really* a witch. You didn't put curses
on people—you tried to help them."

"There are blessing-witches and cursing-witches. Master
Hopkins did think the blessing-witches worse. Give me
your book."

She turned to a page; so quickly and easily I knew she had the whole damn thing off by heart.

"By the laws of England, the thief is hanged for stealing, and we think it just and profitable. But it were a thousand times better if all witches, but especially the blessing-witches, do suffer death. These are the right hand of the Devil. For men do commonly hate the cursing-witch as unworthy to live among them. Whereas the blessing-witch is so dear unto them, they fly unto him in necessity, depend upon him as their god, and by this means thousands are carried away to destruction."

She closed the book with a slap. I thought about the girl I'd given soap to, and her brother who wanted Paul Podgam.

"But you're not *really* a witch—you're a lady."

"Did you not read of Canewdon, Cunning Webster? Where they did always have three witches in silk and three in cotton? Do you listen." She moved her legs together under her skirt, and there was a rustling of petticoats. "Do you hear my silk, Cunning? There are far more witches in silk than cotton. But they are never hanged. Who dares to look for witches in great men's houses?"

"I still can't *really* believe it, somehow."

"Do you look at your fine new watch, Cunning."

I was still wearing my watch, though it hadn't gone for months.

It was going now.

"That's a fluke!" I yelled desperately.

"Try and stop it going, then."

I shook it and banged it. The thing went on going. "I shall stop it, now," she said.

As I looked at the watch, the second-hand stopped moving. I shook it all over again. No effect. It stayed dead.

"I still say it's a fluke. It's like with motorbikes sometimes; they just stop and won't go, for some reason."

Then I thought exactly when the Cub had let me down. When I had tried to escape from the barn. Beside Hopkins' grave at Mistley. . . .

She smiled, and for the first time I felt really frightened.

"I can make you do *anything*, Cunning Webster."

"You bloody can't!"

"I can. I shall make you look behind you."

"Like hell you will."

"I shall call up the Devil to make you."

"Try it."

I settled down, eyes fixed firmly on her face. Her eyes were very large, and bright with excitement. I began worrying about hypnotism, but she shifted her eyes from mine, and looked over my shoulder toward the door.

The door creaked on its hinges; a cold draft came across the floor. I broke out in a sweat, but kept my eyes fixed on her face. Her eyes moved infinitesimally, so I could almost imagine someone creeping up behind me.

The table creaked, twice. Like something was leaning on it. I gritted my teeth and held my gaze.

Then the settle I was sitting on creaked gently, right behind my head. I jumped up and whirled, ready to smash anything that was there.

The room was quite empty. Johanna giggled.

"But . . . the door opened . . . the draft . . . the table creaked."

226

"The door does always make that noise; there are always drafts; the table does often creak. Have you not noticed? I did only direct your mind. What did you expect to hit, Cunning? A man with goat's head and goat's feet?" She giggled again. "You are all the same, you men. You are so sure that God is a man, and the Devil also. Poor Master Hopkins—he did hate the Devil greatly. But he did never insult him by thinking he might be a *woman*."

"Is the Devil . . . female?"

"Men do oppress us every day, Cunning. Men are the masters. Do you think when we creep out into the fields at night, risking our lives, we would do it to be ruled by yet another *man*?"

I brooded.

"So Hopkins was *right*?"

"He was right—for Hopkins. There can be no peace between us and his sort. With their money and their usury, and their furnaces that do make the fields black. For we are green and they are black. They do hate green so much that no woman can wear it for fear she be thought a whore. Yet trees are green, and the grass we all do live from, and quiet pools and cool moss in the warm weather. . . ."

Just for a moment, under her eyes, I belonged with the trees and the roots under the earth. And felt safe and whole and included in all things. But then I thought of yew trees, and gravestones, and bones under the earth. They did bury fresh-drowned kittens in their herb-gardens. . . .

I hurled my mind into a new track.

"The people brought gifts . . . Derek . . . they knew you were coming."

"The people do love me, Cunning. They would take

me for their god. Only Hopkins hated me, and now you. Oh, you do think ill of witches. Just like Master Hopkins. Are you sorry he is dead, and not I? Do you want to hang me, Cunning? Or burn me? Or just strip my body naked, to search for foulness?" She rubbed her legs together again, and again there was the sound of silk.

"But how did the people *know* you were coming?"

"Because *you* did come, Cunning."

"But I came by pure chance!"

"Lady Chance?"

My head whirled. I remembered the surge of traffic that had thrust me onto the Colchester road; the crazy traffic that would not let me turn right for Clacton; the fight with the Roundhead Association.

Johanna began to softly hum a tune. I remembered it. It was called "The King Shall Enjoy His Own Again."

"That girl at Hammer's Field with the lute. . . ."

"I did put it in her mind to sing it—she did know the song already."

"And that storm, when I first came to the barn?"

"Did not Master Hopkins say that when there are gales and thunderstorms, all men do know that witches are about?"

I put my head in my hands. "Why me?"

"You did look for me, Cunning, before I did look for you. What do your friends at the university seek? Drink, sport, the bodies of young women? Why was not that enough for *you*? Why did you set out to look for Lady Chance?"

"Oh, my God!"

"I do not mind you calling upon God. Only Hopkins and his like did think we were against God. Do God be more wroth with us or Hopkins, Cunning?"

I groaned.

"Did I not ask you if you were happy, Cunning? Did I not warn you about asking questions? Art happier now?"

"But how do you *do* it—all your witchcraft and seeing the future?"

"I shall tell you why you *cannot* do it. Because you fill your hearts with thoughts of engines and money. And because you fill your houses with boxes which flicker the same dream over and over again, and benumb your brains. I did see such boxes being sold in a booth in Colchester. In this booth were twenty boxes, and some did have bright colors and some did be white and gray. But they did all have the same face saying the same thing, and that thing did be a lie. You do listen or look at nothing, save what is in those boxes. How can you know *any* thing? Here." She thrust a little twist of cloth into my hand. "Do you sniff that."

"What is it?" I asked, really scared.

She laughed. "It will only make you peaceful."

I sniffed. It was smashing: green and moist, and old and new, all at the same time. I sniffed and sniffed.

"It is but rosemary, that do lift the heart, as Master Gerard do say. It is not better than lying dreams that flicker on boxes?"

I took it with me to my sleeping bag.

25

I felt like hell the following morning. I'd lain awake half the night, in spite of the rosemary. Listening to Johanna walking up and down next door in the lost room. Little feet making a soft *shush-shush-shush* on the brand new floor-covering of Norfolk reeds that Derek had brought her in the trailer.

What was she up to now? I'd never know. If I asked, she'd tell me half the truth. She was far too clever to lie.

Half-awake, I heard her come into the barn, and stir the fire from its ashes. It was really cold that morning; it felt a bit like the start of the autumn term. For the first time in months, I thought about Rugby. I had a chance of the vice-captaincy this term; a chance to tell the selection committee what I thought of them.

Johanna kept tiptoeing over, to see if I was awake. I knew she wanted to get my breakfast; to talk. That made me pretend all the harder to be asleep. Finally, I heard her pick up her new basket, and close the barn door softly, so as not to waken me. Then I felt a rat.

I knew she'd be gone a couple of hours. Each day she wandered farther and farther, collecting herbs. The whole barn was hung with sweet-smelling bunches of green, which she laid on the outside stair every day to dry in the sun. They made the barn smell great. But eerie.

She was looking up her old haunts. Every day she came back with a new tale. Some of her hidden places had gone, to make room for a silo, or a road-widening. But a surprising number remained, so she said, just as she'd left them. Little woods at the corners of fields; little buried lanes full of foxglove and cuckoo-pint.

I got up. Had a lump of yesterday's home-baked loaf for breakfast. Felt like a wash. Found some hot water in the kettle over the fire. That had to be refilled, which meant a walk of two hundred yards upstream. Joh wouldn't let me use the stream where it flowed by the barn. Reckoned something got into the water from a field of turnips that was "not good."

That reminded me. Johanna wanted the well cleared out. It was a sensible move; save both our legs. So why did I resent doing it so much?

But working hard is one way I can get rid of a bad mood. So I set to. The well lay in what used to be a garden behind the barn. Now the garden was just a tangle of briars, growing over low mounds. Couldn't make out what the mounds had been. They were scattered here and there, each about six feet long. Anyway, I soon found a ring of mossy stones, under the dead grass.

The well wasn't hard to clear. Hadn't been filled in properly. People had just chucked things down it; old boots, a rusty pick-ax blade, even the remains of a gold watch that somebody must have nicked, then lost their nerve.

I got down three feet in two hours, and at that point I struck the water level. Felt I'd earned a break. Went and hacked a corned-beef sandwich; put the whole tin in, and went and sat on the outside steps.

"Morning, Cunning!" The voice, suddenly breaking the silence, made me jump. But it was only Matthew Fassett and his son, looking over the wall. They had a shallow basket with them, with a dozen eggs in it.

"We cum for the Paul Podgam, Cunning."

There was plenty of Paul Podgam now; a whole bowl of it, set in the fireplace to catch the woodsmoke. It was the first herb Johanna had prepared. Only trouble, I didn't know how much to give; so I tipped about a quarter of it into a paper bag.

Matthew opened the bag and sniffed appreciatively. Then he took two pinches, put them into an old Swan Vestas matchbox and gave me the bag back.

"Very generous of ye, Cunning. But it don't keep fresh, you see. Not once it's left the yarb mother."

I grinned, comparing my monstrous vision of the yarb mother with the youthful smallness of Johanna.

"Yarb mother out gatherin', Cunning?"

I nodded.

"We'm did think we saw her, down Yearsley's Field." He started for the gateway, and then turned back.

"We'm all glad you've come, Cunning. Yarb mother needs a Master; otherwise there be trouble and gossip. . . ."

"Yes, thank you very much," I stammered. It was the way he said it; like I was going to stay on at the barn for ever and ever. Then I remembered the basket at my feet. I took the eggs out, handling them so clumsily I cracked one. I put them on the ground, and gave him his basket back.

"Thank'ee, Cunning." He looked relieved to get the basket back. Yet if I hadn't offered it, he'd have cheerfully gone off without it. And it was a good basket.

"Thank *you*," I said stupidly, like a shopkeeper.

I sat on, on the outside steps. The sun was at its height now; nearly midday and getting hot. That old Suffolk misty-blue was back under the trees, all the way to the horizon. Not a sound of car or plane or tractor. I felt peacefully buried alive. Did U.C. London exist? Did London exist? Did it matter?

The Cub was my only proof. I went and started her up, and listened to the tappets. Sounded good and sharp, driving the silence from the yard.

I switched off, and the silence same back, only worse. I felt I was dissolving, melting into the green smell and the humming of late bees. The only cure was the Cub, and I couldn't run that all day; I only had half a gallon in the tank.

Across the lane, in the dark of the hedge, something stirred and rustled. Rabbit? It was about rabbit size. I kept very still; I like watching rabbits.

After a long pause, when I'd given up hope, it moved again. Big for a rabbit. Didn't move like a rabbit. Too low to the ground and quick. I caught a sudden prick of pointed ears, in a blue gap in the hedge.

It was a cat. And a cat moving in a way that could only mean one thing. A frightened cat; a disorientated cat. Jumping at every sound, belly ridiculously close to the ground, diving from hiding place to hiding place.

That's the way this cat was moving.

I stayed very still, and at last she came out of cover and stood in a patch of sunlight, one paw lifted for flight.

Instinctively I called, "New-News-News!"

For it *was* her. I recognized the blaze of ginger that ran down to her left eye; the three ginger spots on her left flank, like the letter S in Morse code. And those ridiculous whiskers, half-black, half-white.

Then she gave me that look of cold mistrust that any strange cat gives you, and I knew it wasn't News. She was too big for News. And News' skull lay on the window-sill, gleaming in the sun. The world was full of black-and-ginger cats. Most farm cats have some ginger.

But the cat, stranger though she was, wouldn't go away. She wanted something; but it was not me. She kept creeping out of the hedge, then darting back.

Curious, I got off the steps, and walked through the barnyard to the lane.

Immediately, walking in a deep curve to keep as far away from me as possible, she made for the barn door. She sniffed the outside stair, then rubbed herself against it in ecstasy.

She knew the barn.

Then she sniffed a pair of Johanna's square-toed shoes, washed and put out on the step to dry. She rolled on them, over and over. Pushed them about with her nose and rolled on them again. I could hear her purring, right down the yard.

She knew Johanna.

More than that, in finding the barn and the shoes, she had come home. For she was no longer disorientated. She relaxed on the doorstep and began to wash herself, pushing one paw over her ear. The ear turned inside-out, showing bright pink in the sun. She shook her head to release it, then in the same movement attacked the inside of her hind leg.

It was a movement I knew by heart.

Somehow, beyond rhyme or reason, News had come back. The whitened skull had been some other cat's. The blood on my helmet had not been fatal blood.

I ran to her, crying her name.

She took one terrified look, and fled back to the hedge in a black-and-ginger streak. And as she ran, I could see from the lean depth of her flank that she was a much older cat; one that had had many kittens.

It was then that I remembered Johanna's words:

"You shall have cat; but it will not be the same."

It was News all right. But a News that had never known me. A News plucked, God knew how, from a different, forgotten, fold of Time. Lost, frightened, disorientated. Just to please me. . . .

It did not please me. The cat had been used, ruthlessly, without her consent.

As I had been used, without my consent. Helpless as the cat. Led by the nose all the way. From first to last I had been a puppet. It was no accident that Derek had shown me how to use the shotgun, or the plastic explosive: All had been most exquisitely planned.

For what purpose?

To destroy Hopkins.

Not to kill him. That would have made him a Puritan martyr, to be buried with honor. An honor that would have spawned other Hopkinses, eager to follow in his footsteps. England would have become a hotbed of witch-hunting, like France. Where they burned four hundred witches in one day. . . .

But there had never been another Witchfinder-General in England. Because people had watched Hopkins go mad; destroy himself, caught in his own net.

And I knew I hadn't been the first Devil on the road. There was that name, scratched on the fireplace in the barn. I went to look at it.

John Michael Briarly
Magdalen College Oxford
7.8.1877

Scrawled so triumphantly, a hundred years ago. Had he been on tour like me? A walking tour, perhaps, leaving no forwarding address? He had been allowed to find the fireplace. What else had he been allowed to find?

What had happened to John Michael Briarly?

He had certainly failed. Otherwise Johanna wouldn't have needed me. He wouldn't have had a motorbike to help him, poor sod; or a ready-made Devil fancy-dress. And when he went . . . the barn had been tidied away in a hell of a rush. I somehow felt there had been a nasty accident, back there in the depths of time.

How many nasty accidents? Maybe John Michael hadn't been the only one. There were those low mounds in the abandoned garden where I'd been digging out the well. Long low mounds . . . .

Suddenly, I was grabbing up my gear in armfuls. I had to get clear of the barn before Johanna came back, and she was already overdue.

I cleared the barn of my stuff; I cleared the yard. But I was still a pair of old gauntlets short, and a multispanner. And somehow I didn't want to leave anything of myself in that place.

The only place left to look was Johanna's room; that was where she'd hidden my witchcraft book. I went up the outside stair nervously, and opened the door. But it was very ordinary. The four-poster bed was made. A few clothes were folded neatly on a milking stool. A towel was hung up to dry on a piece of binder twine strung between a bed post and the door. Nothing else. Till I looked under the bed.

There was something under the bed, but nothing of mine. Funny-looking object. I reached under, among the fluff, and pulled it out.

It was the kind of abstract sculpture they do at the Slade School at U.C. Bits of bent wire, with candle grease dribbled all over it. Only there *was* something of mine, embedded in the candle grease. A rusty spark plug. Thieving little so-and-so! But then I always leave spark plugs lying about, like any motorcyclist. My mother once made a collection of thirty; arranged them along the bookcase in my room, just for a laugh.

But, there was also one of my motorcycle gauntlets, or what was left of it. Just the five fingers and palm of the hand, and all the fingers twisted at funny angles to each other. And a couple of gasket rings embedded in the wax, new and unused. What a magpie the girl was! And all ruined to make a feeble little abstract-sculpture.

But Johanna didn't do pointless silly things. I turned the object over and over in my hands.

And suddenly saw what it was.

A motorbike with a rider. The gasket rings were the wheels, and the spark plug stood for the engine. The mangled glove was the body of the rider, the fingers his arms and legs. Even the yellow crash helmet was represented, by the yellow top of an aerosol spray. I lifted the aerosol top, and in the head beneath, a lock of hair was embedded.

My hair; I knew, because my hair's got a reddish tinge.

The rider's hands, fixed round the handlebars, were made of curious half-moon shapes embedded in the wax. I pulled one out.

It was a fingernail.

One of my fingernails; the black grease from the bike was still on it.

I knew then what the object was: a poppet; a poppet of me.

What had the witchcraft book said: "It was alleged that the two women had made wax models of the children. Into these they had stuck pins and needles, before they were burned in a fierce fire. Several impes in the shape of mice were seen running to and from the fire. That same night the two children sickened, and in the morning died. Wheresoever a witch do stick a needle in a poppet, in that same place shall the bewitched person be afflicted with great pains. If a poppet be consumed in fire, then the person shall die."

I looked at the poppet of me. There was one pin in place through the spark plug; where the engine would be in a real bike. And another through the rider's left wrist, where I wore my watch.

I wanted to stamp the thing to pieces. Luckily, I came to my senses in time. I just took out the two pins, and carried the thing downstairs and packed it into my top-box, surrounding it with a padding of sleeping bag. Maybe I'll break it some day. When I've sold the Cub and feel like committing suicide.

When I kicked the Cub over, she started fine. And I set off down the track for the last time.

A cloud crossed the sun. I glanced up nervously; but it was only a little cloud.

But there *was* something the matter with my engine; sluggish, kept missing and picking up again. I had a job getting the bike up the last little slope to the main road.

I looked at the cloud again. Seemed bigger, nearer. Let's say there was not much likelihood of the sun coming out in the near future. Thought I heard a bit of thunder, but it was hard to tell over the racketing of the engine.

Looked left and right and started the right turn toward Sudbury.

The Rover came out of nowhere, doing a ton, head-lights blazing. I thought for a horrible second my engine was going to conk altogether, and leave me right in the Rover's path. But the engine caught just in time, and the car swept past with horn blaring. Its slipstream caught me so hard, I had to put out a foot to save myself.

Funny . . . I've always found Rover-drivers careful guys, who care about machinery. Now if it had been a Vauxhall . . . .

I chugged miserably up the hill in second, then in first. The accelerator made no more difference than if I'd been twiddling with a stick of licorice. And the cloud was bigger; much bigger.

Then a Kawasaki 750 overtook me, going full out. The kid riding it was tanking it, head down behind his fairing, in a world of his own. I felt a tug on my boot as he passed. When I looked, I saw he had clipped my top buckle off, clean as a whistle. And I swear he never even knew I was there.

I'd pulled up to shout insults after him. Then I noticed my engine had died. And it wouldn't re-start. As I kicked and kicked, the first shilling of rain hit the dust of the road.

The barn was still in sight down the hill. There was someone standing in the barnyard. In the gathering gloom I couldn't make out clearly who it was. But the person was small, and its face was turned toward me.

I nearly gave up then. Rain fell in torrents. Cars roared past, throwing the puddles over my leathers and bike. Nobody stopped to offer help. People who'll stop if they run over a bird won't stop for a sodden motorbike-yob.

An infinite despair swept over me. I notice the rust on the Cub's handlebars. Her front tire needed replacing again, after only five thousand miles. Soon, in spite of my endless fiddling and touching-up, she'd be only fit for the scrap yard. The passing cars . . . in less than ten years they'd only be fit for the scrap heap too. The drivers would age and die. I would turn gray and die—gray like Goody Hooper with her wrinkled breasts and lice in her hair. *Kiss me, fine young gentleman . . . I will sing you a song . . . a song to break the spell of venery, put on you by a witch who has been your paramour. . . .*

Break a spell of venery? Paramour?

Without hope, I began to bellow out the words of the song. As a kind of last defiance, shouted at the green of Suffolk, the damp selig green that would never die, but renewed itself; green of hedge and tree, grass and bog and hidden things; green in which Johanna cradled herself and lived forever. She was green, but *I* was black. Black leather. Hopkins in his black cloak and tall black hat. I am Hopkins, I thought, with a kind of cruel drunken glee.

> *"Will you make a fine cambric shirt*
> *Parley with Red Mary in time*
> *Remember me to one who rides by*
> *She was once a true love of mine."*

Something, it may only have been the force of the rain, gave back a little, as if wounded. I kicked the bike, without hope. It started, strong. I mounted, strong. I thought of chimneys belching black smoke, of the armored tracks of tanks, of guns firing, of Honda Goldwings and Harley-Davidsons, of blast furnaces and steam trains. I am black, I thought, fast and strong and black.

I went off like the clappers.

"First there was one and then there were two
Three and six and then there were nine
The Devil make you a fine cambric shirt
Mary was once a true love of mine."

The road was twisting every way. But I saw a road sign pointing left. *Sudbury 10.*

Then it grew dark, like driving at night; only not blue, like night, but the green of thunderclouds. The road was a black shining nothing. Cars coming toward me had headlights that shone like stars, great constellations. I was not riding; I was flying, through outer space. And the waist of my leathers felt tight, as if a small pair of arms was clasped round it. And a whisper seemed to come over my shoulder, through the pandemonium of the rain, and my engine blatting defiance at the hedges.

"Faster, Master Jack. Faster." And I was sad she was not really there, and the cat too, snuggled down the front of my jacket.

Sudbury 14. Besingtree 1.

Somehow, the blasted roads had twisted me round; I was going back to the barn. I did a wild and frantic U-turn, without even looking behind me. If there'd been a car, I'd have died then. Maybe I wouldn't have cared all that much. Been buried in the green of Suffolk.

"Off with her gown and off with her shoon
Off with her kirtle all made of green
Off with her skin and break up the bones
Now she's gone, she's no love of mine."

Lightning lanced down onto the road in front. A little tree crashed in fragments on the tarmac. A little ash tree.

As I pulled up, I could see the fine thin leaves were already drooping, and the thin immature ash-key seeds that would never ripen now.

I tried to think of Johanna as the lightning; but as I sat staring, I couldn't help thinking of her as the ash tree. It was such a little ash tree.

It was a while before I noticed it had stopped raining, and that no car had passed for ages. I looked up, and the rags of thundercloud were being swept away by the wind. A bit like the stage staff clear away the props at the end of a play. Somehow I knew it was all over, and I was sorry.

And immediately I wanted to see her. Maybe some bloody-mindedness in me wanted to be *sure* it was all over. Maybe I thought that now I'd broken the spell, we could go on knowing each other in a matey way. I could run down to see her from London for weekends. . . .

It didn't take me long to get to the barn. In all that tangled struggle on the road, I had actually traveled one and a half miles from it.

But as I reached the lane end I met a funny sight. An old man carrying away a milking stool under his arm. One of my milking stools. I shouted at him, "Hey, where you going with that?"

But he just clutched it tightly to him and hurried past.

Halfway up the lane, I met two women carrying bundles, and they hurried past as well, with down-turned faces.

I pulled in to the barnyard. Derek's Land-Rover was there, and Matthew Fassett and another guy were loading the dismantled four-poster into it. Other stuff was lying about; the table and a bench. The whole scene had the air of people clearing up after a road accident.

"What's happened?" I shouted.

242

Fassett gave me a long look, and then said, "There be some people who want to ask *you* that, Cunning."

There was something in his look that stopped me saying any more.

I went into the barn, to the sound of a hideous scraping. Two more farmhands were just pushing the settle back into the fireplace. Everything else was gone. The barn was a barn again, just the way I'd found it.

My head was in a whirl. I hadn't been gone from the barn more than an hour, and yet these people had come and carved the whole place up, destroying it. It was crazy.

I ran back to Matthew Fassett. I knew he wanted to land me a clout; I think he'd have liked to kill me. But I had to *know*.

"Where is she? Where is she?"

He looked down at his hands; sighed. Like he was thinking how to explain something to a very naughty stupid child who has just made a mess for the umpteenth time.

"She's *gone*. Cunning. And she won't be coming back. She don't stay where she's not wanted. . . ."

"Gone? Gone where?"

"Back where she came from."

I was really frightened then. Had Hopkins got her?

I think he saw the look on my face. He said, a bit kinder, "Don't ee worry, Cunning. 'Tain't the first time 'tis happened. She'll come again. But not in your time, nor mine."

I remembered the name scratched on the fireplace.

John Michael Briarly
Magdalen College Oxford
7.8.1877

Matthew Fassett said, "Why do ee call her, if ee don't want her? You young men do be all the same." There was a lifetime of bitterness in his voice.

So John Michael Briarly had chickened out on her too. Just gone away. I know that's true, because I checked up on him afterward. He became a vicar in Warwickshire, and lived to be nearly a hundred. Maybe he hung on a long time, hoping to meet her again.

How many more had chickened out on her, in three hundred years? Forcing her to knead Time, over and over again? Well, I'd managed more than most. The Devil on the road had done for Hopkins. It was the hard bit I'd chickened out on—loving her. What would she have done to the man who loved her and stayed? I knew one thing—she'd have looked after him. I remembered her saying, "I will keep you safe, Master Jack," and I believed it now. Maybe I'd have lived to the ripe old age of 109, like George Pickingale. Maybe I'd have lived forever. Maybe I'd have learned all the secrets of the universe . . . but it was too late now. I only knew one thing. I wouldn't have come to a nasty end, in a quick-dug grave behind the barn. There weren't any graves behind the barn. The mounds were six feet long; but they were wide as well. They were middens dug for kitchen garbage; or turnip clamps; or something. Only a coward would have ever seen them as graves.

"I will keep you safe, Master Jack."

Johanna loved her men; even when they didn't love her.

But it was too late now. I turned to Matthew Fassett.

"Can I leave a message? I mean, scratched on the wall?"

He sighed; but motioned the other men to pull the settle out of the fireplace again. And there I scratched my name.

John Webster
University College London
21.9.1977

I thought of scrawling something else, but while I was still thinking, Matthew Fassett said, "That'll do," and the other men replaced the settle.

After that, all I could do was ride away.

A seventeenth-century engraving showing Matthew Hopkins
with witches and their attendant demons
(*Radio Times Hulton Picture Library*)

AUTHOR'S NOTE

This book is deeply indebted to Richard Deacon's biography, *Matthew Hopkins: Witch Finder General.* Mr. Deacon is not merely the leading authority on Hopkins; he is almost the only authority. He has rescued Hopkins from oblivion and the horror movie.

Hopkins repays study. For five hundred years after the Battle of Hastings, the English scarcely executed a witch a century. In the two years between 1645 and 1647, Hopkins, a bright young man in his twenties, promoted by a cunning publicity campaign the hanging of about five hundred old ladies on charges of withcraft. His main motive seems to have been money. He made a fortune for himself.

His character and actions in this book needed little invention. Most of the dialogue is drawn from his own writings, or the writings of those of his ilk. His death is popular legend. There is an alternative legend: that his death was faked, his coffin empty, that he was spirited away to New England, where members of his family were already living. Perhaps his pernicious views and methods survived to foster the similar witch-hunt that broke out in Salem, Massachusetts, some fifty years later. Not that they were needed; the social dynamics that Hopkins manipulated remain dormant in our society to this day. Wherever minorities exist, despised, not understood, difficult to live with, there is witch-hunt potential.

I would like to thank Mr. Christopher Westall for his unstinting technical advice about motorcycling. He asks me to stress that Master Jack Webster, like many motor-cyclists, has perhaps an optimistic speedometer.

R.A.W.

24.2.78

248